CON-MANDER-IN-CHIEF

The Trump Years in Satire

By

NED O'HEARN

© 2023 Edward H. O'Hearn

This is a work of satire. Many of the settings and characters mentioned by name or satirical inference are real; the stories are fictional.

Cover and Book design by Laura A. Rodil
www.sophella.com

Front cover photograph:
Donald Trump speaks at a campaign event in Fountain Hills, Arizona, March 16, 2016
by Gage Skidmore

Back cover photograph:
Donald Trump with supporters, October 29, 2016
by Gage Skidmore

ISBN 979-8-35093-768-8

For:

My wife Carol

Remembering:

Rich Feigel

Friend, Humanitarian, Democrat

Decision 2024

Trump and Dame O'Cracy sat on a wall,
When Trump tried to grope her she had a great fall.
Dame O'Cracy scampered back up and gave him a whack
When Trump fell over backwards she heard a loud SPLAT!

Or

Trump and Dame O'Cracy sat on a wall,
When Trump tried to grope her she had a great fall.
Dame O'Cracy scampered back up and gave him a whack
Then she ran away and never came back.

Two different ditties; which will it be?
The choice is all ours, and soon we shall see!

CONTENTS

BOOK ONE
Ascendency: Up the Down Escalator

BOOK ONE

Ascendency: Up and Down the Escalator

On June 16, 2015, Donald J. Trump descended a golden escalator to the lobby of his Trump Tower in New York City to announce that he is running for president. He appeared in front of a pre-selected collection of cheerleaders paid $50.00 to wear T-shirts, hold up placards, and shout their approval. American politics, and America itself, has never been the same.

This is the beginning of that story in satire.

ONE

The Untold Story of Gaspar J. Hoodwink and the Second Continental Congress
(The founding fathers deal with a pompous delegate from New York)

Act One, Scene One

[The setting is the Pennsylvania State House in June, 1776. Delegates from the 13 American colonies have gathered to discuss the war with Great Britain that has been raging for over a year. Prior to President John Hancock opening deliberations, a group of delegates comprised of John Adams of Massachusetts, Thomas Jefferson of Virginia, Benjamin Franklin of Pennsylvania, Roger Sherman of Connecticut and Richard Henry Lee of Virginia are seen engaged in a lively discussion on one side of the room.]

(Adams) "I trust all of you are familiar with Mr. Paine's pamphlet."

(Jefferson) "Indeed, his arguments are wise and well taken."

(Sherman) "It's widely distributed and has stirred great sentiment against the crown."

(Lee) "A worthy title as well. His positions make common sense."

(Franklin) "He's struck a match to dry leaves in a rain-poor forest."

(Adams) "A conflagration to follow is what you foresee?"

(Lee) "Isn't that what we're here for?"

(Jefferson) "Let's not get too far ahead of ourselves, gentlemen."

(Sherman) "Indeed, despite the conflict we remain subjects of the crown, albeit disloyal!"

(Franklin) "The king has no hose long enough to quench this rebellious fire."

(Sherman) "You see no outcome other than independence, Mr. Franklin?"

(Lee) "You will soon learn that my instruction is to make formal such a proposition."

(Adams) "How interesting! But what word from the battleground suggests success?"

(Jefferson) "General Washington is doing well for the little support we've offered."

(Adams) "That must be remedied forthwith. As a leader of men he's like none other."

A man of wide girth is seen approaching the group

(Jefferson) "Hold your talk, gentleman, the other would-be general is upon us."

Enter Gaspar J. Hoodwink of New York into the gathered circle, wiping his brow

(Hoodwink) "Hot enough for you fellows? Philadelphia in June! What a great idea."

(Jefferson) "Would you prefer, Mr. Hoodwink, to be at arms with General Washington?"

(Hoodwink) "Not me *with* General Washington, but General Washington with *me*!"

(Adams) "Ah, yes, Hoodwink. You sought the command in a plea to the Congress."

(Hoodwink) "I did indeed, sir. But for my ailment I'd be upon a steed waving my sword."

Hoodwink demonstrates by waving a fat arm in the air exposing a sweat-stained armpit

(Sherman) "Bone spurs as I recall."

(Hoodwink) "I denote a tone of derision in your voice; they are nothing to trifle with."

(Franklin) "Your boot spurs would irritate your bone spurs was what you claimed."

(Hoodwink) "Bad luck for me as a warrior; but far greater misfortune for the rebellion."

(Sherman) "We'll just have to make do with General Washington, won't we now?"

(Hoodwink) "New York, my beautiful city, has been burned. What say you to that?"

(Adams) "All has not gone well. But, we're gathered here to approve reinforcements."

(Hoodwink) "They'd better come soon. The General has fled across the river."

(Sherman) "A strategic move it was; and well executed."

(Hoodwink) "No movement backwards is well executed in my view of things."

(Sherman) "You disapprove of the decision?"

(Hoodwink) "On further consideration of who's in charge, it was a good decision."

(Sherman) "And but for bone spurs the British would be in full retreat?"

(Hoodwink) "We could well be sipping tea on my island and not suffocating here."

(Jefferson) "A timely interruption is it not, gentlemen? Hancock summons us."

Act One, Scene Two

[*The setting is the same room but the Congress has been called into session.*]

(Hancock) "The honorable delegate from Virginia has requested the floor."

(Lee) "Thank you, my esteemed colleague from Massachusetts."

(Hancock) "Tell us, Mr. Lee, what instruction have you been given."

(Lee) "I'll be to the point. We must declare our independence!"

Rumblings are heard throughout the room as the men react

(Hancock) "Order…order. Why such a proposition at this time Mr. Lee?"

(Lee) "We should not engage in civil war with our king, but be rid of the yoke."

(Franklin) "A fine analogy! The yoke weighs heavy on one yearning to be free."

(Jefferson) "Independence. Dare we declare? It does have a sweet sound to it."

(Hoodwink) "Bittersweet you mean? We'd be unfed chicks in a motherless nest."

(Franklin) "Your suggestion is that the king provides nourishment to his colonies?"

(Hoodwink) "I have great respect for King George. I know him well."

Jefferson aside to fellow Virginia delegate Lee

(Jefferson) "His dealings have to do with property protected by the crown. He has much to lose."

(Lee) "Does he belong here? (*Sounding alarmed*) Is he a loyalist?"

(Jefferson) "He holds no loyalties but unto himself."

(Lee) "Does he know the king as he says he does?"

(Jefferson) "He has traveled to England several times to expand his own little empire."

(Lee) "What empire is that?"

(Jefferson) "We are plantation owners from rural parts; Hoodwink erects buildings in cities."

(Lee) "That explains his dismay at the burning of New York?"

(Jefferson) "I suspect his holdings were known by the torch bearers and spared."

(Lee) "Is he a threat to the cause?"

(Jefferson) "Only men of principle are a threat to our cause. Hoodwink is unprincipled."

(Lee) "Enough. Hancock has taken notice of our private discourse."

Act One, Scene Three

[*The same setting a few weeks later. The debate that ran on since Mr. Lee's motion has finally ended with the delegates voting to declare independence from Great Britain.*]

(Hancock) "Nothing like a good debate among men of varied persuasions, I do say!"

(Adams) "Finally, all the colonies of one mind as to what must be done."

(Franklin) "Even the wolves slept peaceably with the sheep during Noah's flood."

(Sherman) "We think we're aligned in mind, but until the declaration is worded…"

(Hancock) "That is indeed the next step. I am proposing a committee be formed."

(Hoodwink) "Have you ever heard the saying that God so loved the world…"

(Hancock) "…He didn't send a committee. Yes, the trite saying is indeed familiar."

(Hoodwink) "But you choose to ignore it?"

(Hancock, *valiantly suppressing exasperation*) "There will be one main scribe."

(Hoodwink) "Excellent. I volunteer! Shall I and my quill be excused to my quarters?"

(Sherman) "Perhaps, General, your services are more suited to the war…as advisor."

(Adams) "Or as overseer of buildings to properly house our troops in winter quarters."

(Lee) "Or employing your negotiating skills to gain support from sympathetic France."

Franklin aside to Jefferson

(Franklin) "Or as inspector general of the brothels where the war is waged. He's a womanizer, not?"

(Jefferson) "'Tis well known that he's fond of groping the fairer sex. Claims they love it!"

(Franklin) "Likely bedecks himself in military raiment and wags his mighty sword before them."

(Jefferson, *laughing silently*) "More like a stubby dagger I would surmise!"

(Hancock, *interrupting*) "Gentlemen, one conversation please, attended by all."

(Jefferson) "Excuse the distraction. We were discussing Hoodwink's manifest talents."

(Hancock) "As are yours, Mr. Jefferson. I ask of you to draft the important document."

(Jefferson) "Are others not more qualified?"

(Hoodwink) "Indeed!"

(Hancock) "Mr. Jefferson, your artistry with words is well known."

(Jefferson) "This is not a task to be assigned to an artist."

(Hoodwink) "Indeed!"

(Hancock) "The king must understand why this bold initiative is undertaken."

(Hoodwink) "The king is a friend of mine; he'll mark my words."

(Hancock) "You don't declare independence from a friend."

(Sherman) "To be getting on with it, let Hoodwink serve on the committee."

(Hancock, *clearly exasperated*) "Fine…along with Adams, Sherman and Franklin."

(Jefferson) "I have given some thought to the matter and will create a draft promptly."

(Hoodwink) "Why not just say we're cutting ties?"

(Hancock) "The declaration must appeal to freedom seekers around the world."

(Hoodwink) "So be it. Let Jefferson write the mush…I'll insert the meaning."

(Hancock) "We're now adjourned. Mr. Jefferson, inform us when we are to resume."

Act Two, Scene One

[*The setting is a drawing room in the State House where the committee assigned to draft and edit the declaration has assembled, Mr. Jefferson as the author is presiding*]

(Jefferson) "Gentlemen, I trust you have taken the time to review the draft so provided."

All nod in agreement

(Jefferson) "Then, what have you to say about it?"

(Adams) "You are a master of words, Mr. Jefferson. A brilliant beginning."

(Sherman) "I have some comments, but, overall, it's masterfully written."

(Franklin) "You do yourself honor, Mr. Jefferson. A clip here and there and we're done."

(Hoodwink) "Words, words, words, very prettily put...but lacking forthrightness."

(Jefferson) "In what manner does it lack forthrightness? Explain your meaning, sir."

Franklin aside to Adams

(Franklin) "Too many words with multiple syllables – usurpations, magnanimity, unwarrantable."

(Adams) "Consanguinity! (*Titters*) And sentences that extend beyond five words!"

(Franklin) "Perhaps our declaration should be accompanied by a fifth grade reader."

(Adams) "Hoodwink would have it amplified by sketches for better understanding!"

(Franklin) "I doubt he got past the opening paragraph...Contends he doesn't read."

The general discussion resumes

(Hoodwink) "The king would need spectacles and patience to get our drift."

(Jefferson) "So, you're saying it's too long?"

(Hoodwink) "I'd prefer that we speak plainly and get directly to the point."

(Jefferson) "Interpret that for us if you will."

(Hoodwink) "Just say we're bailing. Cutting ties. Shoving off. Going bye, bye!"

(Sherman) "And state no reasons?"

(Hoodwink) "No, include those, all the 'He has' stuff that pads the middle."

Franklin aside to Adams

(Franklin) "The stuff that pads the middle is all the mutton he consumed last night."

(Adams) "It's risen to the upper reaches of the scalp."

The general discussion resumes

(Jefferson) "So, you suggest eliminating the two opening paragraphs?"

(Hoodwink) "Yeah…Forget all the God and Nature nonsense."

(Franklin) "Then from whence do unalienable rights derive?"

(Hoodwink, *appearing confused*) "What rights?"

(Jefferson) "Life, liberty…pursuit of happiness."

(Hoodwink) "Mush. That's all mush. I've already attained those."

Act Two, Scene Two

[*The setting is again the main assembly hall where the delegates have gathered to affix their signatures to the edited and approved document. Their work completed, there's talk amongst them of what will follow if the war is won and the colonies are independent.*]

(Hancock) "Gentlemen, a job well done. The king will soon be aware of our decree."

(Adams) "To gain what we've declared we have a war to win."

(Franklin) "The hound now has a bigger stake in the hunt."

(Hoodwink) "Ben, do you ever speak clearly?"

(Franklin) "Little is clear to the muffled mind."

(Hoodwink) "You're doing it again!"

(Hancock) "Gentlemen, what lies ahead if the British flag is removed?"

(Jefferson) "I envision a Republic – a government by and for the people."

(Hoodwink) "Why not a king? Just tinker with the known system. Make it better."

(Jefferson) "And pray for a benevolent monarch?"

(Hoodwink) "What kind of king is that?"

(Jefferson) "One who doesn't rule with an iron hand and respects the will of his people."

(Hoodwink, *demonstrating with his fist*) "Sometimes an iron hand is needed, is it not?"

(Adams) "If by that reference you mean laws, of course. And fair judges to apply them."

(Hoodwink) "I believe we're thinking too much. Just win the war and choose a king."

Franklin aside to Hancock

(Franklin) "I suspect he has someone in mind."

(Adams) "Is there gold enough to forge a crown around that fat head and starched crop?"

The general discussion resumes

(Adams) "Tom, so people from all the colonies would elect an overall leader?"

(Jefferson) "Precisely, a president, with certain powers entrusted to the states."

(Hoodwink) "Okay, I could be president…I mean, I could go for that idea."

(Hancock) "A true democracy for the world to use as a template."

(Hoodwink) "Temple? You don't mean Jews would have a say do you?"

(Hancock, *speaking as if to a child*) "It means a system worthy of imitation."

(*Franklin aside*) "He still doesn't comprehend…try again."

(Hancock) "A form of government that other nations might use as an example."

(Hoodwink) "Why would we care about that?"

(Jefferson) "No people should live under oppression."

(Hancock) "Are the slaves not oppressed?"

(Jefferson) "They are cared for. It was not I who deleted the reference in my draft."

(Hoodwink) "I still don't see why we worry about anyone but ourselves."

(Hancock) "A topic for another day! Gentlemen, take your leave. Go home!"

Franklin and Hancock remain behind as the gathering breaks up

(Hancock) "That Hoodwink tries my patience to no end."

(Franklin) "Add him to Job's long list of afflictions and he'd cry out for mercy."

(Hancock) "Let's say all goes well. Could a man like that ever be elected president?"

(Franklin) "Not in 100 years. I would like to think the masses aren't that stupid."

(Hancock) "Then how about in 200 years?"

(Franklin) "Will the minds of free men have deteriorated that much in two centuries?"

(Hancock, *breathes deeply*) "He'd be president and then offer himself as king!"

(Franklin) "I don't agree with Tom on every issue, but he trusts the will of the people."

(Hancock) "So, my fears for the future based on him are unfounded?"

(Franklin) "Oh, there'll be some fools; but I don't foresee our nation being hoodwinked!"

TWO

The Once and Would-Be Forever King
(*A kingdom is threatened by its own cowardly king*)

<u>Scene One</u>

[*The setting is a castle in medieval England. The king's inner circle and courtiers have grown increasingly concerned that the king, a pompous man who trusts no one, relying on his own undisciplined instincts, represents a threat to the security of the kingdom.*]

(*Murmurings, then* First Knight) "We must protect the kingdom from the king."

(Second Knight) "Forsooth, I concur it has come to that. Is he mad?"

(First Knight) "No, he's just an idiot. Won't read, listen or heed any advice."

(Second Knight) "How's goes it with his daily briefings?"

(First Knight) "Same. Unless it's new and something he can tweet on his piccolo about he waves it off."

(Second Knight) "Does he understand the threats from other kingdoms? These are real!"

(First Knight) "What I did was lay out a map on a large table illustrating the boundaries of all the known fiefdoms and kingdoms upon each of which I placed either a pearl or a stone indicating whether they were friend or foe. That way I figured even *he* might understand, if you know what I'm saying. It was as simpleminded an approach as I could conceive."

(Second Knight) "And, how did the king respond?"

(First Knight) "He asked for the names of the feudal lords and kings in these territories, and when I added the names to the map as requested, he promptly rearranged the pearls and the stones, making friends of foes and foes of friends. He then declared this official."

(Second Knight) "And what of arms?"

(First Knight) "He demands more and better weaponry; seems to have a warlike spirit. Likes putting on a suit of armor and playing at swords with Baron Bannon, Baron Bolton and Pence, his jester."

(Second Knight) "And how would these more and better arms be paid for?"

(First Knight) "Taxes on the peasantry, of course, and any landholding nobles of the Blue Faction."

(Second Knight) "What actual commands has he given?"

(First Knight) "So many it's hard to count. We mostly ignore them knowing he'll move on to something else and soon forget. Remember the big parade he ordered? King Vladimir is fond of these parades – thousands of foot soldiers marching, archers kneeling on wagons with drawn bows, catapults pulled by horses. All the latest weaponry in a show of might."

(Second Knight, *sighing heavily*) "Okay, it's up to us to save the kingdom. He might be a moron but he's our moron to deal with. Now be gone; this meeting never happened!"

Scene Two

[*The king is meeting in a private chamber with his wife, Queen Melania, as well as Lord Lindsey, Maiden Sarah, his spokesperson, and court jester Pence. The king is just finishing dictating a sentence when the door bursts open and Baron Bolton, fully armed and wearing a suit of armor, his helmet tucked under his arm, rushes in. The startled small group leaps up in anticipation.]*

(King) "Now Maiden Sarah, make it sound as if..." (*Breaks off*)

(Baron Bolton, *breathless from running*) "Your majesty, I beg your pardon but I have to interrupt. A legion of bloody Saxons is on our doorstep to the East. They are well armed and equipped. (*Stops to catch his breath*) I came at full gallop from the front to sound the alarm. The McCain and Kerry clans, led by Sir John and Sir John, are armed and rushing to the scene as I speak. They're gathering an army as they ride. (*Breathes heavily*) I left clear instructions not to engage the enemy until you could arrive and take your kingly position at the front of the charge. That is all I know for now. You must not delay!"

(Queen Melania) "Thank you Baron Bolton! We were just discussing small matters. How exciting is this news! Our heroic king will now mount up to lead his army!"

(King, *fidgeting*) "These were not small matters, Baron Bolton. I was just preparing to head south to oversee the construction of a great wall as we are being overrun from there as well. That's it! We shall divide and conquer – McCain to the East and I to the South!"

(Lord Lindsey) "Sire, the danger seems far greater to the East. The invaders you speak of from the South are mainly women and children seeking asylum from rampant barbarism in their lands -- not warlords as Maiden Sarah purports to tell. You must head east, take command of our armies, and lead the legions to honor and victory!"

(King) "Lady...ah Lord Lindsey, you speak out of turn and foolishly. The southern front is where I must be...ah, and my suit of mail is at the polishers...right my queen?"

(Queen Melania) "Oh no, it was returned yesterday from the forge where it was...fashionably expanded."

(Baron Bolton, *impatiently*) "Time is of the essence, sire. We must be off without delay. Your troops are waiting for you. (*Turns to Pence*) Fetch his armor at once and soon we'll be on our way."

(*Pence runs out and returns fumbling with a suit of armor*) "I think it's all here" (*Drops the bundle noisily to the floor*) "It's very heavy…way too heavy for little me."

(Baron Bolton) "Come forward, sire. Let's begin with the breastplate."

(King) "No, I…I prefer to dress from the bottom up. Sort of a superstition. Pence, hand me that left solleret." (*Pence hands him a metal shoe and the king tugs it on*)

(King, *screaming*) "Ow! Ow! Ow! Ow!" (*Begins hopping around on his right foot*)

(All, *startled*) "What's the matter your majesty? Are you in pain?"

(King) "Oh, yes…Tremendous pain. Terrible pain. More pain than anyone has ever experienced…Pence, remove this solleret from my foot and relieve my agony. Do it quickly…Oh, the pain. Oh, the agony. I tolerate pain more than anyone, but this…"

(Baron Bolton, *to Queen Melania*) "What ails the king?"

(King) "She wouldn't know. This goes way back. Bone spurs. Horrible bone spurs. They're killing me now. I must lie down… From experience, I should be walking in a month's time."

(Baron Bolton) "Then sire, who will lead the charge?"

(King, *pointing at Lord Lindsey*) "He will."

(*Lord Lindsey feints and crumples to the floor*)

Scene Three

[*Two weeks later. The scene is a scarred, smoking battlefield at break of day. Bodies on stretchers are still being removed and the profiles of broken catapults stand hauntingly against the sky. Thirty strong-armed men, fifteen on each side, shoulder a lavishly adorned catafalque atop which sits the king, in royal garb, on his golden throne.*

Following is a full troupe of trumpeters. Pence in his outlandish jester's outfit sits at the back of the catafalque, holding a piccolo, his legs dangling off the end. A knight in battle-torn armor, his visor lifted, limps slowly towards the procession and bows deeply.]

(Knight) "Welcome your majesty to this grim scene. But, I gladly report to you that the battle has been won."

(*The strong men lower the catafalque to the ground and step aside*)

(King) "So we won! That's good. That's real good. I'm pleased."

(Knight) "With high costs, sire. Whole legions were lost. But the men under the McCain and Kerry commands fought very bravely."

(King, *musing*) "As well they should. It's a beautiful thing…a beautiful thing."

(Knight, *bewildered by these words*) "What do you mean, sire?"

(King) "I mean, you know, we make all these wonderful weapons, like these fire throwing cata-things, and they just lie around being wasted. They're never put to use for all the engineering and money that went into making them. It's beautiful to see them, you know, finally put to use."

(Knight) "The weaponry did its job, sire; but it was the brave men who won the day."

(King, *still musing*) "If you say so. Beautiful thing though…How many men were lost?"

(Knight) "I don't know, sire. Thousands, of course. Others, like Sir

John of the McCain clan are missing and presumed captured. They are heroes indeed!"

(King) "McCain? No hero there. I like heroes who don't get captured."

(Knight, *bowing*) "As you say, sire."

(King, *shaking his head*) "Such a shame…such a shame…"

(Knight) "War is a terrible thing, I agree, sire."

(King) "No, no. I was just thinking how different it could have been."

(Knight) "How so, sire? We did all we could. The men fought bravely."

(King) "I mean, it's just a shame that this thing with my bone spurs came up and I couldn't be here to lead the charge. We won in the end, of course, but we could have won big, really big…and quicker. (*Musing*) Just a shame; a dirty rotten shame." (*Long pause*)

(*The strong men take their posts and lift the royal catafalque*)

(King) "Well, I'll be going along. Thanks for the report. See that the men get paid, but only half wages since they had to leave their farms unattended and we might lose the king's share of their crop… Trumpeters, sound the royal salute! (*Toot-toot-a-tooot!*) Henchmen, lift and let's be on our way…I have a wall to build!" (*The procession slowly departs, jester Pence playing "Yankee Doodle Dandy" on the piccolo*)

THREE

The Public Garden
(A fable about bigotry set in a garden where flowers walk and talk)

One day the flowers in the public garden decided they'd seen enough.

"Did you see what's going in along the fence line?"

"At first I didn't believe my eyes...pansies!"

"Just yesterday I saw the groundskeeper digging along the pathways."

"He appeared to be getting ready to plant something."

"I can't believe he's planning on planting roses *there*."

"I think I spotted a load of daisies in his wheelbarrow."

"My God! Daisies? Really? In *our* garden? That's just absurd!"

"We *must* do something about this!"

And so the carnations, lilies, irises and roses began to think and plot.

(All looking up to a tall red rose) "You're the head rose, what shall we do?"

(The head red rose speaks) "We're going to stop this invasion of inferior flowers."

"But, what about the groundskeeper, what if he objects?"

"We'll act at night under the glow of a full moon. No one will see."

"Perfect! That way none of those pesky human gawkers will be around."

"I don't mind them entering the garden," said a fair yellow rose, "but to be sniffed at and touched…oh how I hate that."

"They are *so* insensitive and rude," agreed a beautiful lily.

"Tell me about it! One cuffed me by the neck, pulled me forward, and held me against his snout. I've never felt so humiliated! There ought to be rules!"

"Or banish the humans. They act like Gods!"

(*They all chant in unison over and over*) "Rules…rules…or banish the humans!"

"Now, now," advised a comely iris. "They are important to us. We can put up with a little overzealousness. They do admire us, you know, and say wonderful things."

"And the gardener does look after us," one of them said.

"I suppose so," added a lovely rose, "although I missed my last pruning."

Every night once the gates were closed and the garden was quiet again the inner garden flowers huddled together to make their plans. There was agreement that something must be done; but there was no consensus on exactly what to do.

"They're compromising the desirability of our garden; but is that enough to act?"

(*An iris responds*) "Water is scarce…They'll be using up our water."

(*There were nods of agreement*) "And, they'll need *our* fertilizer."

"To say nothing of the gardener's time…Imagine him wasting time on *them!*"

(*More nods all around*) "You're not thinking straight," declared the head rose.

"What do you mean?" a bold lily dared to ask.

"These low-life plants from shithole gardens bring pestilence and disease."

"That's a real danger! They could kill us!" a fragile, frightened rose loudly exclaimed.

"Exactly, imagine a bee touching down on one of *them* and then landing on *you!*"

"Oh, the horror! *Their* pollen mixing with *mine*! That's scandalous!"

"Murderers and bearers of disease!" (*Someone shouted*)

(*All chanting together over and over*) "Murderers, murderers, and bearers of disease!"

It was then settled that taking action was justified. But, what kind of action still needed to be discussed. Weeks later, days before the full moon, the debate was still ongoing.

"More and more pansies, daisies and daffodils are showing up every day."

"They're brought in on large pallets and nothing is done."

(*The lead red rose finally speaks*) "Something's going to be done. I promise."

"But what? We can't just uproot them or cut them down."

"We're all here in the center of the garden. Right? We need a fence. We'll build a wall!"

"How do we get that done? And, who'll pay for such a wall?"

"Trust me. The humans who are emptying their sorry gardens, sending us the outcast blooms they don't want anymore will pay for it! They will pay. Believe me!"

It was then settled. The flowers had never spoken to the groundskeepers or gardeners, but they knew that the birds, which regularly splash in the central fountain, had a way with them. They'd ask friendly birds to convince the groundskeepers that the inner garden, where only prized flowers grew, should be protected against this dangerous onslaught.

And so it was that the birds communicated with the caretakers and soon a wall was erected, separating the inner garden from the spacious lawns and winding pathways.

"Let's celebrate our success with a procession!" a white rose suggested.

"A splendid idea…That's what we'll do when the full moon rises tomorrow night."

The inner garden's residents could hardly wait for the next day to pass. The sun shone brightly in the sky, promising a cloudless night. Humans passed though the arched gates, some with dogs on leashes, others pushing strollers, still others alone with their sacs of food or birdfeed. A general nervousness spread throughout the inner garden whenever these people passed through openings in the wall. Some alert roses leaned sideways to hide their becoming countenances lest some rogue spectator deign to touch their petals. The irises and lilies likewise protected themselves by feigning a breeze was blowing.

The pansies, daisies and daffodils spent the day like every other day, occupying and adding color along the outer fencing, aside the garden pathways and in small circles surrounding the bases of the garden's stately old trees. They had heard about the procession from some telltale birds and were looking forward to the spectacle.

Nervousness gave way to anticipation throughout the garden as the sun slowly dipped to the horizon and then finally disappeared, varnishing the sky with a burst of vermillion light. The human visitors shuffled off, the gardeners packed up their rakes and hoes, and then the gatekeeper's key could be heard fastening the iron latch. The garden was closed.

Soon the moon, like a golden shield, was seen rising majestically in the night sky. When it was directly overhead, a signal was given, and the inner garden sprang to life. All the flowers behind the wall fell into line, exactly as ordained, the most favored near the back, with the head red rose hoisted on a temporary bed of ferns and soft petals at the very end. Birds hurriedly flew in, perching on the wall, fountains and statues, vying for a better view. It was a splendid sight to behold. The public garden was never so wondrous.

The parade was a spectacle like no other. Every flower from the inner garden marched in perfect cadence, bowing slightly in unison only to acknowledge a venerable member of the garden's avian community. The bees were summoned and swarmed busily overhead.

The carnations were followed by the lilies, followed by the irises and then by the roses. A white lily had been chosen to announce the appearance of the most acclaimed of the flowers and proclaim the arrival of the head red rose who had saved the inner garden.

The procession passed through the opening in the wall as a show of luxury and command. The pansies, daisies and daffodils along the route could only admire what they beheld.

"See how they envy us," a beautiful iris declared.

"Careful, not too close…You don't want anything from *them* rubbing off on *you*."

"Wait 'till they hear that we're going to ration their water supply," beamed another.

"Once a week...and their tiny seedlings will be snatched away from them." (*Laughter*)

"The red rose has big plans to uproot them completely...the garden will be ours!"

"As well it should be; what craziness allowed them in in the first place?"

"They have no place in this garden; send them back to the pits from where they came."

"Have you heard that the head red rose also plans to make the garden private?"

"No...how so?"

"Only members of an elite garden club will be allowed to enter."

"With high fees which means no low-life flowers. No riff-raff humans...How perfect!"

"The red rose as promised is truly making our garden great again!"

The grand procession lasted until the wee hours of the morning. The garden only grew still when the gatekeeper's key was heard turning in the lock at daybreak.

As it turned out, this day was a Sunday, which by chance was also a festival day for the people of the city. Humans filled the streets, turning out in droves to celebrate their own special day. Many brought picnic baskets to the seashore. Others took to the gardens.

The public garden was packed with sun worshipers, flower enthusiasts, and just plain festival frolickers that day. They spread their blankets on the lush lawns, played games with balls, dipped their little ones' feet in the brimming fountains, and feasted on sumptuous meats and vittles of every kind. They drank heavily from flasks and wine sacs, told stories, flew kites, wrestled, and clamorously made the most of their holiday.

By late afternoon the inner garden was in shambles. A statue of Cupid had been knocked off its pedestal, wrappers and food bits floated in the fountains, and hundreds of flowers had been plucked to fill the vases that adorned the people's lavish picnic spreads.

A bluebird and a dove flew over to inspect the aftermath of the people's festival. Those humans had a good eye for beauty, they mourned. An exquisite iris, the very one that had boasted of being envied, was found in a trash barrel. The beautiful yellow rose was wilting inside a tipped-over vase. A prideful carnation had been earlier seen pinned to the bosom of a laughing maiden. The head red rose, the unflinching leader of them all, was missing and nowhere to be seen; a shallow hole indicated it had been uprooted.

At the edges of the garden the pansies were untouched; the overlooked daisies swayed back and forth in the late evening breezes. Because of the wall, they couldn't see the devastation that had torn apart the inner garden. The day seemed like any other.

The daffodils, all but identical in color and height, chatted merrily amongst themselves.

"What a marvelous parade last night," one exclaimed.

"I'm just happy to be anywhere in this garden," said another.

"Maybe one day we'll be accepted into the inner garden," offered a third.

"I wish I could see what's going on in there now."

"They must all be basking in their glory."

(*Sighing*) "I can only dream what it must be like to be them tonight."

The very next day city officials voted to replace the inner garden behind the wall with a paved children's playground, a musical merry-go-round replacing the central fountain.

FOUR

Down on the Plantation with Miss Lindsey Graham: The Hearing
(*A pre-Civil War hearing is held on a Supreme Court nominee*)

Act One, Scene One

[*It's a few years prior to the American Civil War. Miss Lindsey Graham, dressed in southern finery, is sprawled on a swinging chair fanning herself on the veranda of her white-columned plantation house in South Carolina. She summons her Black servant.*]

(Miss Lindsey) "Oh Charles, do fetch me a fresh lemonade. My throat is positively parched from all the speaking I had to do yesterday in defense of poor, mistreated Judge Kavanaugh."

(Charles) "Yesem, Miss Lindsey."

(Miss Lindsey) "Imagine, Charles, that dastardly woman – where did she get her degree? – accusing such a fine man of grinding his genitals over her body." (*Under her breath and fanning furiously*) "I do declah the thought of being in her position just makes me a little feint."

(Charles) "Must o' been somtin ta watch Miss Lindsey…Shameful… Jus shameful."

(Miss Lindsey) "Such an outrage I declah I've yet to witness before. After all, Judge Kavanaugh would be *much* more discriminatory in choosing young women to satisfy his natural boyish urgings."

(Charles) "A straw in da lemonade, Miss Lindsey?"

(Miss Lindsey) "No, Charles, just the tiny parasol on the rim...Thank heavens justice prevailed. I'll have to return to Washington tomorrow for the committee vote. (*Sighs*) Soon it will be over."

(Charles) "I'll see ta pressin' ya new petticoat Miss Lindsey and have da carriage ready."

(Miss Lindsey) "I'm worried, Charles, about Flake. He's not running again and hardly uttered a syllable during the hearing...I worry that he's lost his way."

(Charles) "He da man from out dare west?"

(Miss Lindsey) "Correct, Charles. Arizona. Dreadful place; hardly any trees and that canyon of sorts that could well be better used for uranium mining. I swear, Charles, it never ends what these liberals come up with. Pretty soon the whole country will be one national monument."

(*Charles steps inside the house, making sure the screen door doesn't slam behind him*)

Act One, Scene Two

[*A day later. Miss Lindsey Graham slumps into her seat on the veranda after returning by train and coach from Washington, D.C.*]

(Miss Lindsey) "Oh Charles, my fears about that awful man Flake were realized."

(Charles) "Somtin' go wrong, Miss Lindsey?"

(Miss Lindsey) "Oh Charles the horror of it! I declah I've never seen the like of it. Is there no justice?"

(Charles) "Wahs gonna happen, Miss Lindsey?"

(Miss Lindsey, *sighing deeply*) "There's going to be an FBI investigation into Judge Kavanaugh's background based on what that that awful woman had to say about the poor man."

(Charles) "F-B-I? Wahs dat?"

(Miss Lindsey) "Federal Bureau of Investigation, Charles. A pawn operation of the liberals. They'll make up some facts and stories and try to paint poor Judge Kavanaugh in a bad light."

(Charles) "Did da judge do anathin' wrong Miss Lindsey?"

(Miss Lindsey) "Of course not, Charles. This is all about when he was young and just acting out his boyhood fantasies. Boys will be boys." (*Then, under her breath*) "How *fondly* I remember those days!"

(Charles) "So he did some grindin' on dat woman's body?"

(Miss Lindsey) "Charles, don't ask silly questions...He might have; he might not have. If he did he was probably inebriated; too drunk to see that *she* wasn't worth the trouble. It really doesn't matter. He was young. He's a good man. He'll make a *great* Supreme Court Justice."

(Charles) "Dis gonna de-lay he bein anointed?"

(Miss Lindsey) "*Confirmed* is the term we use. Flake asked for a week. Goodness knows what garbage prowling liberals can make up in seven days. It's all so dreadful...So unexpected!"

(Charles) "I suspect, Miss Lindsey, knowin you, dat it's all gonna turn out jus right."

(Miss Lindsey) "I hope you're correct...It's just that the left doesn't know what's right."(*Miss Lindsey follows Charles into the house letting the screen door slam behind her*)

Act Two, Scene One

[*Judge Brett Kavanaugh relaxes with his wife Ashley at their manor home in a posh Washington suburb after a day of testifying before the Senate Judiciary Committee.*]

(Judge K) "Honey, can you get me a beer?"

(Ashley) "Brett, darling, don't you think eight is enough."

(Judge K) "Look, I like beer! Okay. I like beer! I had a tough day. Eight might not be enough."

(Ashley, *sweetly*) "You *did* have a tough day, darling. But you did just fine…and the president seems to be pleased."

(Judge K, *calming down a little*) "Ya think so? I mean, you *really* believe I did okay? (*Reaches out and grabs his beer and takes a long sip*) "Thanks for the beer, I needed one."

(Ashley) "You did fine…only you might have come across just a teensy bit…annoyed."

(Judge K, *angrily*) "Damn right I was annoyed. My life is, is…ruined." (*Begins to whimper*)

(Ashley) "Don't be so hard on yourself, darling. (*Puts her hand on his trembling shoulder as he purses his lips and dabs his eyes*) You really didn't like coaching that much anyway."

(Judge K) "Even if I'm confirmed people will look at me and wonder – 'was *he* lying?' 'Did he *grind* his crotch against that 15-year old girl's body?' 'Why *didn't* he have sex?'"

(Ashley) "I was very proud when you told everyone that you didn't have sex until we were married."

(Judge K, *stammering and taking a big gulp*) "Well, that's pretty close." (*Now under his breath*) "I said *that* under oath?" (*To his wife*) "I never could understand why girls didn't go for me. I went to Yale you know…Yale University!…I lifted weights…I played sports…I drank beer, so I *was* cool. What did Donkey Dong Doug have that I didn't?"

(Ashley) "You were a wholesome young man. You went to church.

You regularly brushed your teeth. You worked your butt off to finish at the top of your class...You didn't need sex."

(Judge K) "Ah...can you grab me another beer, please! I'm, I'm feeling a little, a little..."

(*Judge Kavanaugh's wife hands him another beer. He quickly gulps it down*)

(Ashley, stroking his head) "Don't be ashamed, darling, that you were studying while other boys were being rowdy. It's alright having been a grinder. Look where it's gotten you!"

(Judge K) "A grinder, yeah." (*Aside to himself*) "NOW I remember." (*To Ashley*) "You're right – just look where it's gotten me!"

Act Two, Scene Two

[*The following evening in the same front room setting only this time Judge Kavanaugh and his wife have been joined by their two daughters, Margaret and Liza.*]

(Judge K, *listing slightly in his chair*) "Hon, would you g...g...get me a-notter beer?"

(Ashley) "Brett, darling, don't you think *eleven* is enough for one night?"

(Judge K) "Hey...I...I like beer. Okay! I like beer...I went to Yale ya know...I worked out...I played sports..."

(Margaret) "Mom, is dad okay?"

(Ashley) "Of course he is, dear. He's fine...He just had another tough day. We learned that the FBI is going to do an investigation... Now be a good girl and get him a beer."

(Judge K) "Yeah (*hic*)...be...be...be a goody g-girl and g-get me a...a...beer."

(Ashley, *gushingly*) "Just think positively, darling. Soon this will all be behind us!"

(Judge K) "Yeah, and I can't wait...Just wait until I'm on the... the..." (*Ashley interjects* "Supreme Court, darling") "Yeah, that! No more 'Save the Planet' bullshit...No more 'gay rights' bullshit...no more 'pro choice' bullshit...And don't even get me started on that... that...'MeToo' bullshit."

(Liza) "But dad! Women have a right to be heard...ah...even if their memory sometimes isn't so good."

(Judge K, *swaying a bit and spilling some beer*) "They all ought to be named Miranda is what I think...They have the right to and *should* remain (*hic*) si-si-lent."

(Liza) "Women need role models too, dad! Women who inspire them."

(Judge K) "I'll sh-sh-ow you a ro-roll model...Mel-an-i-a Tr-Tr-ump...Keeps her mouth shut...Does what she's told...and comes in a great p-p-pack-age...Nice piece of ass!"

(Ashley) "Brett, now *I* think you've had too much to drink! You need to be able to speak with the FBI when and if they come by. You must be able to answer their questions. They're likely to ask more questions about Dr. Ford and that other woman, that Miss Ramirez, who claims that you..."

(Judge K, *wobbling*) "Yeah...yeah...I know. Pulled my pants down and wagged my wiener...I liked girls (*getting sullen*) but...but Donkey D-d-dong (*starts sobbing*)...I remember that Ra- Ra-mirez girl...So ugly I p-probably mistook her for a urinal...(*hic*)...I musta been g-etting ready to have me a pee."

(Margaret) "Mom, are you sure dad needs another beer?...I think he's passed out."

(Ashley) "No dear. Your father hasn't passed out...He's just sleeping; that's all."

Act Two, Scene Three

[*It's the following morning. The Kavanaugh family has gathered in the formal dining room of their manor home waiting for their Black servant Dalia to serve them breakfast.*]

(Ashley) "Feeling better this morning Brett darling?"

(Judge K) "I feel GREAT! Ready to take on the world…Bring em' on!"

(Ashley) "So you're not at all concerned about the FBI talking to your accusers?"

(Judge K) "I have an ace in the hole on that one my dear…and her name is Miss Lindsey Graham. She's not much to look at, mind you, but underneath those petticoats and parasols is one feisty woman. Whatever they come up with she'll shout em' down. Lordy, will she ever!"

(Liza) "Dad, what you seem to be saying is that they might find something but it won't matter because you have it fixed…Is that what I'm hearing?"

(Judge K) "No, Miranda dear, that isn't what I'm saying…exactly. It's just that we all know that this latest hearing was just a left-wing conspiracy campaign backed by the Clintons meant to dishonor me, and Miss Lindsey, ah… knows how to handle such things… Now Dalia, would you bring me my calendar…I still keep it up you know…Every day; just like dad."

(*Dalia leaves the room and returns with Judge Kavanaugh's monthly big block calendar*)

(Judge K) "Thank you, Dalia. Eggs sunny side up this morning to reflect my mood…Let's see now…I need to fill in what happened yesterday." (*Begins writing*)

(Ashley) "Yesterday was quite crazy, darling…What notes are you taking?"

(Judge K) "I'll read it as I write it my dear – 'Turncoat Flake demands FBI investigation. Trump agrees but swears allegiance. Had a couple of beers before bed'…There!…Done!"

(Margaret) "Dad, I think you had more than a couple of beers."

(Judge K) "I like beer, okay? I don't keep count…but that's what I remember. (*Raising his voice*) You're getting old enough…Do YOU like beer? Huh? Do YOU like beer?"

(Ashley) "Brett, darling, don't raise your voice at your daughter. And, besides, she doesn't drink."

(Margaret) "That's right, dad (*beginning to cry*). Don't yell at me…I don't even like your *weak* brand of beer. My older friends call those 'Trainer Beers.'"

(Ashley) "What are you writing on your calendar now, darling?"

(Judge K) "Just getting a jump on today (*begins writing*) 'Happy breakfast with family…FBI begins witch hunt…must remember to send flowers and a new bonnet to Miss Lindsey.'"

Act Three, Scene One

[*Miss Lindsey Graham has been summoned by the president to participate in a strategy session pending the anticipated release of an FBI investigative report on allegations of sexual assault and harassment against Supreme Court nominee Judge Brett Kavanaugh. The scene is the White House where upon arrival Miss Lindsey finds the president talking with his Counselor Kellyanne Conway and Press Secretary Sarah Sanders.*]

(President) "Ah, here she is now. Welcome Miss Graham. How was the carriage ride? Not too bumpy I hope. You can place your parasol in the corner alongside Sarah's whip and Kellyanne's broom."

(Miss Lindsey) "Thank you, Mr. President, but I do declah that the commute from my plantation to this infernal city is wearing down my patience, but I'll do anything to help that poor falsely-accused darling hunk of a judge."

(President) "Well, that's why we're here. This is big. The Democrats will do anything to derail this nomination. Kavanaugh's a good man. I know a good man when I see one and Kavanaugh's a good man. He was made for the Supreme Court. He's my kind of guy."

(Sanders) "Mr. President, reporters – I know, I know, they're all despicable liars who roll in the muck of fake news – but they want to know if you find Dr. Ford's testimony credible."

(President) "Well, she's a bitch trying to ruin the life and career of a very good man…but we can't come out and say that. If the FBI says nothing happened, we can say it then, and we will, believe me, we will, but in the meantime we need to prepare for a different outcome."

(Sanders) "Meaning that he's guilty as charged? I thought we had that handled?"

(President) "I think we do. I really think we do. The FBI doesn't dare cross me too many times or they know I'll take action. It's just a damn nuisance department anyway; a bunch of liberal fags. I should fire the whole lot of them."

(Conway) "But what if the report indicates some wrongdoing, like he might have lowered his pants exposing himself in front of that Ramirez woman, or ground his crotch against the body of Dr. Ford and cupping her mouth to keep her quiet while tearing at her clothes?"

(Miss Lindsey) "Oh, Kellyanne! Please don't be so graphic! I'm beginning to (*sighs*) lose my breath."

(Conway) "So sorry, Miss Lindsey. Please use your fan; it'll help calm the libido."

(President) "Kellyanne, I see where you recently admitted that you were once sexually assaulted. (*Kellyanne nods*) Well, that seems to work in our favor now that I think of it. What you need to do is make your assault sound worse than Dr. Ford's and then say how much you enjoyed it."

(Conway) "Mr. President, that might be going a bit too far. For one thing, the 'MeToo' group will explode."

(President) "Why? If you didn't get a rush like the women I 'allegedly' groped all I can say is that's too bad…But, don't worry, it'll be okay. We'll go with the 'boys will be boys' defense. The Senate will buy into it…won't it Miss Lindsey?"

Act Three, Scene Two

[*Meanwhile, over at FBI Headquarters, investigators Fenton Hardy, Sam Spade and Harry Callahan gather for morning coffee.*]

(Fenton) "You were assigned to this case, too, huh? What did you two do wrong?"

(Sam) "I'm a Republican so they put me on the case. You guys all Republicans?" (*They all nod*)

(Fenton) "Well, it's going on 10:00 so I guess we should hitch the horses and hit the streets. How many people do you have on your list, Harry?"

(Harry) "There's gotta be something wrong because I only have three people to interview and I can't figure how they're even connected."

(Fenton) "That's not a mistake. Word came down from you-know-where that we're only to contact these few. And remember, if they don't want to cooperate just thank them and turn around. This isn't an investigation; just a routine extension of a background check."

(Sam) "Who has Dr. Ford and that Ramirez gal?" (*No one speaks up*)

(Harry) "How did those news reporters find all those character witnesses and we don't have any of them?"

(Fenton) "Don't ask those questions, got it? Step outside the restrictions and we'll have Miss Lindsay Graham poking us in the ass with her fucking parasol. I even heard she sharpened the tip just in case. That's one bitch you don't want to mess with."

(Sam) "I'm already done! I hit the streets this morning, hiring a carriage to get around. One said 'I know na-ting' – must have been a fan of *Hogan's Heroes* (*laughs*) – one said she didn't want to talk because her husband loves Trump, and the third told me to come back next week. Ha! There is no next week! I'm taking an early lunch and then going home."

(Harry) "I've got my boy's soccer game at 2:00 so I'll be leaving early as well. It shouldn't take me but a few minutes to race through the names on my list – all pals of the judge!"

(Sam) "Wait! I think we need to stretch this out a bit. If we file a report too soon it won't look good. Play a game -- see if you can keep people on the doorstep for three minutes with you doing all the talking." (*Laughter*)

(Fenton) "Okay, so we have a plan. We'll meet again at 10:00 tomorrow. The only thing we need to decide is who's going to assimilate the information and write the report. We're to keep it short, after all, it's for the president and senators! No big words. Any volunteers?"

(Sam) "I don't think we need to bother. You'll see that the list of names to contact came with filled in statements. We just need to attach names to the statements."

(Harry) "Works for me! Now who's in charge of doughnuts for tomorrow?"

Act Three, Scene Three

[*Miss Lindsey Graham sits contentedly on her veranda sipping a mint julep a day following the Senate vote in which Brett Kavanaugh was confirmed as an Associate Justice on the United States Supreme Court. Her Black servant Charles enters.*]

(Charles) "Miss Lindsey, a carriage jus come down da drive wit two mens in it."

(Miss Lindsey) "Ah, that must be Orrin and Chuck. How delightful. They hinted they might come by."

(Charles) "I'll be bringin' 'em right along, Miss Lindsey."

(*Charles reappears accompanied by Orrin Hatch and Chuck Grassley*)

(Miss Lindsey) "I do declah this *is* a wonderful day! Two of my favorite senators!"

(Orrin) "Not as fine as day as yesterday, Miss Lindsey, thanks in no small part to you!"

(Miss Lindsey) "I was jus tendin' to my business gentlemen. Serving justice and the country!"

(Chuck) "Judge Kavanaugh, by the way, sends his regards. He's obligin' to ya."

(Miss Lindsey) "Well, gentlemen, he'll have plenty of opportunities to prove it, won't he?"

(Orrin, *as they all laugh*) "They're lining up the cases as we speak, Miss Lindsey. The oil barons have their knives and forks poised, so to speak, itchin' to carve up the Arctic, so don't forget to add them to your campaign appeals list…as if they're not already on it!"

(Chuck) "And LGBT will soon mean "Let's Get Boys Toughened!" (*More laughs*)

(Miss Lindsey) "Gentlemen, what a perfectly awful hostess I've become!…Charles, Charles…there you are, stir up two glasses of mint juleps for my dear friends…and make Orrin's a little extra strong. He's among friends and doesn't have to worry about that Mormon thing."

(Miss Lindsey *continues*) "I will confess, gentlemen, that for an itsy-bitsy minute there I was worried about getting enough votes for final confirmation. We won't be missing Senator Flake, will we? Such an unfortunate name…but so appropriate, don't you think?" (*They all laugh*)

(Miss Lindsey, *breathing deeply*) "Ah me, imagine causing that fine man to break down in tears in such a shameful way in front of everyone… simply uncalled for and utterly outrageous! And all over some loose hussy accusing Judge Kavanaugh of sexual deviancy." (*Blushes and rapidly fans herself*)

(Orrin) "Can't trust those Democrats, Miss Lindsay. "They do have some strange notions."

(Chuck) "Next thing you know they'll be tryin' to abolish slavery… Wouldn't put it past 'em'!" (*Nervous laughter all around*)

FIVE

The King's Parrot
(A fable about a king who's a pathological liar)

The family had gathered for a special holiday weekend. The children's father was watching Fox News while their mother was cleaning up after dinner in the kitchen.

"Can we have Uncle Ned tell us a story?" they asked their father. "Have him invent one of his fairy tales; just don't let him fill your impressionable young ears with his liberal nonsense," he responded. The children found their uncle reading a newspaper, crowded around and begged him to tell them a story, adding "but it can't be about that liberty nonsense."

Their uncle set aside his newspaper and then asked them as they gathered round:

"Have I told you the story of the king's parrot?"

"No you haven't" they all gushingly said together.

"Well, then I'll tell you. Once upon a time in a not so far away land there lived an evil king."

"If he was evil how did he get to be king?" one of the older children interrupted.

"Skullduggery!" their uncle said. "That means using dirty tricks, but that's another story for another time. The fact is that King Potus ruled over a widespread kingdom."

"How big was his kingdom, Uncle Ned?"

"As you've heard it said in a song, it stretched from sea to shining sea."

"What was he like?"

"Well, he was fat [*the children giggle imagining a fat king*] and he wasn't very smart. But he was cunning, which means he could trick people into believing that he was there to help them when that wasn't true at all. All King Potus cared about was himself.

Because he wasn't very smart, he had a hard time with words. He struggled when giving speeches and resorted to repeating simple phrases that his followers liked to hear. There were many good people in the kingdom who laughed at him, but he was king and lashed out at anyone who mocked him. The courtiers in his inner circle lived in fear of him.

There was also a group of special people who made the laws that even the king was to abide by, and another group of special people who ruled on which laws were right or wrong. But, these people also lived in fear of the king and did what he told them to do.

The king had a lovely queen who also feared to question her husband's bad behavior. Behind the king's back she was called a 'kept woman.' But, she felt sorry that he couldn't express himself well in his speeches beyond cheer-raising phrases – pithy little sayings like "Build the Wall!" and "Lock her up!" – and calling people he didn't like childish names. This always resulted in a frightful chant that would go on until he raised a hand. The king loved hearing his little phrases and names repeated by his adoring followers.

The queen had heard about a parrot that had been brought into the kingdom from a foreign land. Rumor had it that the parrot, now up in years, had belonged to a wise, honest and spiritual man who lived on a high mountain top. This man had endowed the parrot over time with his wisdom and the bird could speak openly and clearly.

The queen ordered the king's jester, a laughable little man named Pence, to find the parrot, buy it at whatever cost, and bring it to her. Pence wasted no time and soon arrived back at the king's palace with the bird in a thatched cage.

It didn't take the queen long to discover the great talents of this striking green-feathered bird and on the king's birthday she presented it to him as a gift. "Sire, besides my eternal love I present to you on this special occasion this extraordinary parrot. Carry him on your shoulder so it can speak into your ear. Repeat what it says, and people will marvel at your wisdom and way with words." The king thought this was total foolishness, but to satisfy his wife's wishes he propped the bird on a shoulder and listened as it spoke into his ear.

The king was amazed! The parrot could speak in a manner that would be the envy of the brightest professors in the kingdom. Soon he was strutting about the palace with the bird perched on his shoulder uttering thoughts and ideas that astounded those who heard him speak. The courtiers were amazed, and soon the king felt so comfortable that he was willing to appear on the palace's upper-story balcony and speak to his people.

What the bird wanted him to say, however, wasn't what he had in mind. He still loved hearing his adoring followers chant his trite phrases and repeat the insults he flung at his enemies. So, he started giving his standard speech about all he has done for the people.

"That's a lie!" the parrot squawked loud enough for everyone to hear. Annoyed at the interruption, the king continued but after almost every sentence the parrot squawked "That's a lie!" The queen had neglected to inform the king about the bird's upbringing by a wise, honest and spiritual man who had no tolerance for lies and unjust behavior.

Infuriated, the king had the bird removed from his shoulder. As it was being hastily taken away in its now gilded cage it kept repeating "All lies! All lies! All lies!"

The embarrassing balcony speech was intended as a lead-in for a very important speech the king was to deliver to the people in the great hall of the palace the following day. This was his annual 'State of the Kingdom' speech in which he would brag about all his accomplishments, almost all of which benefited only him and his wealthy allies.

King Potus feared no man because all men feared him, but this seemingly all-knowing bird made him tremble. The queen, feeling guilty for causing her lord such anguish, summoned jester Pence. "I want to change the menu for tonight's pre-speech banquet," she whispered in the little man's ear. 'Tell the chef that instead of the roasted lamb, the king and I prefer parrot stew and bring him the gilded cage containing that awful bird."

Pence did exactly as he was told and presented the royal chef with the parrot in its cage with instructions that it was to be served in a stew as the evening's main course."

At this point in the story horror overtook the faces of the young children.

"They're not going to kill the wise parrot are they?" one shouted. "Don't let it happen!"

"I'm just the story teller," their uncle said. "I can't change the story."

"The chef had heard about this bird but was too frightened to disobey orders so he removed the parrot from its cage, grabbed it so tightly it couldn't fly away, pressed it on a cutting board and with one accurate chop of his glistening butcher knife cut off its head."

The children clutched their chests in disbelief. One of the younger ones began to cry.

"The story doesn't end here," their uncle advised, holding his index finger in the air as another way of saying there was more of the story to come. "Listen up."

"The following day a huge crowd – over 10,000 people – gathered in the great hall to hear the king's annual address. It would be more of the same, but the king wasn't worried that the parrot would point out all his lies and exaggerations; after all, he and his queen had enjoyed a deliciously spiced parrot stew – the only parrot known in the kingdom."

"Yuk!" one of the children exclaimed. "Too bad he didn't choke on it," added another.

"The great hall was lavishly decorated for the event. The king would deliver his speech from a high podium at one end of the hall. As he spoke, a team of people would relay his words down the aisles, ensuring that everyone could hear what was said. The king spoke so slowly and simply that there'd be no problem spreading his words around the hall.

With a blast of trumpets the king entered the hall and took a seat on his throne. After waiting for the thunderous applause to quiet down – servants had been strategically placed around the hall in advance with instructions to bring the crowd to its feet and keep them cheering for a long time – King Potus waddled behind a gold lectern bedecked with precious jewels, removed his crown, and began to speak. His confidence had never been higher. He recognized his wife, his courtiers and the richest among his flatterers.

For a minute the speech went well because it was all fluff. But the moment he uttered his first false claim an extraordinary thing happened – feathers, little green feathers, spewed from his mouth. He lied again in his next sentence and more feathers came forth, floating in the air, momentarily obscuring his startled face. With each new sentence and each new lie feathers poured from his face like bats exiting a cave. The chief justices, who owed allegiance to the king and thus weren't really justice-seekers at all, had been honored with seats up front and were now swatting at a waft of feathers drifting over them like bits of confetti. But the king went on, and soon the entire hall was filled with feathers.

The thing is that the dim-witted king didn't draw the connection between his lies and the feathers spewing from that orifice in his face. He thought it rather marvelous indeed!

King Potus was so comfortable telling outrageous lies about his achievements and the faults of his personal enemies that soon every hill and valley in the kingdom was strewn with little green parrot feathers. It became a widespread joke that could only be whispered among the peasantry because everyone but the king realized the connection.

A legend says that one day a young boy and girl tending their lambs decided to climb the highest mountain in the kingdom that really wasn't all that high. They said they saw an old man with a parrot – describing him as resembling the king's former master chef."

"So the parrot wasn't killed after all?" one of the children asked with anticipation.

"I really can't say," said their uncle. "That's the way the fairy tale ends. You decide."

Just then the children's father entered the room. The look on his face suggested something was wrong. "I hope Uncle Ned didn't feed you any liberal crap," he muttered.

"No, Daddy," they said in unison. "He told us a tale about a king and his parrot."

"What's the matter Bill?" Uncle Ned asked.

"Nothing that would bother you. Rush Limbaugh has stage-four lung cancer."

"Who's Rush Limbaugh?" one of his sons asked his father.

"A courageous man who told the truth, inspiring millions. A man who did great things for the military, police, and 9/11 victims and families. A truly great American patriot."

As their father gathered them up to leave, did the children really see what appeared to be green feathers strewn on the carpet where their father had been standing?

SIX

The Rope Jumpers
(*Children at play mimic their parents' prejudices*)

The setting is the conference room of a private elementary school located in a posh almost exclusively white Maryland suburb outside Washington, D.C. The principal and school administrators are gathered for their weekly meeting. Before addressing their agenda, they're discussing the news that two mass shootings have occurred within 24-hours in El Paso, Texas and Dayton, Ohio. In the playground outside the conference room, sixth grade children are indistinctly heard singing rhymes while jumping rope.

"Two more shootings! My gosh, twenty dead in El Paso and some 26 injured, and then nine killed and 27 others wounded at that Dayton nightclub. What's going on?"

"Drugs...mental illness...foreigners...illegal aliens..."

"All of the above. But, you know the liberals are going to blame it all on guns."

"They always do, but they won't get anywhere. That's not the solution."

The singing outside the windows begins getting a little louder

"Do you want me to close the window?"

"No...no. Why don't you open the others. Let's listen in for fun; might help us get our minds off this terrible subject."

The assistant principal gets up and opens all the conference room windows

"I don't hear anything."

"They're playing jump rope and just now swapping roles. They'll be at it again in a minute. They've got a long rope so three can be skipping at the same time."

"My office faces the playground and I'm used to watching them. One will start with a rhyme, and then a second child will jump in and continue the rhyme, followed by a third so there are three skipping to the cadence all together. They're very clever."

> *O-ba-ma, O-ba-ma*
> *Where we're you born?*
> *Ha-wai-i, Ha-wai-i*
> *It says on the form.*
>
> *O-ba-ma, O-ba-ma*
> *The form looks fake.*
> *Admit it's Kenya*
> *For good-ness sake.*
>
> *O-ba-ma, O-ba-ma*
> *Now that you're free.*
> *Go home to Af-ri-ca*
> *To live in a tree.*

"Looks like our young students are into politics!"

"They're very tuned-in. Tiffany's dad is not only a big donor to this academy, but a big shot in the Republican Party as well."

"The second boy in has an uncle who serves in the Maryland legislature. Nice kid."

> *Hill-er-y, Hill-er-y*
> *Your emails say*
> *You knew about Ben-ghazi;*
> *They died any-way.*

Hill-er-y, Hill-er-y
Did you hear them wail?
If the dead could talk
You'd go straight to jail.

Hill-er-y, Hill-er-y
You should write a book.
We'll name it for you –
"The Life of a Crook."

(*Laughter in the conference room*) "These kids were babes then!"

"I asked Tricia about that. I asked her where they get ideas for their rhymes. She said from dinner talk at home. Her mom and dad are political gurus!"

Mus-lims, Mus-lims
Murderers and creeps;
You don't be-long here
Walking on our streets.

Mus-lims, Mus-lims
We can't see your face.
Are you not part of
The hu-man race?

Mus-lims, Mus-lims
We should send you home.
There's so many rats there
You won't feel alone.

"Josh Philbrook's dad is a minister. He's the one jumping now."

"Candy, the pretty girl in pink, is really smart. Wants to be a lawyer."

"She'll be a good one for sure! She's about to sing. Listen in."

Ammo and A-Ks, Ammo and A-Ks
Hand them to me.

I just saw a lib-er-al
Scamper up a tree.

Ammo and A-K's, Ammo and A-Ks
Take 'em to the shore.
Black rats have in-fes-ted
Bal-ti-more.

Ammo and A-Ks, Ammo and A-Ks
Wanna start a fight?
Just try messin' with
My second 'mendment right!

"Emily's parents belong to a prayer club. They're very religious. You can tell. She's so well-mannered…Ops! She just stepped on the rope!"

"Well, we should attend to business. But, I just can't get these shootings out of my head. How do these things happen in America? What's gone wrong? Why this upsurge?"

Donald Trump, Donald Trump
You're our man.
Fight-ing to make
America great a-gain.

Donald Trump, Donald Trump
Ignore the fake news.
If you say it's true
It becomes our view.

Donald Trump, Donald Trump
To you we sing;
If we had our way
We'd crown you king.

"It's hard to pinpoint what's gone wrong. But, it wasn't like this before. There were mass shootings, of course. But this seems different. These killers aren't just crazy; they're angry. They're mad at something. They're somehow being stirred up into a frenzy."

"These two gunman were in their twenties. And they were white. I think they just want to get back to a time when everyone spoke English and were proud to be Americans."

"Well, there's hope on the horizon. Look at these kids in the playground. They're smart, politically attuned and ambitious. They come from good families. Families that care about their communities. Families that go to church. Families that pray together. They're our future, and so there's a good day coming. In the meantime, all we can do is put up with what's happening and just try to figure out how things got to be so wrong."

SEVEN

The Trump Zone – "The Prize"
(Trump, Putin and Un share the Nobel Peace Prize)

(Rod Serling's voice over theme music for *The Twilight Zone*) "Imagine time, space and matter converging in the tiny prism of one man's brain, from which only dull light emerges and is so distorted as to be indistinguishable from reality, where truth lies in darkness, and where men are free to express shameless intolerances with impunity. A place where women are treated as playthings, where friends are regarded as foes and foes regaled as friends. A place so far beyond the edges of human compassion and dignified behavior that everything real is fake and everything fake is real. Look! There's a signpost just ahead. Brace yourself. You are about to enter...*The Trump Zone*."

Scene One

[*The setting is the first lady's dressing room in the residential quarters of the White House. The hour is late, and Melania Trump, dressed in her silk nightgown, is brushing her hair, preparing to go to bed. There's a knock on the door and Donald J. Trump, the 45th President of the United States, still wearing his work attire – blue suit, jacket unbuttoned, red tie hanging too low – enters the room. He appears to be quite excited.*]

(Melania) "This better be important; I'm about to call it a day."

(Trump) "It's more than important...I have incredible news!"

(Melania) "Okay, what's with this latest 'incredible' news? Did Pelosi resign?"

(Trump) "Better than that!...(*Rubbing his hands*) I've been nominated to receive a Nobel Prize!"

(Melania) "That's very nice, dear. (*Continues brushing*) What in? Chemistry perhaps...for the way you're getting along so well with Congress?" (*Squelches a sarcastic laugh*)

(Trump) "Make all the jokes you want, but this is terrific. I'm nominated for the Peace Prize."

(Melania) "The *Peace* Prize! Are you kidding! Did you hear this on *Fox News*?"

(Trump) "They're even talking about it on *CNN*. This time it isn't fake news. It's for real!"

(Melania, *picks up her nail file and starts filing*) "Don't hundreds of people get nominated?"

(Trump) "I don't know...I suppose that's possible. But who are they going to pick over me?"

(Melania) "In all honesty, darling, what have you done to deserve a peace-maker award?"

(Trump) "Are you kidding? I've done lots of things! Take Iran. They'd probably have more nukes than Frisco has fags if it wasn't for me. They don't dare mess with me like they did with Obama. They know they wouldn't know what hit 'em if they did." (*Uppercuts the air*)

(Melania) "That doesn't sound very peace-like to me."

(Trump) "That's because ex-models and White House wives don't need to know what it takes to make peace. I know it takes big weapons and willingness to use 'em to make real peace."

(Melania) "Isn't that what your pal Kim is saying? Yet you want to disarm him don't you?"

(Trump) "That's different. He's...he's...(*frustrated*) That's just different, that's all."

(Melania *has put down her file and has been studying her cell phone*) "It says here that former winners include Presidents Carter and Obama."

(Trump) "Peanut man! Carter's a born loser; terrible president. What did he ever do? Obama! What a joke! Purely political. They couldn't resist picking a Black man who's president."

(Melania) "He didn't start any new wars."

(Trump) "That's right...but it took *me* to end the war that he couldn't manage. There's no more ISIS, remember? All we're doing now is mopping up...ISIS is no longer a threat."

(Melania) "Didn't you just have a Nobel Peace Prize winner in the Oval Office?"

(Trump) "Yeah, that really surprised me. I knew she had won a Nobel Prize but I figured it was for something like books, ya know. Something she might have written. Said her mother and a zillion brothers were killed by ISIS. I didn't challenge her on that because I didn't want to embarrass her. She should have known that ISIS doesn't exist anymore."

(Melania) "She must have earned the award for something."

(Trump) "Maybe. I'd like to investigate her claim though. Could have been the water heater in their house exploded and she survived and the others didn't. She said something about Yahtzee. Maybe they were playing a game when it happened. Who knows with them?"

(Melania) "Them?...And who might 'them' be?"

(Trump) "Don't play that game with me. You know who I mean. Them women...them...them cover-my-head-with-a-towel types... them refugees. Always bitching; never satisfied."

(Melania, *getting up*) "Well, on that fine note I think I'll go to bed."

(Trump) "You'll see. I'm going to win this prize. You can come with me to Sweden."

(Melania) "Norway…But whatever. I'm going to bed; you go work on your acceptance speech."

Scene Two

[*The five members of the Norwegian Nobel Committee are meeting privately in Oslo to consider the 2019 nominees for the Peace Prize. The Chairman opens the proceedings.*]

"Gentlemen, I trust you have taken time to carefully review the nominations."

(All) "We have Mr. Chairman."

"Excellent. And I see that you have followed procedure and created separate stacks for those considered 'Exceptionally Highly Qualified,' 'Very Highly Qualified,' 'Qualified,' 'Qualified with Reservations,' and 'Not Qualified.'"

"Yes, we have done so, Mr. Chairman."

"I've taken the liberty of examining the stacks, mine included, to determine if certain nominees are considered to be 'Exceptionally Qualified' by the entire committee."

"Very good, Mr. Chairman."

"The findings were most interesting. The names of three nominees appeared in everyone's highest ranking stack – Kim Jong Un, Vladimir Putin and Donald Trump."

"So, Mr. Chairman, are you proposing that we focus exclusively on those three?"

"Yes, I think that's proper procedure since we seem to have some sort of consensus. Would someone care to address nominee Vladimir Putin?"

"I will volunteer, Mr. Chairman. Vladimir Putin is in a unique position to engage in war or peace. His role in Syria can legitimately be characterized as a 'peacemaker' by balancing the forces of President Assad against the Western-backed rebels. Without that delicate balance, one side would overrun the other and create a major catastrophe, likely incentivizing more outside intervention and escalating the violence and bloodshed."

"I will support that summation, Mr. Chairman, and add that President Putin's close relationship with Iran also deters American and European aggression against Iran."

"Any concerns about Ukraine?"

"Mr. Chairman, more than half the Ukrainians consider themselves Russian. By providing an outlet, President Putin has ostensibly prevented a civil war."

"Alright, President Putin appears to have strong support, what about Chairman Un?"

"A bit of an unpredictable sort, to be sure, but for the first time he's open to negotiations to curtail development of a nuclear arsenal. That's a very significant step forward."

"Mr. Chairman, it's also consistent with a critical component of our deliberation instructions. It can unquestionably be argued that Chairman Un can be credited for 'holding and promoting peace congresses.' That's unprecedented behavior from him."

"Which, I suppose, is a natural segue to the nomination of President Trump. You can't have a 'congress' with just one participant. The man on the other side of the negotiating table was the American president. I could well argue (*reading from the committee's mandate*) that President Trump has 'done the most or best work for fraternity between nations.' Never have North Korea, Russia and the United States been more aligned."

"That one statement leads me to the conclusion that all three nominees are most deserving of the Nobel Peace Prize. Shall we award our prestigious prize to all three?"

"Since we have no cause or reason to eliminate any one of them, I would propose that it only represents sound judgment to select all three."

"Gentlemen, do I have a motion?"

"I move that the 2019 Nobel Peace Prize be awarded jointly to President Vladimir Putin of Russia, Chairman Kim Jong Un of North Korea, and United States President Donald J. Trump…I'll add to my motion that this represents our finest work in this area to date."

"All those in favor, say 'aye' and raise your hand." (*Ayes all around and five hands are raised in the air*) "Gentlemen, thank you for your service. You are dismissed."

Scene Three

[*The setting is the Oval Office in the White House. The president, his entire family, Secretary of State Pompeo and Vice President Michael Pence are gathered around a special phone anticipating word from Oslo on the Nobel Prize Committee's decision.*]

(*Suddenly, the phone rings and the president picks it up*) "This is the president."

(Chairman) "Mr. President. This is the Chairman of the Nobel Prize Committee. It is my great pleasure to inform you that you, along with Russian President Vladimir Putin and North Korean Chairman Kim Jong Un, are recipients of the 2019 Nobel Prize for Peace."

(Trump) "I knew it!…I knew it!…I knew it!…Thank you Mr.

Chairman. This is great news. A great decision. Makes up for all the bad decisions you fellas made in the past."

(Chairman) "I beg your pardon. What did you say, Mr. President?"

(Trump) "Oh, nothing. Nothing at all. I'm thrilled and you should be honored. I've gotta go."

(*Trump hangs up the phone and raises his arms in victory*) "I told you so!"

(Pompeo, *looking a little surprised*) "A well-deserved honor Mr. President."

(*The president picks up Pence and twirls him around*) "Pretty good, huh Mikey?"

(Melania) "Is it strange that there are two other winners and they are those guys?"

(Trump) "Not at all! We're the 'gang of three.' Pompeo, get them on the line."

(*Secretary Pompeo dials on a second special phone that does not offer speaker service so only the president's side of the conversation can be heard*)

(Pompeo) "Mr. President, we're lucky with our timing…Putin and Un are on the line."

(Trump, *on the phone*) "Hey guys, what do you make of the news? Pretty sensational don't you think?"

(*After a pause*) "No, I don't think it's unusual. I think it's great!"

(*Another pause as he listens*) "I disagree. I think we should issue a joint statement."

(*Another long pause*) "No, okay, too formal, let's go with 'The Three Amigos.'"

(*More waiting*) "Okay, okay. No joint statement, but let's have dinner in Sweden."

(*Another pause as Trump listens*) "Ah, it isn't? Okay, then the place where we meet to accept the awards, wherever that is. This is tremendous. It'll be just like after World War II with Reagan, Churchill and Lenin. Lots of photo ops. It'll be great."

(*They hang up*) "See everyone…I told you so! That just about seals my re-election!"

Scene Four

[*The setting is Oslo, Norway where the five committee members are seen leaving City Hall by themselves in an unusually mechanical-type march at night after issuing their decision. They then enter an awaiting flying saucer. The setting then switches to the interior of the alien spaceship where the Commander is addressing his crew.*]

(Commander Zoe) "Very nicely done, my fellow comrades from Planet Zenon. You have performed well."

(First Officer Zan) "Thank you Commander Zoe. (*Looking at the five members of the Prize Committee*) What shall we do with them now?"

(Commander Zoe) "Earthling scientists refer to our homeland only as Space Object X3479. But, that's understandable because they have not progressed beyond infighting among what they refer to as 'nations,' driven to confrontations by avenging leaders. You can now reprogram the five cooperating Nobel Prize Committee members' brains from 'Stupid and Diabolical' back to the way they originally tested which was 'Brilliant and Honorable.'"

(First Officer Zan) "And what do we do with them following the reprogramming?"

(Commander Zoe) "We can release them. They will have no recollection of what they have done for us. And, we are now certain from this experiment that we from the great Planet Zenon can occupy and control this planet they call Earth whenever we want with no difficulty given the gullibility and insecurity of their leaders, especially the one they call Trump. *(Begins smiling wickedly)*...We might not even have to bother programming his little brain!"

(First Officer Zan) "But, isn't he the leader of what these Earthlings refer to as the "free world?""

(Commander Zoe) "An odd choice indeed for people who are free which is why our timing is so perfect. A small dose of flattery and one as insecure as he is will be begging to do our bidding!"

(First Officer Zan) "Ah, feed him a sugar cube and he'll be eating out of our hands forever...It's so easy!"

(The scene ends with the crew of the spaceship from Planet Zenon laughing hysterically)

Scene Five

[As the five members of the Prize Committee are seen in the blurry background descending a ladder from the alien space ship, the camera focuses on a man in an ill-fitting dark suit smoking a cigarette.]

"You are witnessing five men returning to a world that will look very much the same to them but will forever be different – unwitting participants in a successful experiment in human behavior modification. What they don't know is that they have played a key role in sculpting human destiny – a destiny now far more uncertain than ever with the valued concept of 'peacemaker' irrevocably redefined. They and their fellow voyagers on Planet Earth have entered into a new dimension of the mind, where good is seen as evil and evil is seen as good. Where world leaders behave as if it's all about them; where peace and war are interchangeable and acceptable. Humankind has just entered...*The Trump Zone.*"

EIGHT

America's Vanishing "Cornutopia"
(Fruits vie for the First Family's Thanksgiving table)

Part One: A Fable

It was the most exciting of days – selections would be made as to who would fill the cornucopia serving as the centerpiece of the president's annual Thanksgiving Day family dinner in the White House. Presiding over the process would be "The Colonel" – the latest in a long line of ears of corn from America's Heartland. He'd be assisted by a bright Naval orange known as "The Captain" from a venerable grove in Florida.

The cornucopia was always so perfect that it became known as the "Corn-Utopia" among inner circles. It was in everyone's dreams. It was what you lived for.

Gathered atop a broad table were all the hopeful applicants from every variety of fruit, vegetable and nut. The morning had been devoted to last-minute preparations, as the contestants feverishly primped and polished themselves to win the judges' approval.

The proceedings began with a toot from a snail's shell that brought everyone to attention.

(The Corn Colonel) "Okay, everyone, quiet now as we're starting. Captain – begin!"

(The Naval Captain *reads from a scroll*) "Will the apple finalists please come forward."

Four red-ripened apples work their way through the crowd and station themselves in front of the Colonel and the Captain, who holds a special scroll with notes.

Whispers around the table indicated there was a clear favorite – a Red Delicious apple from the State of Washington, the nation's top producer.

"Apple Number One, please introduce yourself…followed by the others in order."

"I, sir, am a Red Delicious apple from the State of Washington."

"I, sir, am a 'sweet with a touch-of-tart' Honeycrisp from the State of New York."

"Colonel, sir, I am a cherry-red Gala from California."

"And I am a 'sweet and spicy' Ginger Gold from the State of Michigan."

The Colonel and the Captain confer in private, referring to their notes.

"We have our instructions…*nothing* from New York or California."

"The Red Delicious is clearly the choice…but didn't Washington go…?"

"Yes, with *her*! It was a horrible landslide – 52.6 percent to 36.9 percent."

"Then it's settled…Stall for a bit and then make the announcement."

(The Captain, *addressing the crowd*) "The winner is…Michigan's Ginger Gold!"

Cheers are mixed with gasps of surprise as the Ginger Gold accepts the honor.

"Okay everyone, quiet down please. We'll move on to the peach finalists."

Three beautiful peaches from California, New Jersey and Georgia come forward.

(Colonel *privately to the Captain*) "We'll have to pretend to think this one over."

"Just give all three a long look and tug on your silk beard a while to appear deliberative."

"This might be the biggest no-brainer of the competition." (*Laughing*)

"Maybe not...remember there are cranberries from (*squelching a laugh*) Massachusetts!"

"About as big a chance (*giggling quietly*) as those cherries from Washington, D.C.!"

(The Captain *speaks*) "This was a hard decision, but the winner is... the Georgia peach!"

The crowd applauds politely as the Georgia peach blushingly accepts the award.

(The Captain, *conferring again privately with the Colonel*) "We might have a problem."

"In what category?"

"Pineapple."

"How so?"

"Two things: pineapples have long been held as symbols of 'welcome and friendship.' You know, like the Statue of Liberty as a fruit. That poses an obvious problem with you know who. Another problem is there are only two entrants – one from Brazil and the other, of course, from Hawaii. You remember Hawaii (*checks notes*) – 62.2 percent to 30.0 percent! Widest margin of any state...You'd be roasted and I'd get peeled!"

"Let's convert this into an opportunity to show how 'international' we are."

"Great idea! All he knows about Brazil anyway is that the women are hot."

The event proceeded for a while longer without incident, but as time rolled on uneasiness swept over the table as there were rumblings that things didn't seem to be quite right…a sense that the judging wasn't really fair. An Arizona apricot, for example, had been passed over amidst murmurings from the judges' table about "a McCain" and "a Flake," and no one knew of any connection between those strange names and varieties of fruits, vegetables and nuts. Eventually the restless crowd became more outspoken.

"What about the avocados?" someone in the back dared to shout.

"And, how about strawberries? They should be included!"

These unexpected disruptions alarmed the Colonel and the Captain, who grew angry.

(The Captain, *speaking with a noticeable tone of derision*) "The only avocados entered in the competition are from…Mexico."

(The Colonel *adds*) "Same for the strawberries…also aliens from south of the border."

The contestants were now growing bolder and getting unruly.

"What difference does it make if they're the best of their class?"

"It makes a huge difference! Thanksgiving is an American holiday! There's no room for outsiders in an all-American cornucopia… Besides (*inadvertently*) we have our orders."

"But that's discrimination!" screamed a stalk of rhubarb from Connecticut.

(The Colonel *speaks*) "That doesn't concern me because many fine, upstanding, patriotic fruits and vegetables agree with me."

"But you're infusing politics into what's supposed to be an open and fair competition."

"All I'm saying is that if you disagree with our decisions and want to leave this table now – go right ahead and leave. And as for your baseless accusation, I'll have you know that I don't have a discriminatory hair in my husk. As for you, you're acting like a socialist!"

The rhetoric only intensified and soon a boycott was organized as a means of protest.

(The Captain) "Wow! That didn't go very well."

(The Colonel) "Not a problem. We'll make do. We'll probably be rewarded."

Part Two: A Real Life Fable

The setting is a formal dining room in the White House where the president and his immediate family are preparing to enjoy a traditional Thanksgiving dinner. This time, however, cameras have been called in as the president has stated he'd like to address the nation on this special occasion. The president is seated at the head of the table, his wife Melania on his left, his daughter Ivanka to his right. Next to Ivanka sits son-in-law Jared Kushner and opposite him son Donald Jr. with Baron Trump on his right, and opposite him invited guest Senator Tom Cole, R-Oklahoma. Rounding out the table seated opposite each other are son Eric and his wife Lara.

(Chief Cameraman) "We're close to air time, Mr. President, are you ready?"

(Trump) "I'm ready…should I be standing or remain seated?"

(Director) "It might be a more family-like chat if you remain seated. All we have to do is move the cornucopia aside so there's nothing blocking the camera's view."

(Trump, *to Melania*) "Is that Cole's tribe? Does he have to leave?"

(Melania) "He means the centerpiece, darling…the horn of plenty in the middle there."

(Trump) "Did I order plenty of horns to be played?"
(Melania) "No, there'll be no horns this time. He means that basket of fruit."

(Trump) "Oh yeah, the basket. Funny thing about that. I'm told it's supposed to be full of fruit and all kinds of stuff but this year it's only corn and oranges. Something about some rotten berries from Mexico that spread disease and spoiled the whole lot. Wouldn't ya know!"

A camera crew member removes the cornucopia, setting it aside and the head cameraman stations himself at the end of the table facing the president. As the time for the live program approaches, the director lurches forward in a state of alarm.

(Director) "Mr. President. There's been a glitch. Your teleprompter isn't working!"

(Trump) "Don't worry. No problem. I can handle this. I don't like those things anyway."

(Director) "Okay, Mr. President. As long as you're comfortable."

(Trump) "I'm always comfortable speaking to the great American people."

(Director) "Keep in mind we're celebrating Thanksgiving. You know, the Mayflower story…"

(Trump) "We're there supposed to be flowers in that basket?"

(Director) "No…the Mayflower *ship*…You know…landing at Plymouth Rock."

(Trump) "Okay, okay. Got it. I remember that story. The Indians came to dinner."

(Director) "That's correct, Mr. President. (*Sigh of relief*) Now stand by…3…2…1…We're live!"

The president, who was seated, stands up, the jacket of his blue suit unbuttoned and his red tie hanging way too far below his bulging belly. He begins to speak.

(Trump) "Happy Thanksgiving everyone. As you can see my family and I were about to enjoy a traditional dinner featuring of course a turkey... but Joe Biden couldn't come so we'll probably settle for soup and salad. (*Long silence*)... Just a little joke to get things going."

Melania and Ivanka are seen burying their heads in their hands; Don Jr. laughs.

(Trump) "Thanksgiving is a special occasion in our country. It's an all-American holiday – like the Fourth of July, Presidents Day, and Christmas. It's a day when we express our gratitude to our Founding Fathers – great Americans like George Washington, Thomas Jefferson and Abraham Lincoln – who arrived on the Mayflower... at a rock."

Strange glances and nervous foot twitching at the table. The president resumes.

(Trump) "They came here seeking freedom from Communism, and were welcomed into a new country that would soon be given to them by friendly Indians, including Princess Pocahontas...Not the Pocahontas from Massachusetts who's pretty much a communist herself, but a much smarter and far better-looking Indian girl who presented these future great presidents with gifts of corn and...ah (*glances at the cornucopia that had been set aside*) baskets of oranges. I'll tell you – that first Thanksgiving was a very big deal.

The Indians and the first Americans got along very well you know. During the Revolutionary War they served as code talkers, confounding enemy communications. They joined units that guarded our airports. We owe a great debt of gratitude to our Indian friends who welcomed us to America, which is why I've invited Tom Cole here to join us at our table as sort of a way of more accurately recreating that first Thanksgiving meal. If you didn't know, Tom's an Indian from Oklahoma. (*Directs attention to Cole*) I was hoping Tom that you'd wear your headdress but you must have missed the memo."

Undeterred by the silence and blank stares, and noticing a signal from the director that his time was running short, the president shifts into his rehearsed closing remarks.

"I asked to speak to you today on this momentous occasion to remind everyone in this great country… well, not quite everyone, those who came to America legally in the tradition of Washington, Jefferson and Lincoln… that we have much to be thankful for. The progress we have made in less than three years is unprecedented. Truly historical. The economy is booming; thank you. Never been better. Our borders are being secured against unwanted new arrivals (*Tom Cole rolls his eyes*). We're on friendly terms with former enemies; I'm sending a turkey to Vladimir and Kim as a way of saying 'thank you.' We're fixing bad treaties negotiated by former presidents who had no idea what they were doing that damaged America and Americans…What can I say? *You're* thankful that *I'm* your president because, let's admit it… I'm making America great again."

The camera slowly pulls back as the president proudly takes his seat. He's issuing a closing thumbs up. Melania struggles with a smile. Tom Cole stares blankly at his plate.

Before the telecast ends, the camera pans to a corner of the table where the cornucopia had been moved aside. The horn of plenty is empty. The ears of corn and the naval oranges are nowhere to be seen. No one had taken notice, but while the president was concluding his remarks, the Colonel, the Captain and all the other ears of corn and oranges had quietly departed, overcome by shock, disbelief and despair for cornutopia.

NINE

Moby Don
(The story of a ruthlessly destructive orange whale)

The family had once again gathered to celebrate a national holiday. It was raining outside and the children, growing restless, asked their father if Uncle Ned could tell them another story. "That's fine," he said, "but as always don't let him fill you up with his liberal nonsense. Ask him to stick to some of the literary classics. He can't go wrong."

So the children, the oldest about nine, ran to find their uncle, who was reading the morning newspaper. "Daddy says it's okay if you tell us a story, Uncle Ned, as long as it's a liberty classic. And you can't fill us up with your library nonsense, okay?"

"Let me see. What was the last story I told you?"

"It was the one about the bad king who coughed up feathers for telling all those lies."

"Oh yes, *The King's Parrot*. But now you want a classic tale do you?"

"That's what dad wants you to stick to...whatever classic means."

"Classics are stories written by famous authors that have withstood the test of time."

"Is time something we'll get tested on in school?" one of the boys asked.

"No, it means that readers never grow tired of reading or hearing those stories."

"What old story are you going to tell us, Uncle Ned?"

"Have you ever heard the story of Moby Don, the Great Orange Whale?"

"No, Uncle Ned," one of the girls responded, "but whales aren't orange!"

"That's true. Moby Don was a white whale, making him one of a kind, but in the glow of sunset when hunters came upon him, his enormous head appeared as bright orange."

"I'd like to see an orange whale!" one of children shouted. "That would be so cool!"

(Ned, under his breath) "Well, all you have to do is watch the news." "But I digress."

(He continues) "There once was a young man, a very good and honest young man, who was seeking adventure. His name was Ishmael and he lived right here in Massachusetts. This was at the time long ago when sperm whales were hunted for their oil, before electricity, as sperm oil was used as fuel for lamps. Ships would set sail out of the Island of Nantucket to hunt for whales in hopes of bringing home barrels of oil and becoming rich. Ishmael thought this would be a great adventure and signed on as a deckhand."

"Did they catch a lot of whales, Uncle Ned?"

"Now you're getting way ahead of the story. The name of the ship was the *Constitution* and its captain was named Ahab. Ahab was missing a leg, and he walked around on a stump made from the jaw of a sperm whale. Can you guess how he lost his leg?"

"Did he get bitten by a snake?" one of children asked.

"Did he step on a land mine?" suggested another.

"Those are good guesses. But Captain Ahab had his leg bitten off by Moby Don!"

(*The children gasp!*) "So Captain Ahab knew about the great orange whale?"

"That's exactly right! His ship was wrecked by Moby Don but he survived and his goal on this next voyage was to find the great orange whale and kill it with a sharp spear attached to long line called a harpoon. More than becoming rich that was his main goal."

"Did he find Moby Don?" one of the children asked.

"He did! But it was long ways away from Nantucket. After sailing for many months, and going around the tip of Africa, the *Constitution* entered the Indian Ocean where years before Captain Ahab had encountered the great white whale and seen its head glowing orange in the waning sunlight. Sure enough, near the equator, Moby Don was spotted."

"How do you get close enough to harpoon a whale?" the oldest boy asked.

"It's tricky! The ship is equipped with several smaller boats and a handful of very courageous men get into these boats and row to where a whale was last seen. Whales, as you know, dive deep beneath the surface of the ocean, and you really never know where they'll pop up. When a whale comes to the surface, the men frantically row towards its massive bulk, then hold their harpoons aloft so they can thrust them into its hide."

"What if they miss?" one of the startled children asked.

"They often do! And, as you'll hear, the whale can tip over their boats, which are small compared to such large creatures, dumping the men into the frigid water to die!"

(*At this the youngest children cover their faces and one begins to whimper*)

"But, more often than not, (*Uncle Ned continues reassuringly*) the harpoons, which remember are attached to long ropes, hit the mark and the boat is taken on what whalers call a 'Washington sleigh ride' as the injured whale dives and rapidly swims away."

"That could be fun!" one of the girls exclaimed. "Like water skiing in a boat!"

"I'm not sure if the harpooners saw it that way, especially when the rope runs out and it's either go under or cut the monster loose. But, let's get back to the story; where were we?"

"Captain Ahab, Uncle Ned, had just spotted Moby Don."

"That's right. Whether it would prove to be good fortune or bad, Captain Ahab was now face-to-face, so to speak, with his adversary, the great orange whale. So, he dispatched the first of the smaller whaling boats, this one called *Truth*. The rowers saw Moby Don rise to the surface not far away, but before they could go into their pursuit, Moby Don charged at them, flipping the boat over, spilling the helpless hunters into the water."

(*The children emit a shout and press their hands momentarily against their ears*)

"Ahab then orders the second boat lowered, this one called *Justice*. The brave men in the boat come up on Moby Don who appears to be resting, but just when *Justice* is getting close the great whale stirs to life and with one mighty swish of its tale destroys the boat."

"Oh, my gosh!" one of the children gasps. "That whale is mean!"

"Back on board the ship, Captain Ahab orders the third and last whaleboat prepared for launch, this time deciding that he himself will take charge of the small crew in a personal battle against the beast. This boat, *Integrity*, is lowered into the water as the crew remaining on the *Constitution* look on, helpless to do anything but hope and pray."

"Go get 'im, Ahab...We're all for you *Integrity*," one of the boys urges.

"Moby Don almost seems to recognize Captain Ahab as the small boat approaches the watchful whale, its massive head now ablaze with color as the day was drawing to an end. Suddenly, the whale swims speedily towards the wooden boat. Ahab and his men anxiously prepare to thrust their harpoons, but just when it's almost in range the great whale lunges into the air, momentarily exposing his massive white and orange body, before crushing *Integrity* with its monumental weight. Captain Ahab's one good leg gets snarled in his harpoon line. He's thrown overboard and disappears into the foam."

(The children crouch together, speechless)

"The angry whale then charges at the *Constitution*, ramming it head on, gouging a massive hole in the side of the ship. Ishmael, grasping a floating piece of timber, is able to paddle away, looking back just in time to see the *Constitution* sink into the abyss."

"So, only Ishmael survives?" a timid, disbelieving voice dares to ask.

"Yes, that's the way the classic tale ends. Ishmael is rescued by a passing ship and lives to tell the story. The story of how truth, justice, integrity and even something as seemingly unsinkable as the Constitution can become vulnerable to a menacing force."

"So, even though we don't know what happens to Moby Don, the hero of the story is Ishmael?" the oldest boy asks, exhibiting a level of maturity beyond his age.

"That's a great point! You should shout 'Call me Ishmael!' in a cry for restoring truth, justice and integrity that we know from the story are more at risk than you'd ever think."

As if on cue, at this point their father enters the room noticing his children attentively seated on the floor around the chair in which their Uncle Ned is sitting

"Is the storytelling over?" he asks derisively.

"Call me Ishmael!" the oldest boy shouts, and the others chime in with that chant.

"That's good; very good. A classic American story! I was afraid he'd be delivering more of his leftist drivel against our great president. I congratulate your restraint, Uncle Ned."

(As they leave the room with their father, the youngest of the girls is heard to ask, "Daddy, can we someday go on a Washington sleigh ride to harpoon that awful and mean orange whale Moby Don who smashed the Constitution?")

TEN

America's Emperor
(Trump escapes to Japan to hide from critics)

<u>Act One, Scene One</u>

[President Trump has just arrived in the Oval Office *(a clock on the wall indicates it's after noon)* and is seen tweeting behind his desk. Acting Chief of Staff Mick Mulvaney knocks and then enters the room. The president doesn't look up and keeps tweeting.]

(Mulvaney) "Good morning…ah, good *afternoon* Mr. President. May I have a word?"

(Trump) "Sure Mick, finishing up here soon…P-E-L-O-S-I…I-S…"

(Mulvaney) "I need to confirm your Memorial Day schedule. It's coming up soon."

(Trump, *tweeting*) "C-R-A-Z-I…Is that when the little shits look for eggs on the lawn?"

(Mulvaney) "No, Mr. President. It's when we honor the nation's fallen soldiers."

(Trump) "Oh, yeah. Got it. What am I supposed to do, pick em' up?"

(Mulvaney) "Well, in the morning you'll lay a wreath at the Tomb of the Unknown Soldier."

(Trump, *still tweeting*) "Who is that guy, anyway?"

(Mulvaney) "Ah, we don't know, that's why he's called 'unknown.'"

(Trump) "Gee, I always thought it was one of those secrety-type things, like the nuclear codes and stuff, that the ordinary people don't know but presidents are told about."

(Mulvaney) "No, nobody knows who it is, Mr. President."

(Trump) "So Obama didn't know?"

(Mulvaney) "No sir, he didn't."

(Trump) "Do I get to wear a uniform?"

(Mulvaney) "No sir, formal civilian attire will do just fine."

(Trump) "Why not a uniform? I'm the Commander-in-Chief and I've been in a war zone. Why shouldn't I wear a uniform with medals and ribbons on such occasions?"

(Mulvaney) "Ah…That's not the protocol, Mr. President."

(Trump) "Well look into it. I think it should be done…and lots of ribbons and medals; at least one more than Kelly has."

(Mulvaney) "Yes, sir, I'll look into it…Now about the wreath ceremony."

(Trump, *still busy tweeting*) "Send Pence."

(Mulvaney) "I beg your pardon, sir."

(Trump, *putting down his cell phone*) "Send Pence to do the wreath thing. I need to get out of Washington. I need to be around *friends*. Get away from that bitch Pelosi and that traitor Mueller. Any suggestions where I can go?" (*Buries his head in his hands careful not to muss his hair*)

(Mulvaney) "With your *friends*; well, let's think. From experience we know it's probably too late to set up anything with Vladimir...or Kim (*keeps thinking*), or Viktor (*long pause*) or even the Saudi Crown Prince...But, hey, I've got an idea – there's a new emperor in Japan!"

(Trump) "New emperor (*sighs deeply*)...I like the sound of that."

(Mulvaney) "Better yet, you have an open invitation from Prime Minister Abe."

(Trump) "Memorial Day in Japan...I'm liking it. That's a long ways away, right?"

(Mulvaney) "Yes, Mr. President, about as far away as you can get."

(Trump) "And they were on our team during the big war, right?"

(Mulvaney) "Ah, not exactly. They were fine during Vietnam and everything since. But, the big war...remember Pearl Harbor?"

(Trump) "Oh yeah, got it. D-Day."

(Mulvaney) "Close enough, Mr. President. Shall I make the arrangements?"

(Trump) "You sure they'll put out the red carpet, give me presents, let me pose with the emperor and all that good stuff? If not, let's press Vladimir for a meeting."

(Mulvaney) "I'm sure they'll do all that and more. We can even arrange for you to give a Memorial Day speech to the troops on one of our aircraft carriers...How's that sound?"

(Trump) "Sounds good...But I want that uniform with all the ribbons and medals."

Act One, Scene Two

[*Rear Admiral Gregory Fenton, head of U.S. Naval Forces in Japan, is seated behind his desk in Yokosuta, Japan reading a message that has just been handed to him by his public affairs officer, Lt. Byron Caswell.*]

(Fenton) "God damn it!"

(Caswell) "What's the matter, sir?"

(Fenton) "This just came in from Indo-Pacific Command in Washington. Here, read it." (*Hands the paper over to his PA officer*)

(Caswell) "So POTUS is coming here over Memorial Day, huh?"

(Fenton) "Yup, and he's going to give a speech to the troops on the Wasp. We have to set it up."

(Caswell) "That shouldn't be too difficult, sir."

(Fenton) "Did you read further down? Did you get to item #3?"

(Caswell, *reading*) "Holy shit!...How are we gonna manage to do that?"

(Fenton) "The *McCain* is in for repairs so we can't ship 'er out." (*Shakes his head while thinking*) "But, as the order says, somehow we have to keep the *USS John S. McCain* 'Out of Sight' while the president's here. Any thoughts on how to do that? (*laughs*) We can't sink it!"

(Caswell) "Did the order come from the White House?"

(Fenton) "Hell, I don't know. Wouldn't be surprised. But, my best guess is that the Pentagon brass got wind of the trip and are just taking precautions; covering their asses. The last thing they want to do is piss off POTUS. He really has a hair up his ass about McCain."

(Caswell) "We can throw a tarp over the name on the stern and pull a tug up alongside."

(Fenton) "That'll help I suppose...But what about the sailors? They'll all be ordered onto the deck of the Wasp for the ceremony and you know McCain's name is on their caps?"

(Caswell) "No problem! We'll give 'em the day off. Let 'em hit the beach. They'll be thrilled."

(Fenton) "They'll miss the president's speech."

(Caswell) "As I said…They'll be thrilled."

(Fenton, *sighing*) "And read me again the part about a uniform with loads of medals."

Act Two, Scene One

[*The president is in a closed-door meeting with Japan's Prime Minister Shinzo Abe and Emperor Naruhito in the posh surroundings of the Akasaka Palace.*]

(Abe) "Welcome, Mr. Pwesident…Let me inorouce you to our new emperor."

(Trump, *shaking hands with Naruhito*) "Glad to meet you Mr. Emperor. Happy Memorial Day."

(Abe) "Ah, yes, Mr. Pwesident. It is your Memorial Day. We are honored."

(Trump) "Thanks." (*Off to the side to Abe*) "Does the emperor here speak English?"

(Abe) "Not so much, Mr. Pwesident. He, too, says he is honored."

(Trump) "Well good…so am I. Here's to D-Day!" (*President offers a 'thumbs up'*)

(Abe) "Did you hear latest from North Korea, Mr. Pwesident? It is wery disturbing."

(Trump, *sounding alarmed*) "Kim's okay isn't he? Some health issue I should know about?"

(Abe) "No, not like that. He's fired off some missiles."

(Trump) "Oh, yeah, they did brief me about that. Nothing really. Short-range stuff."

(Abe) "Mr. Pwesident. They are close neighbor and our enemy. We are werried."

(Trump) "Don't be bothered. Some of my people are disturbed, as well as others, but not me. Kim has given me his word. He promised no more big launches. These are just (*pinches his small fingers*) little missiles."

(Abe) "Are you shu Mr. Pwesident? Little missile can deliber big wallop." (*Raises his arms as if a big blast is going off*) "We in Japan don't need any more big wallops!"

(Trump, *upper-cutting the air*) "The only big wallop you're going to see is me knocking out China. They're sucking wind over my latest tariffs (*chuckles*). The ol' President of the United States Donald J. Trump K.O. punch. KA-POW!"

(Abe) "But, you also imposing tariffs on us. We're friends. We're not China."

(Trump, *throwing another mock punch*) "Well, you'd just better duck... I'm getting hungry (*patting his bulging waistline*). Is it time for lunch? I'd kill for a burger."

Act Two, Scene Two

[*The president and first lady are seated at ringside at Ryogoku Kokugikan Stadium in Tokyo to watch a championship sumo wrestling contest. The first lady speaks.*]

(Melania, *whispering to her husband*) "These men are disgusting! Why are they wearing diapers?"

(Trump) "Hush! Someone could hear you. They're wrestlers. You'll see."

(Melania) "I've seen too much of them already!"

(Trump) "Don't you and Mrs. Abe have some shopping to do?"

(Abe, *interrupting*) "Mr. Pwesident. This championship match. You need to watch."

(Trump) "Is this fixed like our wrestling? I mean, do they know in advance who's going to win?"

(Abe) "Oh no! This centuries old tradition. No fix in advance!"

(Trump) "So, it's not rigged so guys like Hulk Hogan can get their own TV shows and comic books. That's unusual." (*Aside*) "I kind of like it when things are fixed in my favor."

(Abe, *excited*) "Look! It's over. We have champion. You can pwesent you Pwesident's Cup now."

(*Trump, wearing slippers, gets help carrying a 4.5 foot high, 70-pound silver-coated trophy into the ring and presents it to the winner who easily holds it aloft*)

(Trump, *to Prime Minister Abe*) "Can this big dude speak English?"

(Abe) "No, Mr. Pwesident. What you want me tell him?"

(Melania, *shouting from ringside*) "Tell him you're thrilled to be around someone fatter than you are!"

(Abe) "What she say?"

(Trump) "Um…she said she was surprised at how *fast* these wrestlers are for such big men."

(Abe) "Yes, they are strong and fast. Can winner keep trophy?"

(Trump) "No, I had that specially made. I'd like it to be recognized as the official sumo championship trophy for centuries to come. I've engraved my name in big capital letters at the top, of course, like on my buildings, and now you can list the names of all the champions year-by-year in smaller print beneath it. Sound good?"

(Abe) "I will tell him you congratulate him and his name go on trophy. (*Abe leans over, speaks and then listens to the wrestler*)…Him acknowledge congratulations and want to say that you could be sumo wrestler too, maybe even champion."

(Trump) "Of course I'd be champion!" (*Trump grabs the announcer's microphone, moves to the center of the ring, looks up to the rafters and begins speaking as a completely disinterested crowd starts filing out*) "I could be a sumo wrestling champion. Big time! I could the best all time at whatever I set out to do. I'm already the best American president of all time…I could take over the Federal Reserve and send those know-nothing imposters back to school…I know more about warfare than all my generals combined…I know how to win trade wars…I know how to improve our aircraft carriers…I, Donald J. Trump, can and will make America great again!"

(Abe, *who was all the time talking to the sumo wrestling champ*) "Did you say someting, Mr. Pwesident? We should move on. Car is waiting for us outside."

Act Three, Scene One

[*Trump is back in the Oval Office joined by acting Chief of Staff Mick Mulvaney, Senator Lindsey Graham and Press Secretary Sarah Sanders. He's acting moody and obviously isn't happy, so Lindsey Graham speaks up.*]

(Graham, *clapping vigorously*) "Wonderful, Mr. President! A great trip. Lots of good coverage on *Fox News*."

(Trump) "Bullshit, Lindsey! All the news coverage has been bad. How Bolton – who let him out anyway? – says that Kim has broken the accord; how our shit-covered farmers are suffering so terribly from the tariff wars; how Iran is snubbing its nose at us; how the Navy was instructed to keep that McCain ship out of sight during my speech; and now Mueller – an awful man, a true anti-Trump guy since he didn't get the job he wanted – goes on television to question what Barr has said and what I'm telling everyone. Now, tell me Lindsey, just how wonderful should that make a returning president feel?"

(Mulvaney) "Maybe so, Mr. President, but the American people, the *real* American people, the true patriots, don't pay any attention to that crap. It's fake news to them."

(Sanders) "You're being much too hard on yourself, Mr. President. Who can name the bitch who testified against Judge Kavanaugh? She was a one-day wonder. Stormy Daniels is ancient history. The people I talk to laugh when they hear that Kim Jong Un said Biden has a low IQ, and they laugh even harder when they learn that you agreed with him. Cheer up! Mueller came and now he's gone. Hell, those who watched him on TV just wanted to hear what his voice sounded like."

(Graham) "Sarah's right, Mr. President. She just needs to stay on point – vindication! No collaboration; no obstruction; no cover up! The people believe you. You could tell them that Pelosi was found in bed with A.O.C. and the tabloids would lap it up. Both would deny it, of course, but, trust me, true blue-blooded Americans would believe *you!*"

(Trump) "Interesting. Nice find. Should I instruct Sarah to bring up this steamy Pelosi-A.O.C roll-in-the-hay thing at the next press conference?"

(Mulvaney) "No, for chrissakes; Graham was just making a point! We did enough damage to Pelosi running that doctored video clip. People ate it up! Mueller has gone into hiding. The Democrats running for president are stumbling all over themselves trying to get headlines. Except Biden. Biden's his own worst enemy. He'll fumble his way into the nomination and melt like hot butter in the debates. We're golden. We should be happy!"

(Sanders) "And the whole world has seen Prime Minister Abe eating out of your hand like a park pigeon."

(Trump) "Okay, okay! I'm listening. We'll see what happens. The trip really wasn't that bad. They served some great French food –

imagine, Japs serving French food! There's even a new sumo cup that's named after me...Oh that reminds me. How'd McCain ever get his name on a Navy destroyer? Someone get a hold of the fucking war department and find out if they're building any more aircraft carriers. I'm going to show them how to build a better plane launching system and I want it implemented right away and I want my name, Donald J. Trump, emblazoned in big letters on the ass end of that carrier. Go!"

Act Three, Scene Two

[*That same night in the residential quarters of the White House. Melania Trump, wearing a silky nightgown, is brushing her hair at a dressing table while her husband paces back-and-forth in the room dressed in a Superman T-shirt and Sponge Bob boxer shorts.*]

(Trump) "I'm feeling a bit better about the trip. Lindsey's convinced that all the garbage that happened back home won't amount to anything. Sanders says the world saw the prime minister eating out of my hand like a parked car. It wasn't bad; we'll see what happens."

(Melania) "I found the prime minister's wife to be a terrible bore but I did my duty as always."

(Trump) "You didn't have to call me fat in front of the whole goddamn arena."

(Melania) "That's what you get, darling, for telling me to go shopping!"

(Trump) "Okay, truce. Do you think that Mueller's statement will set the public against us?"

(Melania) "Lindsey doesn't seem to think so."

(Trump) "Lindsey's a toady...Of course, he's my toady, so I like him."

(Melania, *removing her lashes*) "They're all toadies – Mulvaney, McConnell...Especially Pence."

(Trump) "Christ! Pence told the cadets at West Point that they'll be going to war. But, then again, he'd eat grass if I told him to. Takes care of wreath laying and all that crap."

(Melania) "Did *you* get anything out of the trip besides *your* name on a big silver cup?"

(Trump, *pacing, then turning to his wife*) "You know, I did. They have an emperor who serves until he dies and we have a president who's limited to two terms – eight years. And, those eight years can be tormented by liberal scumbags who just want to bring you down. They won't let go. They won't let me get things done. (*Pauses to think*) I know how to get things done. I'm the only one. I can fix things. I'm Donald Trump! (*Raises an arm in the air with a pointed finger and begins to stalk around the room*) I need to be above it all. I need to be permanently *above* the presidency. America can learn something from Japan. We need an emperor! Not a figurehead numbskull like Naruhito – God, the man's clueless. He wants to *shepherd* his people. Fuck shepherding the people. The American people need a leader! The American people need an emperor as in the glory days of Japan before all this prime minister shit! If America is ever going to be great again they need ME! They need an American emperor. They need Emperor Trump!"

(Melania, *putting down her hairbrush*) "Okay, emperor, I've had enough. I'm going to bed. Don't stay up all night tweeting and you should get a new nightshirt – that one's way too short and shows your big tummy. You look more like a sumo wrestler than an emperor. Good night."

ELEVEN

The Cracker-in-Chief Visits NASCARland
(Trump makes a surprise appearance at the Daytona 500)

[Note: Buck Laughlin is not an original character. Fred Willard played Buck Laughlin in the fabulously funny 2000 film *Best in Show*. In it, Laughlin is a wise-cracking commentator at the Mayflower Dog Show sitting alongside straight man Trevor Beckwith, played by Jim Piddock. Our dialogue is modeled after their exchanges.]

It's February 16, 2020. The setting is the Fox television booth high above the track at the Daytona Motor Speedway, site of today's Daytona 500 NASCAR race. It's raining, but the stands are filling and preparations for the broadcast continue in hopes that the rain will let up and the race will proceed as planned. Seated behind the main microphone is veteran announcer Buck Laughlin; next to him is racing expert and former NASCAR chairman and CEO Brian England. The show's director instructs them to "stand by."

"Good afternoon racing fans and welcome to Daytona, Florida for the opening race of the 2020 NASCAR racing season. I'm Buck Laughlin; sitting next to me – not too close of course – is former NASCAR Chairman and CEO, Brian England…Well, Brian, it's raining but we're up here in the booth high and dry so that's something positive, huh?"

"Well, yes, Buck, but things are going to have to dry out a bit if we're going to have a race today. Unfortunately, the weather outlook isn't too promising."

"I drove over here in the rain. Are you saying Brian that these professional drivers can't drive in the rain? Aren't these expensive cars equipped with windshield wipers?"

"It's not the cars, Buck, but track conditions. These boys are going to be flying around that oval at speeds up to 200 miles per hour and they'll need a dry track to run safely."

"Two hundred m-p-h you say? That's mighty fast. I was doing just under 90."

"You need to slow down a bit, Buck, on those freeways. This of course is a controlled track and built for speed. But, it takes more than a good car to win the Daytona 500. Like most everything in sports, it's a mental game and a lot of strategy is involved."

"That's interesting, Brian. I guess that will give us something to talk about. I was wondering what we might tell our audience throughout the day if all that was happening was cars racing in circles. You know, 'the blue car is ahead right now but watch out for the red car.' That sort of thing. Can get pretty boring after a while if you ask me."

"So this is your first Daytona 500, Buck?"

"Oh yeah; and my first car race! I'm pretty excited. Up until the call came in at the last minute I was pretty much assigned to dog shows, spelling bees and stuff like that."

"You received a last minute call?"

"That's what happened. The guy who was scheduled to call the race got word that the spotter in our booth was Chinese and he was afraid of catching that coronavirus thing."

"You mean Harry Chang. He's been spotting for us for years. He's never been to China."

"I haven't either. Heard they have quite the wall over there. I bet I can name someone who'd like a wall like that, huh? The Chinese built it like they did our railroads. Not sure who paid for it, though. But, we know it wasn't the Mexicans, don't we?"

"Just because Harry's Chinese, Buck, as you know, doesn't mean he has the virus."

"I told the boys back at *Fox* that when I was a kid growing up in Minnesota I had all them viruses – mumps, chicken pox, measles, herpes, gono – the whole shebang! I'm immune, so I don't care if a Chinese guy is in the booth as long as he doesn't smell like curry."

"Raised in Minnesota, Buck? That's not what I'd consider NASCAR country."

"No, Brian, but we had demolition derbies. Wouldn't you agree it's about the same thing, only on a smaller scale? Had more crashes though. Isn't that what people come for?"

"Crashes are inevitable in the sport, Buck, with all the nudging and bumping that goes on at super high speeds. It adds a dimension of danger and provides thrills, but safety is our Number One concern... Maybe it's the rain but the fans are coming in very slowly."

"About these NASCAR fans, Brian, is it true that they're all sort of related? You know, cousins marrying cousins and that sort of thing. Happens in the South a lot I hear."

"I can't comment on that, Buck... Let's try to focus on the Daytona 500 if we can."

"You're right, Brian. I guess I was thinking more like the crowd at Talladega over there in Alabama. But still, if I were to lean out of the booth right now and shout 'Hey Bubba!' how many heads do you think would turn? "

"Buck, that's an old stereotype. But, I will say NASCAR attracts its good 'ol boys.'"

"Lookin' at the crowd that's here, Brian, I'm not seeing any Black good 'ol boys.'"

"Um…moving on, Buck, even with the rain letting up the drivers are nowhere near the pits. All the officials are gathered around the grand marshal's box for some reason."

"I might have the answer right here, Brian. I was just handed a note letting us know that Air Force One would be doing a low flyover moments from now."

"Air Force One! Wow! That's special. The president must be on his way to Mar-a-Lago."

"That's his plane, huh? He'll be all pissed off, Brian, if his golf game gets rained out."

Just then with a mighty roar Air Force One completed a low flyover of the track. People in the stands started cheering in unison. The noise quickly becomes deafening. Suddenly, dozens of fans sprint onto the wet infield carrying "Trump 2020" flags. Other fans are wearing them as rain-protecting capes in the garage area. It's pure pandemonium!

"There's even better news, Buck. The president is coming *here*! He's going to be the Grand Marshall! No wonder it's taking so much time for the fans to file in. Security at the entrances must be incredibly tight – like TSA airport checks on steroids."

"I haven't seen anything like this scene, Brian, since a few weeks ago when that standard poodle won Best in Show at Westminster. The place went nuts! Fifth time a standard poodle took the honors, breaking a tie with lots of breeds for fourth overall all-time."

"The president's motorcade is now on the track, Buck."

"Some of the other owners and trainers were pretty upset. Can't blame 'em. I mean, you ever seen one of those fancy poodles? If it's a male dog it has to be upset. No real dog would put up with being sheared to look like pom poms were attached to its feet."

"The president, Buck! The president!"

"If the president was a dog he wouldn't go out looking like that. But, then again, this president sports an orange bird's nest hairdo. Brian, do you think that's his real hair?"

"Buck, let's tune in. I think he's about to begin speaking."

The broadcast then features the president delivering written remarks, picking up with "A legendary display of roaring engines, soaring spirits and the American skill, speed and power that we've been hearing about for so many years. For 500 heart-pounding miles, these fierce competitors will chase the checkered flag, fight for the Harley J. Earl trophy and make their play for pure American glory. That's what it is: pure, American glory."

"That was some great speech, wouldn't you agree, Buck?"

"He certainly has the crowd stirred up. Seems like everyone's standing up and cheering."

"Buck, I'd say conservatively that 95 percent of NASCAR fans are Trump supporters."

"You don't say? Why is that Brian?"

"The president is in tune with their way of looking at life, Buck. Things like putting in an honest days work to earn a decent living, promoting family values, going to church on Sundays to thank their lord and savior Jesus Christ for what he offers us every day…"

"Sorry to butt in Brian, but, if I must say so, Trump doesn't seem to me the perfect model for those things. I'd say almost quite the opposite based on his behavior."

"Keep in mind that what counts most is not what a man does, but what he says. How he inspires us. We're all sinners, Buck, but this man is God's chosen one for America."

After finishing his remarks, the president and first lady return to their limousine which executes a triumphant lap around the big track, avoiding the high-banked turns and staying on the apron through the corners. The half-filled grandstands emit a roar.

"It's really a shame, Buck, that with the rain and the back-up at the entrances there weren't more people in the stands. This would make a great reelection ad."

"I wouldn't worry too much about that, Brian. This isn't my first rodeo with *Fox*. What they'll do is show the limo on the track and dub in crowd footage from another race."

"Now that the president and first lady have departed, these stands are really beginning to fill up, Buck. I just hope they'll see a race today but the rain seems to be picking up."

"Some fans just got seated in the row below us. Wanna hear what they have to say?"

"Great idea, Buck! Fan interviews are a terrific way to fill in time during delays."

"Hey, Bubba! Yeah, you. What did you think of seeing the president today?"

"Seeing the president? Are you s_ _ _ _ ing me? We just got here! Got stuck in that goddamn f _ _ _ ing line for two f _ _ _ ing hours because of that a_ _hole!"

"Whoa! I'd say, Brian, that you need to revise your estimate down to 94 percent."

After two lengthy delays totaling more than three hours, the race was postponed until Monday for the first time since 2012. During the delay prior to the postponement, Fox ran a replay of the 2019 Daytona 500. Buck Laughlin did not call the race on Monday.

TWELVE

Please Welcome the New Supremes
(Trump's trio pays tribute to the high court's most famous hits)

[The setting is Liberty University. TV's Inside Look is there with Buck Laughlin reporting behind-the-scenes as the DCTown singing trio, The New Supremes, is about to take the stage for its premier performance in a large auditorium packed with young Republicans.]

(Buck) "Welcome to the latest edition of *Inside Look.* Tonight I'm behind-the-scenes at Jerry Falwell's Liberty University to witness the historic opening performance of the New Supremes. This should be a fabulous show and we're just about to get underway."

(Announcer) "Ladies and gentlemen, you're about to meet Neil Gorsuch, Brett Kavanaugh and lead singer Amy Comey Barrett in the debut performance of…The New Supremes!"

(Buck) "Amy, I know you're just about to take the stage. What will be your opening number? There's been all kinds of rumors about the remakes. What's your lead song?"

(Amy) "Well, Buck, as you know, there's a lot of concern about the Court rolling back gun rights. We're here to let Americans know that their Second Amendment rights will never be taken away or even tampered with. Owning lethal firearms is a constitutional right."

(Buck) "Does that go for automatic and semi-automatic weapons?"

(Amy) "It goes for *all* weapons. We Americans have a right to protect ourselves."

(Buck) "So, I can own a missile launcher? Aren't there *any* restrictions?"

(Amy) "I gotta go. Look, I wanted to be a Supreme. To be nominated you had to answer certain questions correctly, okay? I got this one right, among others, so here I am."

(Announcer) "Ladies and Gentlemen, please welcome – The New Supremes! (*Applause*)

(Amy) "Neil, Brett and I are thrilled to be here tonight. (*More applause*) We know you're a lovely crowd of gun and Trump supporters, so here's our undying salute to you."

The band begins the intro to the original "My World is Empty Without You, Babe"

My world is empty without A-Ks
My world is empty without A-Ks

And if I go my way unarmed
I find it hard for me to carry on
I need your steel
I need your trigger touch
I need a magazine
That can kill so much

My world is empty without A-Ks
My world is empty without A-Ks

And when I see a Black man on the run
I know its time to go and get my gun
I hear moms cry 'No more Sandy Hooks'
But for every kid that dies I'll stop ten crooks

My world is empty without A-Ks
My world is empty without A-Ks

Loneliness I'll never feel again

Knowing that there's no better friend
With my A-K I have no fear
There's no more right that I hold dear

My world is empty without A-Ks
My world is empty without A-Ks
(*Fade*) Without A-Ks
(*Fade*) Without A-Ks

(Announcer) "How about that! (*Thunderous applause*) The New
Supremes will be back on stage in a moment but first let's bow our
heads in a minute of silent prayer for the patriots who are unjustly
being put on trial for their peaceful demonstration on January 6[th.]"

(Buck) "I'm here with Brett Kavanaugh. Brett, you really rocked the
house with that one. That's going to be a tough number to follow.
What song have you lined up next?"

Brett: "This concert is a tribute to the Court's greatest hits. None
was more impactful than its refusal to allow a recount of the Florida
election that resulted in George W. Bush becoming the 43rd President
of the United States. That decision truly was historic."

(Buck) "I should say! He's reading a children's story, the 9-11 attack
takes place, and Bush, Rumsfeld and Cheney go start a war chasing
those WMDs that didn't exist."

(Brett) "Sure enough, but what a great boost for our economy.
There's nothing like a good war fought by blue collar kids to give
a needed shot in the arm to American corporations. They keep
Americans in jobs and through covert donations keep Republicans
in office."

(Buck) "So, what you're saying is that the decision along straight
party lines to put Bush in the White House was a great moment in
the Supreme Court's history. Is that right?"

(Brett) "You bet it was! Hey, if Gore had won there probably
wouldn't have been a war. That's why this next number shows
how little things – tiny things to be more precise – can change

the course of history…Gotta go now. The song's called 'Hanging
Chads.'"

Announcer (*as the band begins the tune of the original "Baby Love"*) "Once
again ladies and gentlemen, put your hands together and welcome
the fabulous New Supremes!"

Ooooh…hanging chads, O hanging chads
Thank you, bless you, hanging chads
Without you Gore would have won
Something we couldn't get undone
But you came and saved the day
Sent the outcome up our way

Ooh, ooh, hanging chads, O hanging chads
Thank you, bless you, hanging chads
That's a vote for Gore they claim
But see how that bit does hang
We can't let that stay in play
Best to just throw it away

Toss it! Toss it! Toss it!

Ooh, ooh, hanging chads, O hanging chads
Thank you, bless you, hanging chads
They left it up to us
Saw no reason to make a fuss
We were already on the bus
Knowing Bush was just like us

Ooh, ooh, hanging chads, O hanging chads
Thank you, bless you, hanging chads
We've had the final say
Votes for Bush O they can stay
But throw Gore's votes away
Don't worry it's okay
(*Fade*) Just throw his votes away
(*Fade*) Don't worry it's okay

(Announcer) "Aren't they fantastic! (*Loud applause*) Don't worry, they'll be back for one final song, but now its time to open your purses and wallets and give every cent you have to the Donald J. Trump defense fund. You might have noticed that former first daughter Ivanka and first son Don Jr. are with us tonight and they'll now be passing around baskets to help defray the legal costs of defending our great former (and next!) president from scandalous false tax evasion accusations coming from that liberal cesspool known as the State of New York. Please be generous. He helped us; now we need to help him."

(Buck) "Could have seen that one coming! I'm here with Neil Gorsuch. I see you're busy writing a check, Neil. I guess you feel more than a little obliged to the former pres."

(Neil) "The thing is, Buck, that we have no jurisdiction over the State of New York. You know, we're all for pushing issues like abortion down to the state level. The Constitution is very clear about the separation of federal and state authority, but every once in a while that comes back to...ah – I guess I can say this – bite us in the ass. Anything that Congress comes up with to embarrass or injure the former president we can overturn with our majority, but New York is a different matter. That's why I'm writing a big check."

(Buck) "Nothing like judicial impartiality as they say! But, say, now that you're done writing, tell us about your final number. What landmark decision will be celebrated?"

Neil: "That's a no-brainer, Buck. That would be the January 21, 2010 5 to 4 decision by the high court along party lines in favor of Citizens United allowing corporations and other outside groups to funnel unlimited funds into Super PACs supporting political candidates. It really was a breakthrough allowing wealthy donors to spend freely."

(Buck) "If I understood it correctly, that decision reversed century-old restrictions on campaign financing and led to huge sums of dark money being channeled into shadowy nonprofits that don't have to declare their donors. So that's a good thing is it?"

(Neil) "Of course! What the liberals overlooked was that the old law represented a clear infringement on freedom of speech. That right belongs to corporations as well."

(Buck) "If you say so, Neil. I guess what Citizens United did was prove that money talks!"

(Neil) "It also sings! I gotta go. This number is dedicated to friends at Citizens United."

(Announcer) "Ladies and gentlemen. I see the baskets are still being passed around and have had to be emptied several times. Thank you all for your generosity. Still, I hope this is just pocket change compared with your undisclosed donations to our PACs in 2022 and 2024 when order will be restored in Washington...Let's bring back the New Supremes!"

(*The band begins playing the music for the original "There's No Stopping Us Now"*)

There's no stopping us now
Now that we've found a way
There's no stopping us now
Our good 'ol boys are here to stay

Foolishly they were kept apart
No place for their millions to park
But all that has changed for our donors
They can now be our PACs secret owners

There's no stopping us now
Now that we've found a way
There's no stopping us now
Watch as big money comes our way

Corporations and tycoons are now clear
To buy our elections without fear
Their names and their causes obscure
We're citizens united once more

There's no stopping us now
Now that we've found a way
There's no stopping us now
Dark money is here to stay
(*Fade*) Here to stay
(*Fade*) We found a way

(Announcer) "There you have it ladies and gentlemen. (*Thunderous applause*) And the good news is…they'll be with us for a lifetime! It's so true, fellow Republicans, there's no stopping us now…Hold on! I see they're coming back on stage for one more song."

(Amy) "Not really a song. We just want to tell all of you wonderful patriots that *Everything is Good About You*. (*Applause*) We want you to know that we'll give liberal lawmakers *Nothing But Heartaches* (*Louder applause*). We love you fellow conservatives, and speaking for President Trump, *You Keep Me Hangin' On*. And, as far as the future is concerned, with socialist votes from liberal bastions being suppressed in states throughout the country – don't worry, we won't intervene (*Uproarious applause*) – let me tell you what I'm hearing… Do you want to know what I'm hearing my fellow Americans? (*The crowd chants "yes"*) I'll tell you! Listen. *I Hear a Trump Symphony!*"

(Buck) "Well, you just witnessed it. The high court unmasked…Wait, hold on; there are big guys with guns wearing Oath Keepers jackets coming towards our filming crew. They're grabbing the cameras. They're confiscating the film. I haven't seen anything like this since the January 6th insurrection. My microphone is being ripped…"

THIRTEEN

Trumpland Vacation
(The Griswald family visits a renamed theme park)

Act One, Scene One

[*The setting is the Griswold household in suburban Chicago. The extended family that includes Uncle Eddie and Aunt Edna has gathered in the living room as Clark Griswold is about to announce plans for their summer vacation in August, 2020. His wife Ellen, son Rusty and daughter Audrey are also standing by, anxiously awaiting the decision.*]

(Clark) "Okay everyone, listen up. The moment you've been waiting for has arrived!"

(Rusty) "Dad, please no more tours of Civil War battlefields."

(Ellen) "He's right, Clark. We've got pictures of every monument in the country."

(Audrey) "Promise there'll be no mountain hikes."

(Ellen) "Clark, Audrey's right. Remember, she almost got bitten by a rattlesnake."

(Clark) "Calm down, everyone. This year is going to be special."

(Rusty) "That's what you said when we went to see Grandma Grace on her deathbed."

(Clark) "Well, that was very special...for her. And, you got to see her die."

(Uncle Eddie) "Yeah, I wish I coulda been there to see that...the old bag!"

(Ellen) "Eddie, hush!"

(Uncle Eddie) "I was just tellin' the truth."

(Clark, *opening an envelope*) "Aren't we all a little off topic? Listen up now."

(Aunt Edna) "This better be good, my angina's already acting up."

(Clark, *with great flourish*) "Family, we are going to...Trumpland!"

(Rusty, *ecstatic*) "Really, dad? Are you really serious?"

(Clark) "Son, how could I be kidding about something like this?"

(Ellen) "Clark, can we really afford such an expensive trip?"

(Clark) "No problem this year, darling. No worries at all. The company made a simple $100,000 contribution to a certain dark money fund to reelect a certain someone and we just received an Economic Recovery stimulus check in the amount of $3.0 million."

(Ellen) "That's wonderful, Clark. Does that mean your firm can bring back all the assistants and staff workers who were furloughed or laid off during the shut down?"

(Clark) "Well, that's a little unlikely. Three other guys and I got to split $50,000. The boss used the rest to pay off the mortgage on his yacht. I doubt there's anything left."

(Audrey) "That doesn't seem fair, does it dad?"

(Clark) "Sweetie, I don't make those decisions...And we're all going to Trumpland!"

Act One, Scene Two

[*The setting is the same living room only later in the day. After the evening meal the family is sitting around, relaxing, and talking excitedly about the upcoming trip.*]

(Clark, *with enthusiasm*) "Excuse me everyone, I have to go get something."

(Rusty) "I wonder what dad's up to now?"

Clark returns holding a big cardboard box with both arms

(Clark, *setting the box down*) "No Griswold goes to Trumpland without being prepared."

(Uncle Eddie) "What ya got there big guy?"

(Clark) "Oh, just a few little items to get us in the proper frame of mind."

Clark opens the big box and pulls out a cloth sack that he hands to Rusty

(Clark) "Here, Russ. Open this up and pass 'em around."

(Uncle Eddie) "What ya got there boy?"

(Rusty) "Wow! (*reading label*) "Authentically-styled Donald Trump orange hairpieces."

Rusty passes the wigs around and they all try them on

(Clark) "Wait! There's more. (*Clark hands a wrapped box to Rusty who quickly opens it*)

(Rusty) "Wow! It's a model of an aircraft carrier…The USS Dwight D. Eisenhower."

(Clark) "Not for long! I have the inside word that in 2021 it'll be renamed the USS Donald J. Trump. That is, until a newer, faster, bigger one can be built in his honor."

(Rusty) "Look! It even comes with a Trump action figure in full military dress with all kinds of fancy badges and medals on his uniform. How neat!"

(Ellen) "Clark, I didn't think Trump served in the military?"

(Clark) "Not as a serviceman. The Pentagon apparently awarded him these honors for his battles against the Taliban, Al-Qaeda, Isis, and House Democrats."

(Aunt Edna) "Let's keep this movin' okay? What else ya got in there?"

Clark rummages around in the box and takes out several bottles and cans

(Clark) "For the ladies, Ivanka Trump perfume and, as a bonus, a can of Goya beans!"

(Uncle Eddie) "Good one, Clark. The perfume can offset the aftermath of the beans!"

(Clark, *to himself*) "Or, the other way around!" (*to Eddie*) "But, here's something for you."

(Uncle Eddie) "Ah shucks, Clark. Ya didn't have ta…But, lemme see!"

Clark hands Uncle Eddie a wrapped box that he quickly tears open

(Uncle Eddie) "By golly, Clark, you musta known how I like playin' with this stuff."

(Aunt Edna) "What the hell is it, Eddie?"

(Eddie, *reading*) "A COVID-19 Chemistry Kit! Comes with 30 vials of liquid chemicals none of which have been combined and tested as a possible vaccine."

(Clark) "Have at it. Just don't do your experiments in the back of the station wagon."

(Uncle Eddie) "I won't, Clark. I'll wait 'till we get a motel room." (*then aside to Clark*) "But, how will I know if I've found the cure? Don't I need to test on someone?"

(Clark, *aside to Uncle Eddie*) "That's one of the reasons I've invited Aunt Edna along."

(Ellen) "Clark, all this is wonderful, but is it safe to be around so many people coming from all over the country to visit Trumpland. Some states are still in lockdown."

(Clark) "Ellen, darling, think where we're going! We're going to Trumpland. Everything is great in Trumpland. Just the way it used to be. The virus is completely under control."

(Ellen) "If you say so, Clark. When will we be leaving?"

(Clark) "Right away! We have to. School starts in a couple of weeks."

<u>Act Two, Scene One</u>

[*The setting is Trumpland just beyond the grand archway over the moat and through the castle leading into the magical kingdom that the Disney Corporation recently sold to Trump Enterprises. The Griswold entourage is gathered excitedly around Clark who is studying a map displaying the locations of all the rides and attractions inside the park. All are present except for Aunt Edna who suddenly and mysteriously died of suspected poisoning while traveling through northern Arizona where she was hastily buried.*]

(Clark, *pointing at some speakers above the entrance archway*) "Before we head out, let's take a moment and all listen and mouth the words to the Trumpland theme song."

When you wish upon a star
It really matters who you are
Everything your greed desires
Will come to you

If donor money backs your dream
No request is too extreme
Even if against the law
We'll get it done through William Barr

The stars above know who's red or blue
And grant to those who to Trump are true
All things that set their hearts aflame
Riches, power, and everlasting fame

(Uncle Eddie) "Just tugs at the heartstrings doesn't it Clark?"

(Clark) "I guess it still does Uncle Eddie, although I sort of miss the Disney version. But, hey, I made my wish and it was granted, just like in the song!"

(Rusty) "Dad, let's get on with it, times a-wastin!"

(Clark) "Well, let's see. We can start with 'Pirates of the Potomac,' 'Star Wars: Rise of the Socialists,' or even take a ride through 'It's a Small World.' Audrey, you choose."

(Audrey) "Those rides seem sort of familiar but they're not exactly what I remember."

(Clark) "That's probably because of the ownership change. They made adjustments."

(Audrey) "Read me what it says about the 'Pirates of the Potomac' ride."

(Clark, *reading*) "A hair-raising adventure through the Halls of Congress where you'll witness swashbuckling House Democrats steal your tax money and waste it on illegal immigrant healthcare, welfare moms, environmental safeguards and housing subsidies."

(Ellen) "Whatever happened to the fun 'Yo, ho, yo, ho, a pirate's life for me?'"

(Clark) "It's probably the same ride only with politicians dressed as pirates."

(Audrey) "What's it say about the Star Wars ride?"

(Clark, *reading*) "A thrilling space odyssey where the United Powers of Justice under Space Admiral Jared Kushner intercept an alien invasion of Democrats intent upon destroying capitalism and instituting a socialist government on American soil."

(Rusty) "Dad, didn't you once call Kushner the poster child of shameless nepotism?"

(Clark, *chuckling*) "You're right, Russ, I did...We'll just scratch that attraction."

(Uncle Eddie) "Clark, it seems to me that the 'Small World' ride ain't been changed."

(Clark) "Very astute, Uncle Eddie. It's still called 'It's a Small World.'"

(Uncle Eddie) "You could've agreed without insulting me."

(Ellen) "Uncle Eddie, 'astute' is a complimentary word. Clark was being nice."

(Uncle Eddie) "Well, okay. It's my favorite ride, ya know. I pretty much used up all my tickets when we came here as squirts and that song has been in my head ever since."

(Clark, *aside to Ellen*) "Plenty of room for it to rattle around for 50 years."

(Audrey) "So it's settled; we start with 'It's a Small World?'"

(Rusty) "Can we get something to eat first, I'm starving."

(Uncle Eddie) "I had my eye on one of those Pelosi stuffed sausages myself."

Act Two, Scene Two

[*The Griswold clan is in a long line at the Mar-a-Lago Cafeteria. Clark has gone ahead and picked up a menu so they'll have their minds made up when their turn comes up.*]

(Clark) "Okay gang, listen up. I'll read the 'Specialties.'"

(Rusty) "Dad, all I want is a hot dog."

(Clark, *checking*) "Looks like you have two choices, Russ. There's a USDA 'Unapproved' no-beef Demodog served on a stale bun with fake fries."

(Rusty) "Yuk! What's my other choice?"

(Clark) "How about a plump, 8-inch, four-pound all beef wiener that comes with a special sauce tucked between hot buns and served with a bag of big tasty corn balls."

(Ellen) "Clark! Are you making that up?"

(Clark) "No, it's written right here. It's called the 'Stormy Satisfier.'"

(Uncle Eddie) "While the boy is thinking I've changed my mind. I'd like a burger."

(Clark) "They offer a one-eighth pound U.S. Grade 'D' Past-Prime Biden Burger or a half-pound, all-beef AG Barr Burger that breaks all the laws of judicious restraint."

(Uncle Eddie) "Clark, I'll have me one of them Barr Burgers if ya don't mind. I read on an overhead sign that the AG Barr Burger comes however you want it made to order."

When they finally reach the head of the line Clark places their orders and prepares to pay. The bill comes to $419.95. The top of the tab reads: "Welcome to Mar-a-Lago."

Act Three, Scene One

[*The setting is the Griswold station wagon the following morning as the family, plus Uncle Eddie, cruise down a California freeway on the first leg of the drive home.*]

(Clark) "Okay gang, what did you think of Trumpland?"

(Rusty) "To tell you the truth, dad, it sucked."

(Audrey) "We had to wait an hour for a bobsled ride on Dem Debt Mountain, the Haunted Mansion with those dumb cutouts of Democratic House members was sorry, and the parade with all those tanks and mobile missile launchers was so Soviet Union."

(Ellen) "I know you meant well, Clark. But how were you to know that Trumpland wasn't the fantasyland it was built up to be? The way it was promoted seemed so attractive, so different, so welcome a change. You weren't the only one fooled."

(Uncle Eddie) "All I can say is I've got that damn 'It's a Small World' tune in my head again only with the new lyrics. I'd like to blow that ride up with all my chemicals!"

(Clark) "I think one casualty is enough for this trip, Uncle Eddie. Put your kit away."

(Rusty) "It's in my head, too, Uncle Eddie. I think we all picked up that earworm."

(Clark) "Why drive ourselves nuts fighting it? I say we roll down the windows and sing!"

(Ellen) "That might be a good idea, Clark. But I'm not at all happy with the new lyrics."

(Clark) "I know, I know. But, let's face it. It's where we are as a country right now."

With the windows rolled down, they break into song, singing all the way to Chicago:

It's a world without blue states
It's a world without gays
It's a world of tax loopholes
Where the little guy pays
It's a world where the poor
Live on a far distant shore
It's a small world that we want

[Refrain]
It's a small world that we want
It's a small world that we want
It's a small world that we want
It's a small, small, world

It's a world without Muslims
It's a world without Jews
It's a world where a woman
Has no right to choose
It's a world where my trades
Are by insiders made
It's a small world that we want
[Repeat Refrain]

It's a world built on privilege
It's a world lily white
It's world where I sleep
On my yacht every night
It's a world where a bribe
Keeps the lawyers off my hide
It's a small world that we want
[Repeat Refrain]

It's a world of oil drilling

It's a world crossed by pipes
It's a world where a clear cut
Is a beautiful sight
It's a world where the bears
Are best seen through crosshairs
It's a small world that we want
[Repeat Refrain]

It's a world free of science
It's a world without profs
It's a world where books
Are used mainly as props
It's a world where family pride
Includes a mistress on the side
It's a small world that we want
[Repeat Refrain]

It's a world without unions
It's a world of corporate perks
It's a world where welfare moms
Are told: "Go back to work!"
It's a world where my gun
Is like a be-lov-ed son
It's a small world that we want
[Repeat Refrain]

BOOK TWO

Presidential Pandemonium: The "China Virus"

"We have it totally under control. It's one person coming in from China. It's going to be just fine."
(President Trump, January 22, 2020)

"The 15 [American cases] within a couple of days is going to be down to close to zero."
(President Trump, February 26, 2020)

"It's going to disappear. One day, it's like a miracle, it will disappear."
(President Trump, February 27, 2020)

By March, it was evident that his predictions were dead wrong as Covid-19 cases, hospitalizations and deaths were escalating dramatically.

"I don't take responsibility at all."
(President Trump, March 13, 2020)

FOURTEEN

The Wreck of the Hesperus
(A sea captain refuses to seek shelter during a storm)

Act One, Scene One

[*The setting is a busy dock on the west side of Manhattan in 1830. The schooner Hesperus is being outfitted for a short voyage to Portland, Maine, on the New England coast. Three sailors, two raw recruits, Jonas and Marley, and a seasoned salt named Falspar are huddled in conversation as the last of the cargo is being hoisted on deck.*]

(Jonas) "That appears to be the last of it; we'll be sailin' soon."

(Marley) "Tis a good voyage for a novice like me; just long enough to learn the ropes."

(Falspar) "You'll learn 'em quickly, lads, or this will be your first and *last* voyage."

(Jonas) "Would ya be willing ta help us along? Show us the ropes?"

(Falspar) "Ya both look strong of the arm and sharp in the eye. I'll see to it."

(Marley) "Have you sailed on the *Hesperus* before?"

(Falspar) "No lads, I have not. I thought I'd put up my sails, but that didn't last."

(Jonas) "Born a mariner; die a mariner…Is that what you mean?"

(Falspar) "Think you so? Naw! A man must eat. I drank and gambled away my earnings. I had no choice but ta come back before the mast."

(Marlay) "Perchance, are you our skipper?"

(Falspar) "You might wish it so. The skipper is no more qualified than a squid."

(Jonas, *alarmed*) "How can that be? Reassure me! For sure he's been to sea?"

(Falspar, *lighting his pipe*) "Maybe on the ferry to Staten Island." (*laughs derisively*)

(Marley) "Aren't you concerned?"

(Falspar) "We won't stray far from land's edge and I'll command the sails."

(Jonas) "Pray that the weather will be fair."

(Falspar) "An honest prayer, lad. Keep your eyes on the Southeast where troubles tend to loom."

Act One, Scene Two

[*The setting is aboard the Hesperus which is under full sail at night in the Atlantic north of Boston. The wind has picked up and the waves, which had been calm, are rising.*]

(Falspar, *to the captain*) "We need to lower the sails. I sense a storm brewin'."

(Captain, *scornfully*) "Nonsense! Tis nothing. We have a timetable to keep."

(Falspar) "I've sailed the China Main and know an evil sky when I see one."

(Captain) "Understand this, Falspar. I have *total* authority on board this ship. That's the way it is and that's the way it's going to be. As captain, my authority is *total*."

(Falspar) "Last night the moon had a golden ring, and tonight no moon we see."

(Captain) "And that's supposed to mean something? Return at once to your post!"

Act Two, Scene One

[*Many hours have passed and the wind is blowing harder and the waves are battering the hull of the schooner struggling to make headway. Falspar, after pounding on the door to the captain's quarters, is finally awarded entry. The Captain is seen playing his violin.*]

(Falspar) "Sir, I fear a nigh hurricane is upon us. We must put into yonder port!"

(Captain, *dismissively*) "It's a hoax. Old Poseidon is just splashing in his tub."

(Falspar) "I warn you, Captain, there's not a moment to lose."

(Captain) "I'm ordering you to stay the course. This storm will shortly pass."

(Falspar) "You're risking the lives of every sailor on board!"

(Captain) "That's my responsibility, not yours. Now tend to your duties."

Act Two, Scene Two

[*The time is the following morning. The setting a high cliff in Gloucester, MA. A crowd has gathered as word spreads that a wreck was sighted on the Reef of Donald's Woe.*]

(First Citizen) "It must have run aground in last night's ragin' storm."

(Second Citizen) "No God-fearing captain would be out in that gale. There were so many plain-ta-see signs of danger, and our coast is blessed with countless sheltering coves!"

(Third Citizen) "Hark! Here's the lad who spotted the wreck running towards us now."

(Lad, *breathlessly*) "Come quickly! Bodies have floated ashore and some are breathing!"

The crowd quickly disperses and reassembles on the shoreline

(First Citizen) "It's a miracle that anyone survived. Boy, who is alive amongst them?"

(Lad) "Two deck hands, Jonas and Marley, who floated ashore gripping the main mast."

(First Citizen) "Is that all?"

(Lad) "No, sir. The captain. He rowed ashore in the ship's lone dingy."

Act Three, Scene One

[*The setting is the Gloucester Assembly Hall. Bodies of the drowned sailors are lying in rows under white sheets awaiting identification. The town magistrates have assembled.*]

(First Magistrate) "How tragic! The Reef of Donald's Woe has claimed more victims."

(Second Magistrate) "Every savvy mariner should know of it! It needn't have happened!"

(First Magistrate) "You would think so. The signs of this storm were so evident."

(Second Magistrate) "The lighthouse keeper reports that the beacon was illuminated."

(First Magistrate) "Totally senseless. What captain wouldn't have sought a cove?"

(Second Magistrate) "We'll soon know. He's to appear in court to explain his actions."

Act Three, Scene Two

[*The time is a month later; the setting the Gloucester courthouse. The captain has been summoned to answer lingering questions about the wreck of his ship, the Hesperus.*]

(Judge) "You, sir, were the captain of the ill-fated schooner the *Hesperus*, correct?"

(Captain) "That is correct, in a way."

(Judge) "Please explain that statement."

(Captain) "This was my first voyage. I was inexperienced and thus instructed to follow the advice of the more experienced seamen, particularly one named Falspar."

(Judge) "And this fellow Falspar did not survive?"

(Captain) "That appears to be the case. No body was found."

(Judge) "How was it that only you found refuge in the ship's lone dingy?"

(Captain) "As captain, I was the last to abandon the ship. The others leaped overboard in fear. I valiantly held true to the helm until all hope passed to save my ship."

(Judge) "Were you not warned of the imminent danger?"

(Captain) "Rather the opposite. Falspar considered it a 'minor squall.'"

(Judge) "When and where did he tell you that?"

(Captain) "A few hours before the wreck; in my quarters."

(Judge) "What were you doing there?"

(Captain) "Playing with my instrument."

(Judge, *aside to himself*) "That's his first answer that makes any sense!"

(Judge) "You are aware that many sailors perished needlessly."

(Captain) "Tremendous loss."

(Judge) "Leaving behind grieving families."

(Captain, *aside to himself*) "It's the lost cargo and support of my benefactors that really distresses me."

(Captain) "As I've said, it's a tremendous loss. I've offered my thoughts and prayers."

(Judge) "And you claim no responsibility?"

(Captain) "I don't take responsibility at all."

FIFTEEN

The Vaccine Experiment
(Cabinet members are used as guinea pigs to discover COVID remedies)

[*The setting is the White House where President Trump has called an emergency meeting of cabinet members to address the ongoing lack of a vaccine against the coronavirus. Also attending is Chief Coronavirus Expert and Senior Advisor, Jared Kushner.*]

(Trump) "Thank you all for coming on such short notice. Please remove your masks. This is a Lysol-safe environment, Jared saw to it, and besides, with masks I can't tell one of you from another... except for you Ben (*nodding to Ben Carter*), of course. Jared, it's now your meeting."

(Kushner) "As you all know, the so-called scientists are taking way too much time coming up with an effective vaccine against coronavirus. And, every time they think they might be onto something, the Food & Drug guys call for prolonged testing. As you are all well aware, we simply can't wait that long. Time definitely isn't on our side."

(Secretary Pompeo) "Because the death rate is much higher than anticipated?"

(Kushner) "No, Mike. Get with the program. Finding a vaccine is central to the *election*."

(Secretary Esper) "Okay, Jared, how do you propose *we* can speed things up?"

(Kushner) "Mark, I prefer Dr. Kushner. But, the answer is simple: experimentation!"

(Secretary Esper) "*Doctor* Kushner?"

(Trump) "Mark, you must have missed the memo. Because of his tremendous work I've awarded my son-in-law a medical degree from Trump University."

(AG Barr) "And I declared it valid!...Now, getting back to the matters at hand, isn't experimentation, Dr. Kushner, precisely what the scientists are doing?"

(Kushner) "In laboratories! Now how real world is that? They inject infected rats and mice with their drug concoctions. Then they try a promising drug on rabbits and guinea pigs. Bill, there's just no time for all that fooling around. *We* must take action!"

(Secretary Perdue) "Y'all got a'notter plan do ya?"

(Kushner) "We'll cut out the 'middle man' – in this case the 'middle mouse.'"

(Secretary Bernhardt) "Are you suggesting, Jared, er, excuse me, Dr. Kushner, human experimentation from the outset?"

(Kushner) "Precisely, Dave. You're quickly catching on."

(Secretary Ross) "How many Democrats do you think we can round up?" (*laughter*)

(Kushner) "Frankly, Wilbur, that's a great suggestion but...there's just no time."

(Secretary Scalia) "Dr. Kushner, where precisely are you heading with this?'

(Kushner) "Glad you asked, Gene. Whoever comes up with the vaccine will be a big hero, right? I say there are no bigger heroes than those sitting in this very room!"

(Secretary Azar) "I might be Secretary of Health and Human

Services, but I'm hardly qualified for the job, never mind identifying the drug that's gonna curb this disease."

(Secretary Carson) "I'm a neurosurgeon by profession and even that's no qualification."

(Kushner) "Look, no qualifications are required. These are *simple* experiments."

(Secretary Chao) "How simple might that be, Dr. Kushner? Please explain."

(Kushner) "You all have a mug in front of you. You'll note that each mug contains a different liquid identified on the bottom. The president and I have a hunch that the perfect vaccine is something that's in plentiful supply, can be bought off the shelf, and doesn't even cost a lot to buy. The president has already proposed Lysol injections that…"

(Trump) "If I can interrupt here. Lysol has been shown to be an effective drug for dealing with Melania. (*snickers*) And if it can do *that*, I think it might have other possibilities."

(Secretary Azar) "Don't you mean malaria, Mr. President?"

(Trump) "No, not that country. This coronavirus thing came from China, believe me."

(Kushner, *impatiently*) "Okay everyone. Hoist your mugs and take a big gulp!"

(Secretary DeVos, *belching*) "Mine's labeled 'Windex'…Can that be right?"

(Trump) "I figure if it can clean glass it can probably cleanse your lungs."

(Secretary Wilkie) "I'm supposed to drink motor oil?"

(Trump) "Don't worry; I'm told it's the new synthetic stuff. Good for 5,000 miles."

(Secretary Wolf, *gasping*) "I swallowed before checking…brake fluid? Really?"

(Trump, *big smile*) "Could bring the virus to a quick stop!"

(Secretary Mnuchin, *doubling over before dropping down*) "Ah…ah… Drano?"

(Trump) "If it can open up a clogged drain it might open up your lungs. We'll see."

(Secretary Perdue) "This he'a tastes a helluva lot like my own white lightnin'."

(Kushner) "That's indeed what it is! Imagine the jobs created in your Georgia in still manufacturing and moonshine production if that proves effective against COVID-19."

(Secretary Scalia, *spewing on Secretary Perdue's shirt*) "This tastes like warm piss!"

(Trump) "Very perceptive! And you can thank my dear daughter Ivanka for the sample!"

(Secretary Chao, *barfing on her dress*) "Ethanol!"

(Trump) "Perfect pairing with the Secretary of Transportation, don't you think?"

(Secretary Wolf, *sputtering*) "Billy Beer?"

(Kushner) "Let's hope that's not it. They stopped brewing that shit decades ago."

(Secretary Brouillette, *gagging*) "Mr. Kushner. If I have the voice left to ask (*putting down his antifreeze-laced Red Bull*), how will we know if any of these familiar products are effective cures if we don't have the disease to begin with?"

(Kushner) "Dan, you're confusing a 'cure' with a 'vaccine.' We're experimenting to identify a preventative 'vaccine.' What we're doing today is only half of the experiment."

(Secretary Scalia) "So, I'll ask again. Where precisely are you heading with this, doctor?"

(Kushner) "Presuming you all recover" (*aside to Trump while observing Mnuchin twitching on the floor*) "I think we lost the Drano guy." (*again to the assembly*) "You'll next penetrate places where the virus is known, like nursing homes with high death rates. Kiss a few cheeks; shake a few hands. If you don't get it, bingo! You're the hero!"

(Trump) "I have another suggestion. I've apparently been creating the perfect environment for this experiment in my tweets. This is where my tremendous base plays a role. Amongst us girls, let's face it, the base, particularly the good 'ol boys and gals at the bottom of the base, aren't the sharpest knives in the church. I tweet 'Liberate' and they storm their state capitol buildings demanding that 'stay-at-home' orders be removed."

(Kushner) "They're even dumb enough to bring their kids along if you can imagine. (*pause*) What the president is getting at is that these rallies by diehard (*aside*, albeit imbecilic) supporters, standing shoulder-to-shoulder while waving American flags, holding up makeshift 'Trump 2020' signs, while not wearing protective masks or taking any other precautions, are bound to be massive Petri dishes for coronavirus."

(Trump) "Did someone just order a large plate of hors d'oeuvres?"

(Kushner) "We'll dispatch each of you to one of these rallies and see what happens next."

(Secretary Esper) "You mean, what happens next to *us* now that we're '*vaccinated*'?"

(Kushner) "Exactly! Russian roulette, maybe. But, think of the upside of being hailed as a hero. One of you might get all the credit for identifying the elusive coronavirus vaccine!"

(Trump) "Don't get too far ahead of yourself, Jared my boy. Call it 'partial credit.' Most of the credit will go to *me* of course as well it should…And, a moment ago you mentioned the Russians. Are they helping with this plan as part of my reelection?"

At this moment Chief of Staff Mark Meadows opens the door and peeks in

(Meadows) "Mr. President. You're daily media briefing begins in five minutes."

(Trump) "Thank you, Mark. We're just wrapping up."

While his cabinet members stagger around the room disoriented or in great distress, being respectful to step around Treasury Secretary Mnuchin's still twitching body, the president and his son-in-law Jared Kushner leave to join Dr. Anthony Fauci and coronavirus coordinator Dr. Dorothy Birx outside the White House.

(Reporter) "Dr. Fauci. When is the earliest we can expect to have a COVID-19 vaccine?"

(Dr. Fauci) "I wish I had that answer. As you know, scientists are working day and…"

(Trump *belly-bumping Dr. Fauci away from the lectern*) "I'll give you an answer. I just left a tremendous meeting of my cabinet. Tremendous people willing to make tremendous sacrifices in the face of this tremendous crisis. All I can say for now is that we're well underway with some promising remedies, all of them already available."

(Reporter, *with a sarcastic laugh*) "Like ingesting Lysol?"

(Trump) Don't laugh. We're experimenting with similar promising products – items that you all have around the house or in the garage." (*notices out of the corner of his eye a team of medics wheeling a gurney with a sheet-covered body out of the White House, then resumes talking*)...but it seems we can now eliminate Drano as a possibility."

(Dr. Deborah Birx, *who is observed wincing repeatedly in the background*) "My God!"

(Reporter) "So, Mr. President. What is the next step you'll be taking?"

(Trump, *observing the ambulance slowly drive away*) "Finding a new Treasury Secretary."

SIXTEEN

The Voice
(A hospitalized Trump is tormented by his conscience)

<u>Scene One</u>

[*The setting is President Trump's private bedroom at Walter Reed Medical Center where he's being treated by a team of doctors for COVID-19. He's resting comfortably in bed, eyes closed, half-awake, half-asleep, when he hears a voice, presumably a doctor's.*]

(Voice) "How are you feeling?"

(Trump, *eyes still closed*) "I've felt better."

(Voice) "I know how you feel; I'm asking how are you feeling... about yourself?"

(Trump, *sleepily*) "How do you know how I feel?"

(Voice) "That's easy...I'm you!"

(Trump, *opening his eyes*) "Where are you? Who are you?"

(Voice) "I'm right here with you...I'm your conscience."

(Trump) "I don't have a conscience."

(Voice) "You don't believe you have a conscience but you couldn't just will me away."

(Trump) "I did too!"

(Voice) "Oh, I remember it so well. Your father urged you to chase me away."

(Trump) "He did. I remember his words, 'Son, if you're going to succeed in business, especially in our family business, you can't have a conscience.'"

(Voice) "So, you think I just went away for good?"

(Trump, *now quite alert*) "I certainly haven't been bothered by you; you know that."

(Voice) "Yes, you've spent a full lifetime operating without me. But now…"

(Trump, *anxiously*) "What about now?"

(Voice) "Now things are a little different, wouldn't you agree?"

(Trump) "You mean catching the China Virus and being in here?"

(Voice) "Most people in your position begin to reflect on things."

(Trump) "Whadaya mean 'people in my position?'"

(Voice) "I mean, people who have a near-death experience."

(Trump) "Near death! I'm told I'm doing just fine."

(Voice) "Is that what *they* told you or what *you* told them?"

(Trump, *after a pause*) "A little bit of both, I guess."

(Voice) "You know, Donald, you can't cheat death and you can't lie to your conscience."

(Trump) "Who says I'm dying; and who says I'm lying to you?"

(Voice) "I didn't say you were dying. But, at your age and with your weight and anger issues testing positive for COVID-19 can be regarded as a near-death experience."

(Trump) "How near?"

(Voice) "Donald, I'm not a physician, I'm your conscience. But, this is a close call."

(Trump) "What's the saying? Close only counts in horseshoes and hand grenades."

(Voice) "You'd better consider this more like hand grenades than a game of horseshoes."

(Trump) "So, Mr. Conscience, what am I supposed to do?"

(Voice) "Lay back; relax. I'll come back tomorrow. We have some things to go over."

Scene Two

[*The setting is the same only it's the following night. From his bed, President Trump has finished dispatching a flurry of angry tweets aimed at China and Democrats and now he closes his eyes looking forward to sleep overtaking him. But then he's interrupted.*]

(Voice) "Donald!"

(Trump, *stirring*) "Not *you* again."

(Voice) "I told you I'd be coming back."

(Trump) "I tried to will you away. It worked once before."

(Voice) "Times have changed, remember? You're a sick man."

(Trump) "Dr. Conley says I'm coming along just fine."

(Voice) "That's staying positive. But, let's discuss your military service."

(Trump) "I didn't have to enlist. I had bone spurs."

(Voice, *sighing*) "Donald, who do you think you're talking to? You can't lie to me."

(Trump) "Okay, so my father and his doctor got me a deferment. So what?"

(Voice) "Close your eyes; we're going on a short trip."

(Trump) "Where are you taking me?"

(Voice) "To visit the Vietnam Memorial on the Mall."

(Trump) "Never been there."

(Voice) "It's a wall with the names of soldiers killed in the war etched on it. Let's go."

Trump now finds himself standing in front of the Vietnam Veterans Memorial Wall.

(Voice) "The tapered wall symbolizes a closed wound that is healing. Walk up to it."

(Trump) "This is kinda spooky. I've seen it. Can we go now?"

(Voice) "Look at the names…Now, imagine their faces. They're talking to you."

(Trump, *shaking*) "Talking to me? What are they saying?"

(Voice) "They want to know why they had to serve and die while you got to stay home."

(Trump) "Tell them about my bone spurs."

(Voice) "You can't lie to the dead. They know all about you. They're talking to you."

(Trump, *trembling*) "What do they want from me? Tell them to back off and go away!"

(Voice) "Admit to them that you were afraid; that you're a coward and a draft dodger."

(Trump, *shouting*) "Okay, I am! Go away! Go away! Please have them go away!"

Hearing Trump scream, a nurse rushes into the room.

(Nurse) "Mr. President, are you all right? I thought I heard you scream."

(Trump, *waking up*) "Oh my God! Thank goodness I'm back. Just a bad dream."

Scene Three

[*The setting and circumstances are the same only it's the following night.*]

(Voice) "Donald."

(Trump) "Can't you leave me alone? Wasn't yesterday enough for you?"

(Voice) "We have so much more to cover."

(Trump) "Where are you taking me now?"

(Voice) "To a familiar setting -- your office in the Trump Tower."

(Trump) "What are we doing there?"

(Voice) "Some people are coming to meet with you."

(Trump) "What people?"

(Voice) "The hundreds of people you swindled during your business career. Let's go."

Trump finds himself behind his desk in his office. He can hear a rowdy crowd outside.

(Voice) "Be patient; they're on their way. Look out the window. See, there are contractors, sub-contractors, workers of all kinds carrying the tools of their trades – saws, hammers, rivet guns, welding torches. They're very anxious to meet with you."

(Trump) "Alert the security guards! Block the doors! Close the stairwells! Shut down the elevators. Red alert! Get Giuliani and Barr on the phone! I need my lawyers now!"

(Voice) "Donald, in your conscience there's nobody to protect you. You stole from these good people. You refused to pay them what they were owed for their honest work. You ruined their businesses and many livelihoods. They couldn't afford to meet you in court."

(Trump, *cowering in a corner*) "Send them away! Please, tell them to go away! I'll go back and look at the books and pay them all they're owed. Just don't let 'em get to me."

The doors to all four elevators open and the avenging throng storms into the office.

(Trump, *shouting frantically*) "No! No! Go away! Go away! Dear God send them away!"

Hearing him scream, a nurse rushes into the room and throws on a light.

(Nurse) "Mr. President, are you all right?"

(Trump, *shielding his eyes*) "Are you unarmed? Are you alone? Is it just you?"

(Nurse) "Why, of course. Unless you want me to summon Dr. Conley."

(Trump, *perspiring but visibly relieved*) "No, there's no need for that. Good night."

<u>Scene Four</u>

[*The setting and circumstances are the same only it's Trump's third night in the hospital. After sending his final tweet, he leans back in bed, afraid to close his eyes, but nods off.*]

(Voice) "Donald."

(Trump) "I hate you! Go away! Why are you tormenting me like this?"

(Voice) "It's just you tormenting yourself for the way you used and mistreated others."

(Trump) "Where are you taking me now?"

(Voice) "I've reserved a suite in a luxury hotel. You can leave your night clothes here."

Trump finds himself lying naked on his back atop a king bed with the covers pulled back.

(Trump, *peering down at his bulging belly*) "This is a bit awkward; what happens next?"

(Voice) "We're expecting some visitors. They should be along shortly."

(Trump, *alarmed*) "Visitors? Can you hand me a robe? There's one in the closet."

(Voice) "A robe? But, why? These are the women you raped, groped and spied upon."

(Trump, *struggling but unable to move*) "I swear they all wanted it. Most loved it."

(Voice) "Donald, there you go again. You can't lie to me, I'm your conscience."

The bedroom door opens and 20 women enter, including Miss Teenager contestants.

(Trump, *red face contrasting with orange hair*) "This is an outrage! I'm being violated!"

(Voice, *as the women surround Trump's bed*) "What goes around comes around!"

(Trump, *over the titters of the women who point at parts of his body*) "How dare you!"

(Voice, *to the women*) "He set the rules. Play all you want but leave no telltale bruises."

(Trump, *howling*) "No! Hey, leave that alone! Get out! Get out! Please get out!"

Hearing him scream, a nurse rushes into the room where Trump lies naked on his bed.

(Nurse, *flicking on a light*) "Oh my God! Excuse me, Mr. President. Am I interrupting?"

(Trump, *hastily covering himself*) "No, I'm fine…It's just that Voice again."

(Nurse, *recovering herself*) "A voice? What voice?"

(Trump, *disoriented*) "I don't know. Supposedly *my* voice. The voice of my conscience."

(Nurse) "I see. Don't move. I'm going to call Dr. Conley."

The nurse exists and returns with his lead physician who had planned to spend the night.

(Trump) "I'm happy to see you, doc. I've been having some awful nightmares."

(Conley) "Nurse Cantwell says you've been hearing voices and shouting."

(Trump) "Yeah, well, I guess she's right. This having a conscience thing is new to me."

(Conley, *writing on a notepad*) "Can you ask this voice to come to you now?"

(Trump) "I can try. I'll warn you though; he's a mean son-of-a-bitch."

(Conley, *continuing to take notes*) "Close your eyes and give it a try."

(Voice, *whispering*) "You want to move up tomorrow night's lesson, do you?"

(Trump, *aloud*) "Yes, why not? Who else have I violated who wants to meet me?"

Dr. Conley, listening to Trump talk to himself, scribbles frantically on his notepad.

(Conley) "Mr. President, did the Voice give you an answer?'

(Trump, *to Dr. Conley*) "Quiet!" (*then to the Voice*) "I'm listening."

(Voice, *whispering*) "Two hundred thousand coronavirus victims."

(Trump, *his voice quivering*) "Where do they want to meet?"

(Voice) "On the other side."

At this moment, a team of hospital aides hastily enter the room wheeling a gurney. Trump is loaded onto it and they proceed to a nearby elevator bank. Dr. Sean Conley, accompanying them, pushes a button marked "Fourth Floor Psychiatric Ward."

BOOK THREE

Descendancy: Run-up to the 2020 election

The months leading up to the 2020 election were chaotic with COVID-19 deaths mounting and support beyond his hardened base diminishing.

SEVENTEEN

The Ordinary Man
(Trump campaign strategists plan a trip to Mayberry)

<u>Scene One</u>

[*The setting is the sheriff's office in the small rural town of Mayberry, North Carolina. It's late August of 2020. Sheriff Andy Taylor is sitting behind his desk sorting through some papers. His deputy, Barney Fife, is sweeping the floor. The only other person in the room is Otis Campbell, the loveable town drunk, who's sleeping off a binge with the bottle in the town jail in the office. Suddenly, the quiet is broken when the door opens, the warning bell jingles, and two men wearing dark suits and ties enter carrying briefcases.*]

(Sheriff Taylor, *looking up*) "Howdy there, gentlemen. How can we help you?"

(Suited man #1) "We're looking for a Sheriff Andy Taylor."

(Andy) "Well, you've come to the right place. I'm Sheriff Taylor."

(Suited man #2, *extending his hand*) "Pleased to meet you, Sheriff. Some law enforcement officials up in Mt. Pilot suggested that we talk to you."

(Andy) "Is that right? Good folks up there...Everything's okay I hope."

(Suited man #2) "Yes, of course. There's no problem at all. (*looking around and seeing Barney and Otis*) Do you mind if we have a word with you in private?"

(Andy) "Barney, see if Otis is asleep, will you? (*now to the suited men*) Otis spends the night with us every now and then after he's found a little moonshine. (*Otis can be heard snoring in the background.*) It'll be a good two hours before he'd hear a gun go off."

(Suite man #1, *looking into the cell*) "He seems dead to the world. Now, your deputy…"

(Andy) "Fellas, I don't know what you're here to talk about, but anything you have to say to me you can say to Deputy Fife. That's the way we operate here in Mayberry."

(Suited man #2, *looking Barney over with a look of skepticism*) "If you say so, Sheriff."

(Andy) "Now, how can we help you gentlemen?"

(Suited man #1, *displaying a badge*) "We're with the Secret Service. We can't share our names with you but you're free to make some inquiries if you think you need to."

(Andy) "Around here we like to believe that folks are who they say they are. And, I wouldn't think that if you two fellas were up to no good you'd start off by visitin' the sheriff's office, would you now? So, what brings you down to Mayberry?"

(Suited man #2) "Sheriff Taylor, I don't know your politics, but you might be aware that the President has been criticized for being too aloof, not being in touch with the little… (*pauses*), ah, the ordinary citizens of America. There's a new plan on how to fix that."

(Andy) "Are you talkin' about the President of the United States?"

(Suited man #2) "Yes, indeed. President Donald J. Trump."

(Barney) "Did ya hear that, Andy? Did ya hear that? The President knows about us!"

(Suited man #1) "Not exactly. Not yet, that is. The plan is to bring the President to a small town like Mayberry to film a series of short political ads showing him, you know, mixing and mingling with the local residents. We want to show him as an ordinary man."

(Andy) "And you think that Mayberry might be a good place to do this filming?"

(Suited man #2) "That's correct, Sheriff. It seems to have everything we're looking for."

(Barney) "You better believe we have everything…What *are* you lookin' for?"

(Suited man #1) "We're hoping that you might help with some ideas. Maybe he could attend a church picnic, visit the school, drop by a few of your fine local shops…"

(Andy) "Well, we don't have any picnics planned; gets a bit hot, sticky and buggy around here this time of year as you might expect. I'm sure we can come up with other ideas."

(Barney) "Sure we can! When he arrives, we could have his limo stop at the filling station for gas and the President could get out to stretch his legs and bump into Gomer and Goober. They work at the station. Can't find more ordinary types than them two."

(Suited man #2) "Gomer and Goober, you say? Central casting couldn't do better!"

(Andy) "Here's an idea. He could come by Floyd's barber shop right next door to here and be seen talkin' to some of the boys. Maybe even ask for a little trim around the ears."

(Suited man #1, *taking notes*) "Hanging out with the local boys…that too sounds good."

(Andy) "Now school ain't in session, but I'm sure Miss Crump would be more than happy to walk him around the classrooms. We could hang his picture next to Lincoln's."

(Suited man #2) "This is going to be easier than we thought. Any more ideas?"

(Barney) "We could take him fishin' at the lake and then skeet shootin' at the club."

(Suited man #1) "Those sound like fine ideas as well…Anything else come to mind?"

(Andy) "Well, my Aunt Bea, she sure does make the best fried chicken. My goodness does she ever! Now, the President looks like he's a good eater, doesn't he? We could invite him over to my place for dinner. Maybe even have boysenberry pie for dessert!"

(Barney, *shuffling his feet and sulking*) "Ah, Andy…"

(Andy) "Barney, of course! You and Thelma Lou could be our other guests."

(Suited man #1) "Thelma Lou? Really? We thought we might have to change a few names but it appears that won't be at all necessary…I think we've found our town!"

Scene Two

[*The setting is the Oval Office of the White House the following day. President Trump is being briefed by Chief of Staff Mark Meadows and political ad producer Hal Workman about plans for him to spend a full day filming next week in Mayberry, N.C.*]

(Trump) "This sounds pretty hokey. Are you sure this isn't going to backfire?"

(Meadows) "Mr. President, there's no place more down-to-earth than this Mayberry."

(Workman) "It's been thoroughly vetted. Once the crews are on site we're set to go."

(Trump) "What am I supposed to do?"

(Meadows) "Just be yourself...Well, on second thought, for these ads try *not* to be yourself. I mean, you can't act like you're the President stooping down to their level."

(Workman) "What Meadows is trying to say is that you need to pretend that you're an ordinary guy just enjoying time with some old buddies. No polo shirts. No knife-cut creases in your slacks. No white belts with brass buckles. No Gucci loafers."

(Trump) "Will Melania be in on this filming?"

(Meadows) "No, she said she'd rather shop at a Tiffany than with a Thelma Lou."

(Workman) "You'll first meet Gomer and Goober. They run the local filling station."

(Trump) "The local what?"

(Workman) "Filling station...Gas station. Where cars get gas."

(Trump) "I knew they ran on gas but I never knew where it came from."

(Workman) "In the opening scene, you'll drive up to the pumps and..."

(Trump) "What? No driver? I don't know how to drive...Never had to."

(Meadows) "No problem! Like all great stars in dangerous roles we can use a stuntman."

(Workman) "We'll shoot from a ways off and have someone made up to look like you drive up. We'll use a 2010 Chevy Caprise and a stand-in driver wearing an orange wig."

(Trump) "What happens then?"

(Workman) "We'll edit the film, and it'll look like it's you getting out of the car."

(Trump) "And then what?"

(Meadows) "Were going extemporaneous from that point."

(Trump) "What's that mean?…I'm wearing clothes aren't I?"

(Workman) "It means that your conversation with Gomer won't be preordained."

(Trump) "Is this Gomer a priest?"

(Meadows) "No, we mean that there won't be rehearsed lines. Just natural talk."

(Trump) "Okay, tremendous. What else is planned?"

(Workman) "We'll probably film a scene at the school with Miss Crump."

(Trump) "A nice piece of ass?"

(Workman) "The girlfriend of the sheriff."

(Trump) "Doesn't matter. I'm the President. I can grab her pussy. She'll like it."

(Meadows) "Not on camera, Mr. President. And *not* in front of the sheriff!"

(Trump) "What's this about staying for dinner?"

(Workman) "A wonderful scene! You're enjoying a meal with the sheriff's family."

(Trump) "What's on the menu?"

(Meadows) "The secret service agent says she makes a mean batch of fried chicken."

(Trump) "Isn't that what the Obamas might order? How about Beef Bourguignon?"

(Workman) "We'll look into that. But remember, these are very ordinary people."

(Trump) "I'll tell you what. Gimme that list of shooting sites and the notes on what you have planned, I'll look it over, and get back to you on how I want things handled. Mark, you can then call this Taylor guy in the morning and go over the changes. Got it?"

(Meadows) "We'll see you first thing tomorrow. We have a tight schedule to keep."

Scene Three

[*The setting is Mayor Pike's office in Mayberry late the following morning. Sheriff Taylor has left the room to take a phone call in his office. Awaiting his return are Mayor Pike, Barney Fife, Aunt Bea, Gomer Pyle, town barber Floyd Larson and Helen Crump.*]

(Mayor Pike) "I do declare it could be the most momentous day in our town's history!"

(Barney) "You can say that again. Imagine, a visit to Mayberry by the President."

(Floyd) "Yes. Yes it is. So nice. A visit from the President…president of what?"

(Barney) "Floyd! The President of the United States. The big kahuna; the top dog…"

(Mayor Pike) "When he arrives I'll formally present him with the keys to the town…"

(Aunt Bea) "Clara as Lady Mayberry can recite our history. She does it so beautifully."

(Mayor Pike) "And my Juanita can serenade him with a welcoming song…"

(Barney, *looking through the window blinds*) "He's coming this way right now."

Sheriff Taylor enters the room and remains standing

(Mayor Pike) "Sheriff, we've just been going over some of the planned festivities…"

(Andy) "Sorry to interrupt, Mayor, but I need to bring you all up to date."

(Mayor Pike, *alarmed*) "He's still coming isn't he, Andy? Please say he is."

(Andy) "Yes, Mayor, I believe he's still coming…but there's been some changes."

(Barney) "What kind of changes, Andy? C'mon. Spill! Fill us in!"

(Andy) "Well, for starters, when he arrives at the filling station he won't be driving, someone else will, but they'll make it look like he's been behind the wheel…"

(Gomer) "Shazam! Shazam. The President's gonna come to Wally's filling station!"

(Andy) "That's right, Gomer. And when he's out of the car he's gonna say 'howdy' and ask you to have a look under the hood because he's hearing a strange noise under there."

(Gomer) "Gol-lee, Andy. I get to fix the President's car besides fillin' his tank?"

(Andy) "Not exactly, Gom. You see, the way they want to do it is have you pop open the hood and listen to the strange sound but tell the President you don't know where it's comin' from. Then he's gonna ask for a tool kit and pretend to fix it himself."

(Gomer) "If you say so, Andy. But there's nothin' about an engine I can't fix by myself."

(Andy) "I know that Gomer. They just want to show how handy the President is with a bunch of tools and stuff so it looks like he can solve just about any kind of problem."

(Barney) "Are we still going fishing? I hope we're still going fishing."

(Andy) "Yes, Barney, we are. But it's gonna be a very short clip. All they're gonna film is the President reeling in a big bass. Opie will be holdin' a net so the president doesn't have to touch the fish. I guess he's a little squeamish about touchin' scaly things."

(Gomer) "Gol-lee, Andy. How long's it gonna take for him to catch a fish like that?"

(Andy) "Good question, Gomer. Here's the thing. Opie and I will go to the lake a couple of days before the President arrives, catch us a big ol' bass and keep it alive in a bucket."

(Barney) "So then you're gonna put the fish on the hook at the end of the President's line and all he has to do is reel it in. That's brilliant, Andy. Just brilliant."

(Andy) "The same sort of thing's gonna happen at the skeet shootin' range. President Trump will be shown firing a shotgun and I'll be off to the side with my shotgun to make sure the skeet gets shot to bits. It'll look like the President's a genuine sharpshooter!"

(Aunt Bea) "Is the President still coming to the house for dinner? I sure do hope so."

(Andy) "Yes he is, Aunt Bea, but there's been a few changes to that as well. You see, you'll be filmed in the kitchen workin' on the fried chicken while the rest of us are sittin' in the parlor doin' small talk with the President when all of a sudden he gets a whiff of what you're cookin' and he leaps on up and marches straight into the kitchen."

(Aunt Bea) "Into *my* kitchen, Andy? You know I don't like people in my kitchen."

(Andy) "I know that, Aunt Bea. But, just this once, okay?"

(Aunt Bea) "And what's he going to do in my kitchen?"

(Andy) "Well, Aunt Bea. Now don't get all hot and bothered; this is the President you know….Aunt Bea, he's gonna tell you how to change your recipe and make it better."

(Aunt Bea) "No, he isn't! Andy Taylor, you know better than to agree to that. I won't have it. President or no president, he's not telling me how to make fried chicken!"

(Andy) "I was afraid you'd feel that way, Aunt Bea. I'll see what I can do about it."

(Aunt Bea) "I'll tell you what you're going to do about it. He's staying in the parlor chit-chatting and out of my kitchen until I'm ready to serve dinner…The nerve of the man!"

(Andy, *to Helen*) "Helen, you've been quiet as a church mouse. Can you help me here?"

(Helen, *angrily*) "Andy, the man is a misogynist pig!"

(Andy, *frustrated*) "Helen, why did you have to go on and say somethin' like that?"

(Helen) "Because it's true, Andy...I don't want that predator within 100 yards of our school...Do you know how many women have accused him of molesting them?"

(Andy, *really frustrated*) "No, Helen, I haven't been countin.'"

(Helen) "A lot. Do you recall him being with a porn star soon after his child was born?"

(Barney) "Yeah, Andy. That was big news..."

(Andy) "Barney, will you stay out of this!"

(Mayor Pike) "Yes, Barney. You stay out of this. We can't lose this opportunity."

(Barney) "Now just everyone hold on a minute. Hold on. (*pauses*) I'm beginning to think this is all wrong. It's just not right what we're doin.' It's not right at all."

(Mayor Pike) "What's not right, Barney?"

(Barney) "The whole thing's not right. Him pretendin' to fix a car that Gomer can't fix. Him catchin' a fish that's put on his hook. Him lookin' like he's an expert marksman when Andy's the one hitting the targets. Him tellin' Aunt Bea how to fry chicken."

(Floyd) "I'd like to ask him what happened to the mailbox that used to be in front of the shop. A real shame. People tell me it was taken away on his orders. Some men showed up one day from Raleigh and just took it away. They say the post office might be next."

(Helen) "Andy, Barney's right you know. I realize it's a big deal to have a president come to town. That's fine. Even him. Just keep him away from me and my girls. But, not the way you're telling us it's going to happen. We might be the ordinary folks that he wants to be seen with. But, we have our pride as well. He's making us look like fools."

(Andy, *quietly*) "What say you, Mayor Pike? Seems to me I got a bit carried away."

(Mayor Pike) "I know Juanita will be heartbroken, but Mayberry is an honorable town. We're not going to be used. (*pauses*) I think you should tell them to find another town."

Scene Four

[*The setting is the Oval Office in the White House the following morning. Mark Meadows and Hal Workman are meeting with President Trump about the filming project.*]

(Trump) "Mark, did you hear back from Taylor? Are we set to go?"

(Meadows) "Not really, Mr. President. We're looking at alternative opportunities."

(Trump) "What's wrong with Mayberry?"

(Meadows) "They were honored, of course. But, um…they we're overwhelmed."

(Trump) "That's a surprise but understandable. I intimidate a lot of little people."

(Meadows) "That's one way of looking at it."

(Trump) "What's the alternative? Any other ordinary places and people for the shoot?"

(Workman) "We're thinking about having you visit a family rather than a town."

(Trump) "That could work, I suppose. Maybe something closer than Mayberry."

(Workman) "Precisely. You just drop in for a friendly chat with ordinary folks."

(Trump) "Do you have any ordinary family in mind?"

(Meadows) "Actually, yes, Mr. President. The Archie Bunker household in Queens."

EIGHTEEN

One in the Family
(Archie Bunker prepares for a presidential visit)

<u>Scene One</u>

[*The setting is the living room of the home of Archie and Edith Bunker at 704 Hauser Street in Queens, New York. It's late August of 2020. Archie is smugly sitting in his easy chair smoking a cigar and sipping on a beer. Suddenly the front door opens as daughter Gloria and son-in-law Michael Stivic arrive home, first removing their COVID-19 masks before entering. Edith, in her apron, immediately rushes to the door to greet them.*]

(Edith) "Come in…Come in! Have we eva got some big news ta tell ya."

(Gloria) "What is it, Ma?"

(Archie) "Now Edith, don't you be spillin' the beans…Make 'em guess."

(Edith) "Someone's comin' ta visit and you'll neva guess who it is."

(Michael) "The way Archie's acting you'd think it was Donald Trump."

(Archie) "Geez Edith! Did you say somethin' about it bein' Donald Trump?"

(Edith) "No, Archie, of course not. They jus walked in the door jus now."

(Gloria) "Daddy's kidding, isn't he, Ma? Is it Aunt Maude who's coming?"

(Archie) "No, Aunt Maude ain't comin', thank the Lord…but the President is!"

(Michael, *holding his head*) "Ma, please tell me this is all a cruel joke."

(Edith) "No it ain't, Michael. Two men came by today to talk ta Archie an' me."

(Archie) "Two men from the Selection Soyvice no less."

(Michael) "You mean the Secret Service don't you, Arch?"

(Archie) "Whateva…These two guys come by to set it all up. He's comin' tamorra."

(Edith) "See, Michael, they left these cards and this letter and package."

(Gloria) "What's the letter say, Ma?"

(Archie, *handing Gloria an official looking paper*) "Here, read it fer youselves."

(Michael) "Gloria, I think this is for real…Oh, my God. What are we gonna do?"

(Archie) "Yous twos ain't gonna do nuttin' because yous twos ain't gonna be around."

(Gloria) "Whadaya mean, Daddy? We live here. Of course we'll be around."

(Archie) "Nose you won't, little goil. And without sayin' that goes for the Meathead too."

(Michael) "You want us to leave the house so you can meet alone with the President?"

(Archie) "No! Edith will be around, ya know…to soive him lemonade and cookies."

(Edith) "No, Archie. It says that we'll all be sittin' around havin' small talk with him."

(Archie) "You don't have 'small talk' with the President, Edith. You talk about…"

(Michael) "Go on, Archie. What will you and Trump talk about? Your golf game?"

(Gloria, *giggling*) "Maybe our upcoming family trip to Russia to meet with Putin."

(Michael) "Or Archie's nominees for the Supreme Court, including himself!"

(Gloria) "Our ideas on how to mass move all the Muslims out of Queens…"

(Archie, *riled*) "There ya go! These are the very reasons yous liberals can't be here."

(Michael) "Calm down, Arch. Seriously, do you really want that man in our house?"

(Archie) "Of course! It's a nice house. Where else ya wan us ta meet? Kelsey's Bar?"

(Michael) "I wasn't referring to our house, Arch. Do you really want *him* in our house?"

(Archie) "Of course! It's a real honor to have a little sit-down chat with the President."

(Michael) "True, Arch. If it's Obama or even "W"…but this president, no way!"

(Archie) "Now see here, Meathead. What's wrong with this president?"

(Gloria) "For starters, Daddy, he's a misogynist."

(Archie) "Well, maybe he can work on my sore back a bit while we're talkin.'"

(Michael) "Archie, Gloria means that he disrespects women."

(Archie, *turning to his wife*) "Edith, does Trump disinfect women?"

(Edith) "Well, Archie, you know…"

(Archie) "See there! Your mother doesn't think so."

(Gloria) "Daddy, you didn't give her a chance to talk."

(Archie) "She doesn't need to talk, little goil. Dat's my job aroun' here."

(Michael, *throwing his hands up*) "Arch, you're as bad as he is!"

(Gloria) "Look what he's done to those poor immigrant children."

(Archie) "You mean sendin' 'em back 'cause they were here illegibly?"

(Gloria) "I mean separating them from their parents and putting them up in hotels!"

(Archie) "Bein' put up in a hotel sounds pretty good ta me…I don't stay in hotels."

(Edith, *nervously*) "Suppa should be ready. Why don't we talk about all this later on."

(Archie) "There's really nuttin' ta talk about other than these two figurin' where ta hide."

(Michael, *rolling his eyes*) "What's for dinner, Ma?"

(Edith) "'Cause of the big news, I made Archie's favorite dinna –

meatloaf with mashed potatas an' canned green beans with plenty of ketchup on top of the meatloaf."

(Archie) "Edith, you'd better soive myself, you and Gloria foist. There'll be no meatloaf left if the Meathead here gets foist dibs... We'll all eat, then yous two can go upstairs and do whatever you do – but not that! – an' we'll continya this here conyersation tamorra."

Scene Two

[*The setting is the same room the following morning. Archie is sitting in his regular chair; Edith is in the kitchen. Michael and Gloria are seen coming down the stairs.*]

(Archie) "Well, look who's finally arrived. Come ova here now and sit yourselves down so we can discuss where ya can be off to while the President and me are meetin'."

(Michael, *holding the package*) "Arch, did you read what it says in here?"

(Archie) "Didn't have to. Them fellas 'splained it all."

(Michael) "Well, the President might be coming by this afternoon, but he might not. It says in here that about two dozen households in the area have been identified for a possible visit and he's only going to have time to stop by a few of them."

(Archie) "No problem there with that. Them fellas made it sound we was a sure thing."

(Michael) "Did you get to the part where they talk about what's going to happen?"

(Archie) "The President sits down – he can sit in Edith's chair – and I'll be sittin' here in my chair and he'll ask me about a few things and I'll give him the all the right answers."

(Gloria) "Daddy, did you read the list of questions he might ask? It's all rigged!"

(Archie) "Whadaya mean 'rigged?' We're supposed ta talk like we're old buddies."

At this point Edith enters from the kitchen wiping her hands on her apron

(Michael) "Let me read you a few of these, Arch, and you tell me what you think."

(Archie) "Sure, have at it…Edith, sit down and listen to the Meathead here."

(Michael, *reading*) "Do you believe the China Virus was released intentionally from an experimental lab in Wuhan or simply escaped due to lack of precautions?"

(Archie) "Dat dere virus come from rats cooked in a lab, don't ya know. What's next?"

(Gloria) "Daddy, there's absolutely no evidence that COVID-19 came from a lab in China. That's just another conspiracy theory. It originated from a bat in an open market."

(Archie) "What's the difference if it's a rat or bat? They eat 'em both in China, ya know."

(Michael, *exasperated*) "Try this one, Arch. "Do you believe in the slogan *Black Lives Matter* and should local police and federal agents be authorized to use tear gas and other non-lethal weapons on roving gangs of young Blacks, hippies and druggies who are setting fires, breaking into stores to steal merchandise and generally inciting riots?"

(Archie) "Ya know that that Floyd Mayweather guy who caused all this trouble was resistin' arrest, don't ya? He was; I saw it on TV. I jus don't know what it is about them coloreds. They get all this free taxpayer money, have babies like they don't know where they come from, and then get all riled up because one guy says he can't breathe. Geez!"

(Gloria) "Daddy! How dare you say things like that! What about Mr. Jefferson?"

(Archie) "Jefferson ain't Black like all these other people causin' all the riots."

(Michael) "What is he, Arch? Orange...Purple...Chartreuse...?"

(Archie) "No, Mr. Socialist. What I means ta say that he's a Black guy who don't, you know, act like your regular Black guy."

(Gloria) "Daddy! Are you saying that most 'regular' Black people steal and cause riots?"

(Archie) "No, not *all* of 'em, little goil. Jus the ones havin' all them babies ta support."

(Michael) "Arch, you're one of a kind, you know that?"

(Archie) "Not at all, Meathead. The country's full of smart people like me. You'll learn that in this here upcomin' 'lection when your socialist party gets its butt kicked."

(Michael) "I'll just read you one more, Arch. But, these aren't open ended questions that lend themselves to conversation and debate. They're prompts to get guys like you to start spewing back all the garbage you pick up on *Fox News* and right-wing talk shows."

(Edith) "Mike has a point ya know, Archie. You only watch *Fox News*."

(Archie) "Would you stay out of this, Edith. What do you know about these things anyhow? And, shouldn't you be makin' lemonade for me an' the President?"

(Gloria) "Daddy, don't talk to Ma like that! She has every right to say what's on her mind. That's the problem with men; they're chauvinistic pigs."

(Michael) "Gloria!"

(Edith) "I don't think she meant you, Michael...She meant Archie."

(Archie) "Edith!"

(Edith) "Sorry, Archie, but it's true. You shouldn't have those feelin's about Black people and women and even China. What about Mr. Yang our grocer? And Mrs. Chung who's so nice as to give you extra fortune cookies when you don't like the ones ya got."

(Archie) "What is this here? A shootin' gallery? Here you are gettin' me all worked up before the President comes into this house to have an important kinda chat with me."

(Michael) "One more to practice on and then we'll let up. 'Who do you blame for the hoax of climate change? Democrats, scientists, professors or all of the above?'"

(Archie) "That one's easy; all of the above. Did you know that where we are right now was once covered with ice? That was a long time ago, I know that, but did the Romans or the people around back then blame themselves or did they jus accept that Mother Nature was either foolin' around or jus doin' her thing? They had no more ta do with the ice comin' than we have watchin' it melt away. Add Mother Nature to that there list."

(Gloria) "What about all the greenhouse gasses we let loose into the atmosphere?"

(Edith) "And the polar bears starvin.' I saw this documentary about how all the ice is meltin' around 'em and they can't catch seals ta eat so they might soon be all gone."

(Archie) "Well boo hoo! Get them bears out of the way and the bleedin' hearts who won't let us drill in that Arthritic Zone won't have nuttin' to complain about no mores!"

(Michael) "I will say this for you, Arch, you've done your homework for this meeting."

(Archie) "Well, thank you. Sometimes you ain't such a injuramus, ya know that?"

Scene Four

[*The setting is the same room only it's getting on in the afternoon. Michael and Gloria are playing checkers and Edith is knitting. Archie is seen pacing back-and-forth.*]

(Archie, *nervously*) "What time is it gettin' ta be?"

(Michael) "A little after two o'clock, Arch."

(Archie) "Shouldn't they be callin' by now?"

(Michael) "The instructions in the package the Secret Service guys dropped off say that they'll call thirty minutes before the President is to arrive if we're selected. It also says that the last call will come no later than 3:30 p.m. You still have an hour and a half."

(Archie) "I don't get it. They made it sound like we was a sure thing."

(Michael) "Maybe they're saving the best for last."

(Archie, *sitting down*) "You could be right wit that. I'll jus sit an patently wait."

Suddenly the phone rings

(Archie) "Edith, answer the phone! And tell 'em I'm ready any time."

(Edith, *talking to the caller*) "I see...I see. You can maybe find a substitute."

(Archie, *alarmed*) "No substitutes! No substitutes! We're ready now."

(Edith, *cupping the phone*) "It's Harriet Bleacher. She wants ta know if we have any rice wine she could borrow for a recipe she's makin'."

(*to the caller*) "I'll check but you can get away with white wine vinegar if I can't find any in the pantry…Hold on a minute."

(Archie) "Edith! For chrissakes get off the phone! We're expectin' a call, remember?"

(Edith, *back on the phone*) "Harriet, I'll run it ova if I find some. Do you have white wine vinegar if I don't? I believe I might also have some red wine vinegar…"

(Archie) "Get off the phone right this minute! You hear me? Off the phone!"

(Edith) "I gotta go now, Harriet. Archie's expecting an important call from the President who's supposed ta be comin' over this afternoon but so far we haven't heard…"

(Archie, *tormented*) "Edith, please…GET OFF THE DAMN TELEPHONE!"

(Edith) "I think I should get off the phone now, Harriet. Good luck with the recipe."

(Archie) "Edith, what we're ya doin'? What if they called when you was on the phone?"

(Michael) "Archie, if they were planning on coming they'll call again."

(Archie, *slumping into his chair*) "I guess so…What time is it now?"

Scene Five

[*The setting is the same room occupied by the same four people. It's now 3:45 p.m.*]

(Michael) "Well, Arch. It looks like he went someplace else."

(Archie) "I just don't understand it. Those fellas all but gave us a guarantee…"

(Michael) "Not all is lost, Arch. You're better prepared if some poor liberal sucker chances to pop into Kelsey's for a beer while you're there. You're loaded for bear."

(Archie) "I jus don't get it…I jus don't get it. I think I'll get myself a beer."

Archie slowly gets up and shuffles muttering to himself to the kitchen

(Edith) "You'd betta move fast, Mike. He won't be gone long."

(Gloria) "She's right, Michael. What if he decides to go for a walk?"

(Michael, *moving quickly toward the front door*) "I'm on my way."

The camera now shows the exterior of the home of Archie and Edith Bunker. From a close up of the front porch, the camera pulls back to show the front yard and the steps leading up to a short walkway to the house from the sidewalk. On the grass just to the side of the walkway beyond the steps is a small but highly visible sign that reads:

JOE BIDEN
For
PRESIDENT

NINETEEN

The Devil and Donald Trump

(Trump sells his soul to gain favor with liberal commentators)

<u>Act One, Scene One</u>

[*The setting is the president's bedroom in the White House. Melania Trump, the president's wife, knocks on his door (she sleeps in a different room) having heard some sniffling sounds coming from within. The president is seen sitting on the edge of his bed, his head in his hands, moaning quietly. Recognizing the knock he grants her entry.*]

(Melania) "Darling, what's the matter. You seem very upset."

(Trump) "What isn't the matter?"

(Melania) "Are things getting you down?"

(Trump) "This wasn't the way I planned to spend the summer."

(Melania) "You mean stuck in the White House because of that China Virus?"

(Trump) "That's a good start."

(Melania) "You mean because of the protesters calling you a racist?"

(Trump) "Among other things I suppose they're calling me."

(Melania) "They do call you a lot of things."

(Trump) "And how would you know that?"

(Melania) "Oh, it's a little game I play with my maid. Every night we write down all the names they call you on TV or in the newspapers. She says it will improve my vocabulary."

(Trump) "I only watch *Fox News* because they only say nice things about me."

(Melania) "Then you should take up reading and watch different channels."

(Trump) "And how would that make me feel any better?"

(Melania) "I don't know, but it might help improve your vocabulary."

(Trump) "Melania, if you came here to comfort me you're not doing a good job."

(Melania) "Then maybe we should play the name-game. It's fun."

(Trump) "How is calling your husband names fun?"

(Melania, *encouragingly*) "You can start by picking a letter. Any letter will do."

(Trump) "What happens after that?"

(Melania, *opening a composition book she'd brought with her*) "You'll see."

(Trump) "Okay, I'll play along. How about 'C'? I'm thinking of words for me like charming, courageous and charismatic."

(Melania, *flipping through the pages then stopping*) "I don't see those words, but there are lots of other words that begin with 'C.'"

(Trump) "Lots of words? Like what words?"

(Melania, *reading*) "Crass, cowardly, conspiratorial (I like that; it's a big word), corrupt, compulsive, creepy, contemptible, culpable, conniving, cheap, cheater, combustible..."

(Trump, *interrupting*) "Enough!"

(Melania) "Enough for the 'Cs?' Okay. But there's plenty more… Shall we try a vowel?"

(Trump) "I can't believe this is happening."

(Melania) "That's wonderful, darling. See, you're having fun. Let's do 'I.'"

(Trump) "As in this little game, which is 'insane?'"

(Melania) "Very good, darling, you're catching on; that's one of them! There's also insecure, insincere, irascible, irrational, incendiary, inept, insolent, impolite, impressionistic, impossible, illiterate, immature, irremediable, incoherent, indecisive, irresponsible, irritating, immoderate, incomprehensible, icky, illegitimate − that only referred to your election, darling − irritating, illusionary, imbecilic, idiotic, incorrigible, immoral, insensitive, inflammatory …"

(Trump, *exasperated*) "I think I've had enough of the 'Is.'"

(Melania) "There are plenty more, but let's do the 'Ds.' Let me see, we have dumb, delusional, deceitful, despicable, deplorable, detestable, dickhead, dorky, divisive…"

(Trump, *impatiently*) "Is *every* damn letter of the alphabet covered?"

(Melania) "Oh, yes dear. Even those tough 'Qs' (*flips pages*) like quixotic, quirky, quarrelsome, and quack; and for the 'Zs' page we have zombie, zero, zealot…"

(Trump) "Stop, please! It's enough to make a man want to sell his soul to the devil!"

Act One, Scene Two

[*It's the following morning and the setting is the Oval Office in the White House. The president sits behind his massive desk all alone, trying to concentrate, but his mind keeps trying to come up with positive words beginning with each letter to describe himself. His reverie is interrupted by a knock on the door as Chief of Staff Mark Meadows peeks in.*]

(Trump, *to himself*) "Okay 'Ts' – tough, talented, terrific, tremendous." (*he then looks up*)

(Meadows) "Mr. President. There's a Mr. Snatch here who insists on seeing you."

(Trump) "Snatch? (*tittering*) And it's a guy?"

(Meadows) "That's correct. The thing is that the guard at the gate never granted him entry or even saw him go by, and the doorman swears the front entrance was locked."

(Trump) "What's he look like?"

(Meadows) "Wiry, a bit red-faced. Ordinary sort, but with sharply pointed ears."

(Trump) "Did he say why he wants to see me?"

(Meadows) "Not specifically. Something about a deal and your... could it be soul?"

Act One, Scene Three

[*The same room; Mr. Meadows has been dismissed with orders to admit no one.*]

(Snatch) "It's a pleasure meeting you in person, Mr. Trump."

(Trump) "Why not call me Mr. President like everyone else?"

(Snatch) "In my business, titles don't matter. We deal in souls."

(Trump) "You want to sell me shoes?"

(Snatch) "I want to *buy* your *inner* soul."

(Trump) "So, you want my insoles but not my shoes? Isn't that kinda kinky."

(Snatch) "You misunderstand. I'm here at your request to buy *your* soul for *my* services."

(Trump) "Oh, that soul! (*chuckles*) Some people claim I haven't got one."

(Snatch) "They are wrong. Everyone has a soul; yours is a lot like my master's."

(Trump) "And who might that be?"

(Snatch) "Why Beelzebub, of course!"

(Trump, *looking up*) "Bells above?"

(Snatch, *aside*) "I was warned he was stupid." (*to Trump*) "You might know him better as Satan, or, as you referred to him last night, as the Devil."

(Trump) "So there *is* a devil? By golly, that Joel Osteen is a pretty smart guy."

(Snatch) "On with business, Mr. Trump. You said your summer wasn't going well."

(Trump) "Not at all like I imagined it."

(Snatch) "And how would that be?"

(Trump) "You know, me standing in huge arenas overflowing with my adoring fans with me whipping them into a frenzy with my speeches. It's a tremendous feeling."

(Snatch, *aside*) "Like in the 1930s at the Sportpalast in Berlin. How well I remember…"

(Trump, *continuing*) "And trips to friendly countries where me and my family would be lavishly dined, entertained, and given expensive presents. I was hoping to make it to Saudi Arabia and Russia this summer but then China released that virus from its lab."

(Snatch, *aside*) "My master has many friends in those places as well."

(Trump) "And then the simple pleasures: golf at Mar-a-Lago with Tiger Woods and NASCAR races with all those 'TRUMP 2020' signs and Confederate flags. Come to think of it, I'm happiest being anywhere where thousands and thousands of people are cheering me, shouting my name…and *not* calling me the names I heard last night!"

(Snatch) "That was awful. But, you can thank your wife for you calling on us."

(Trump) "It was nasty. All those nasty words, although I'll confess I didn't know what most of them meant. I just assumed it wasn't good."

(Snatch) "So, you'd like to fix that?"

(Trump) "If people would only say nice things about me that would be tremendous."

(Snatch) "But, you wouldn't be changing your ways would you? I mean, the master likes you just the way you are. You just want the liberals, socialists, do-gooders, gays, lesbians, Black people, Hispanic people, poor people, educated people…well, more simply, everyone who's *not* part of your base to begin speaking highly of you. Correct?"

(Trump) "Is that possible?"

(Snatch) "Mr. Trump. For the right price, everything is possible with the Devil."

(Trump) "After the election, they can go back to what they were saying before. I sort of like it, especially when I know that they can't touch me for four more years, or even longer if things go the way I'd like to see them go with changing the Constitution and my owning the Supreme Court. They can call me all the names they want. They'll regret it."

(Snatch, *aside*) "He brings back more wonderful memories. So many countries; so many of my master's servants. I was especially fond of Mao with whom I cut my first deal."

(Trump, *continuing*) "My point is I only need your help for the time between now, the middle of June, and the day of the election, November third. How does that work?"

(Snatch, *surprised*) "You can set any duration you want; but the price remains the same."

(Trump) "You want my soul in exchange?"

(Snatch) "That's the only way we leverage our contracts."

(Trump, *thinking*) "Okay, from now until the election everyone speaks nicely of me."

(Snatch) "Not exactly. My master is good – wait, bad choice of words – my master is adept at many things, but he can't change what some people say. What he can do, and this is the deal, he'll change the way people respond to what *you* say. You'll see."

(Trump) "I'm not sure I get it. Give me an example."

(Snatch) "Easy enough. Pick up your phone and tweet something. Something timely."

(Trump) "I'll tweet about that Black fellow, you know, Boy George or Floyd George or whoever it was, sending presidential thoughts and prayers to his family and friends."

(Snatch) "Don't forget to mention thoughts and prayers for the officers who killed him."

(Trump, *beginning to tweet*) "Great idea!"

Act Two, Scene One

[*The setting is CNN's television studios where Anderson Cooper is live and on-the-air with three liberal commentators: Van Jones, David Axelrod and David Gergen.*]

(Cooper) "Gentlemen, have you seen the president's latest tweet?"

(Jones) "I'm not sure. Why don't you read it to us."

(Cooper, *reading*) "Great day for Floyd George looking down from above and for all Black Americans as unemployment just dropped by the biggest margin in history."

(Jones) "I did see that. Great to see the president reaching out to the Black community in these tumultuous times. He's making sure Black Americans get back to work. Love it!"

(Axelrod) "In his haste he got the name reversed but that's excusable in his rush to display sympathy. This is a sensitivity we haven't seen before from the president."

(Gergen) "I agree. This is exactly the kind of leadership we need in a national crisis."

Act Two, Scene Two

[*The setting is again the Oval Office in the White House the following morning. The president is alone, anxiously awaiting the arrival of Snatch with whom he has a scheduled 9:00 appointment. Chief of Staff Meadows announces the arrival.*]

(Meadows) "Mr. President, Mr. Snatch has arrived for his appointment."

(Trump) "Send him in right away." (*Snatch enters and Meadows leaves*)

(Snatch) "Convinced?"

(Trump) "I can't believe it. This is tremendous. Where's that contract?"

(Snatch) "Are you sure?"

(Trump) "Of course I'm sure. Five months of nothing but praise even from my biggest detractors and enemies. How could I ever possibly lose the election?"

(Snatch) "That would indeed be highly improbable given your newfound across-the-board popularity." (*Hands Trump a document to sign*) "I think you'll find this all in order. It's the standard form. The only entry is the date of collection – November 3, 2020."

(Trump, *signing with great flourish*) "You must have read my book, The Art of the Deal. See how you whittled me down to five months? I could have asked for five years!"

(Snatch) "That was a surprise to me as well. I'll see you on November 4th. Good day."

Act Two, Scene Three

[*The setting is a huge arena, the site of the Republican National Convention, and the date is August 27, 2020. Donald Trump has been unanimously nominated by his party to serve a second term. As the confetti flies, he's just wrapping up his lengthy acceptance speech.*]

(Trump, *from the high lectern*) "Before I close, I want to say a few words about my opponent, Joe Biden (*loud boos shake the arena*), yeah, Sleepy Joe. He's had a tough summer. I can't tell you how many of his supporters have texted me to let me know how my message has turned their heads. Scientists, you know, the pointy-headed guys from Harvard and the other poison ivy schools, the ones who want to tell us that the world is heating up, that global warming is something we should be worried about, they're now getting behind the Trump campaign. (*Loud cheering*) Same with the tree-huggers who fret that we're chopping down forests too quickly; they now realize that loggers need those jobs. (*More loud cheering*) Plus the 'Save the Whales' softies. And the bleeding heart socialists who want to see your insurance premiums skyrocket so people with bad existing conditions, like cancer, who aren't doing anything good for society anymore, can live a little while longer – all at your expense. Well, too bad. If they can pay for it themselves let 'em do it, although their children would probably prefer they just let go. Anyway, more and more people are seeing it *my* way, seeing it *your* way, letting you keep your hard-earned money and not have it snatched away and handed over to others."

(*The president stops to take a sip of water, and then continues as the crowd roars*) "I'm telling you, we're going to win big time, big time, in November. The greatest landslide in history. All Americans will be holding hands and shouting my name (*the crowd starts chanting 'Trump, Trump'*). And I mean *the* Americans, the true Patriots that is, who honor our flag, defend our freedom by buying and bearing arms, and who recognize that China and the Muslim nations are our true enemies, and the way to deal with them is through developing the biggest weapons arsenal the world has ever known, ripping up trade agreements that aren't in our favor, and, building the highest border walls to keep the undesirables, the murderers, the rapists and the teary-eyed socialists OUT!"

(*The president raises his arms in a victory salute as the crowd in the arena goes wild*)

Act Three, Scene One

[*The setting is the White House on election night. The president's immediate family and hundreds of guests, including Vice President Pence, Attorney General William Barr, and Secretary of State Mike Pompeo have arrived to celebrate his reelection. Because of reporting delays in several states, an outcome has yet to be projected by the networks.*]

(Trump) "It's sure looking good; just a matter of a few hours before it's official."

(Pompeo) "In June I was more than apprehensive, I was doubtful."

(Barr) "I have to agree. COVID-19; race riots. This comeback is absolutely unworldly."

(Trump, *aside*) "You've got that right!"

(Pence) "Who would have expected the NAACP to make a late endorsement?"

(Barr) "Or the Sierra Club?"

(Pompeo) "How about Reverend Sharpton, Sean Penn and Michael Moore?"

(Pence) "It's unreal. Out of the world. God intervened to save his country!"

(Trump, *aside*) "You're on the right track…but think lower, ha ha!"

Act Three, Scene Two

[*The setting is the president's private bedroom just after midnight. Confident that the outcome will fall his way, Mr. Trump has retired to his quarters to rest and reflect. Suddenly, seemingly out of nowhere, he receives a visit from Mr. Snatch.*]

(Trump, *startled*) "Snatch, what are you doing here?"

(Snatch) "I'm coming to collect."

(Trump) "Collect what?"

(Snatch) "Your soul. It's all in the signed agreement." (*handing Trump a document*)

(Trump) "How you gonna do that?"

(Snatch) "Simple, you're coming with me."

(Trump, *nervously*) "Now?"

(Snatch) "Of course. November 3rd expired two minutes ago. It's now November 4th."

(Trump) "All that means is that people can say bad things about me again, right?"

(Snatch) "No, the contract has expired. You set the date yourself. Frankly, I was quite surprised; shocked you might say. Most of my clients negotiate that we take their souls at the end of their natural lives in exchange for our favors. You insisted on November 3rd."

(Trump, *trembling and stuttering*) "B…But I didn't understand. Am… am I to die?"

(Snatch) "The body and soul are united. We've found that the soul is inflammable. It's the body that burns wretchedly in the fires of hell. That's what we're seeking."

(Trump) "But, I'm healthy. Look at me. A bit overweight but…"

(Snatch) "The coroner's report has already been prepared. Cardiac arrest due to excessive jubilation in anticipation of election results and a preexisting condition."

(Trump) "What preexisting condition?"

(Snatch) "Bone spurs. That was the first time my master, the Devil, was introduced to your family and its deceitful ways. You've been on our watch list ever since."

(Trump) "So, this is it? What if I call my personal attorney?"

(Snatch) "Are you kidding me, Rudy Giuliani versus the Devil? How about a three-legged horse versus Secretariat? Or, Mike Pence in the ring versus Mike Tyson?"

(Trump) "I meant my *real* personal attorney, William Barr."

(Snatch) "Billy? I know him well. How do you think he became Attorney General?"

(Trump) "The Supreme Court?"

(Snatch) "Two words for you – Brett Kavanaugh, a client of mine."

(Trump) "So I'm doomed?"

(Snatch) "I'm afraid so. Trust me, Daniel Webster in all his eloquence couldn't save you. Most of my clients read the contract from top to bottom. You, the so-called 'great negotiator' and author of *The Art of the Deal*, in your great haste didn't take the time to read it. I must say yours was the shortest term for collection that I've ever negotiated."

(Trump) "Okay, I give in, but one last thing. Did I win the election?"

(Snatch) "That's what I love about my master. Not knowing is part of your hell."

TWENTY

Trump & Goring

(Goring greets Trump at the gates of hell)

[*The date is November 4, 2020. While word rapidly spreads around Planet Earth that President Donald Trump of the United States expired shortly after midnight on November 4th, prior to final election returns, he is now seen sitting on a rustic plank in a dark, smoky and foul-smelling room in an uncertain location, naked and by himself. The only light, fiery red, emanates from a space beneath a large iron door that is closed shut. Suddenly, the door opens, filling the room with a blast of furnace-like heat while allowing a lone figure to enter. Silhouetted against the light, the entrant appears to be a man, also naked, who, like Trump, is remarkable in the darkness only for his great girth.*]

(Trump, *startled and shaken*) "Who are you?"

(Goring, *slowly lowering himself onto a plank opposite Trump*) "Hermann Goring."

(Trump) "The name sounds familiar. Do I know you?"

(Goring) "Perhaps as Der Fuehrer's Senior General, among many other titles."

(Trump) "Da Fewer...I'm not getting it."

(Goring, *shaking his head*) "Does Adolf Hitler ring a bell?"

(Trump) "Now you're making sense. The guy who gassed all the Jews."

(Goring) "A mere procedure; our goal was global Aryan supremacy."

(Trump) "So you wanted to have all the planes and own the skies?"

(Goring) "That was part of my job. But, you misunderstand; Aryan refers to a race of people, superior people, white people predominantly. People like you."

(Trump, *pleased*) "Well, my oh my. Thank you! But you failed?"

(Goring, *taking a deep breath, then coughing and waving at the air*) "Yes, ultimately because of your country getting involved. You Americans put up a great resistance."

(Trump) "We are a nation of great fighters. People of tremendous courage."

(Goring, *sarcastically*) "Like you?"

(Trump, *obviously missing Goring's sarcasm*) "We all have a role to play."

(Goring) "So, you were a fighter, a warrior, a combatant in uniform?"

(Trump, *proudly*) "I was the Commander-in-Chief."

(Goring) "Of course, as president. And before that?"

(Trump) "I couldn't serve. Medical dispensation. Bone spurs."

(Goring) "Ah, yes! A terrible debilitating condition."

(Trump) "And yourself before you became Hitler's right hand guy?"

(Goring, *straightening up, he had been leaning towards Trump*) "I was a flying ace during World War One. Highly decorated. Perhaps second only to The Red Baron."

(Trump) "Well, someday they're gonna name an aircraft carrier after me. They better!"

(Goring) "Such a shame you'll never know."

(Trump) "I was hoping you could tell me if I got reelected last night."

(Goring) "I understand that's part of your hell. Trivial matter anyway in this place."

(Trump) "I meant to ask about this place. Where are we?"

(Goring) "This is what is referred to as the antechamber to hell."

(Trump) "Help me; I don't understand."

(Goring) "Consider it a lobby or waiting room. You sit while they assess your case."

(Trump) "Who are they?"

(Goring) "Why, the Devil and his cohorts, of course."

(Trump) "Are they discussing whether I belong here? All I did was to sell my soul."

(Goring) "You only wish, Mr. Trump. Like me, it was only a matter of time."

(Trump) "You didn't sell your soul to Mr. Snatch?"

(Goring) "If I dare use the term, 'heavens no!' I did this all on my own. I was cruel, ruthless, vain, arrogant, pleasure-seeking…to say nothing of the people I had killed."

(Trump) "So you weren't tricked like I was?"

(Goring) "Trump, you weren't tricked. You'd have ended up here anyway."

(Trump) "But, I didn't kill anybody."

(Goring, *chuckling*) "Oh come now, Trump! I read your dossier before coming here. You're responsible for hundreds, maybe thousands of innocent people losing their lives, or their livelihoods. Like me you were a liar, a cheat, a manipulator who'd do anything to get what you wanted. Don't for one minute consider yourself a victim of trickery."

(Trump, *flustered*) "I didn't kill anyone. I don't even own a gun. People loved me!"

(Goring) "In your business dealings you ruined lives and small enterprises by refusing to make good on perfectly legitimate billings. You sued those who protested knowing they couldn't afford to match your legion of corrupt lawyers...You grossly inflated the value of your real estate assets to obtain loans then deflated the values by as much or more on your tax filings...You sent thousands of desperate immigrants back to their lawless homelands where they faced retribution, torture and some even death...Your ruthless rhetoric unleashed a wave of violence against Muslims, Hispanics and Black people so supremacists – people like me -- suddenly felt free to expose their once self-contained bigotry and hatred knowing you, the president, had their back. They even proudly unfurled the flag of my Third Reich! You have no grounds to protest your presence here."

(Trump, *trembling*) "Lies, all lies! I want my legal counsel! Where's Barr? Bring him here to defend me. God knows the Supreme Court would find me innocent of these charges. This can't be happening to me. I'm Donald J. Trump. I demand justice!"

(Goring, *calmly*) "No, Trump, you're demanding that justice be overruled. What I see is another king on a lost battlefield crying out for a horse: 'A horse! A horse! My kingdom for a horse.' (*chuckles*) This is no Shakespearean tragedy. This is a tragedy of your own making. There are no hand-picked jurors to proclaim your innocence. Time to man up!"

(Trump, *whimpering*) "I can't man up. I've never manned up. You were a top fighter ace. A man of courage. I hear that. My family made sure I never would be exposed to the danger of war. I've always had protectors. I shouldn't be judged the same way as you."

(Goring) "Am I hearing that a weak man like you should not be condemned for his failings simply because he was born rich and led to believe from the cradle that the world was his handmaiden? That privilege accrues benefits that absolve one's bad behavior?"

(Trump) "What you're saying is too complicated for me to understand. I'm just saying that it never occurred to me that what I was doing was wrong. I was just following in the footsteps of my father, doing what I was taught to do, acting the way I was brought up to act. I never had to step back and think about what I was doing. People knew all about me when they elected me president. They loved me. They didn't care about this other stuff."

(Goring) "I was loved as well. People overlooked my excesses, my coarse behavior, my suspicious accumulation of art and wealth because they saw me as a real man, a war hero, but also a down-to-earth man. They saw in me what they wanted themselves to be."

(Trump) "So, it doesn't matter how we got here?"

(Goring) "I charted my course upstream, knowingly, determinedly, with ruthless resolve against the current. You floated down the stream, pretty much rudderless, your oarsmen doing the work. Then we met at a midpoint. It didn't matter which route we had taken."

(Trump) "Again you're talking over my head. What happens to me now?"

(Goring) "They will decide where you should be placed. There are tiers. What doesn't help you is that you were a leader. You controlled a fairly vast business empire. You became president of the world's biggest economy and military power. You were in a position to do good things or evil things. You seemed to have preferred the latter."

(Trump, *pleading*) "But I thought I was doing good things!"

(Goring) "Did you never turn around and look at the wreckage you left behind? The broken businesses, the ruined lives, the Black man dying under his protector's knee."

(Trump) "I didn't will any of those things to happen. I mean it."

(Goring) "Then you were seated too high up on your throne to either notice or care."

(Trump) "You keep confusing me."

(Goring) "I don't know which tier they'll deem you worthy of. I'm on a pretty low tier, just one up from Hitler, Mao, Idi Amin, Pol Pot and others of their ilk. Your problem is that, like them, you were the top guy. You gave the orders. I was second in command, thus never in complete charge. I'm not saying you'll be cast with them, but then again…"

(Trump, *pensive and suddenly resigned to his fate*) "If I could only do it over again…"

(Goring) "Let me tell you something. We'd both be just the same. It's who we are."

(*Just then the iron door swings open flooding the antechamber with blinding light, infernal heat and noxious fumes. A hand with long crooked fingers beckons them to come forward. Goring and Trump, blackened with soot that streaks down their rotund naked bodies on beads of sweat, creating the appearance of them wearing prisoners' striped uniforms, slowly hoist themselves up in resolute response to the eerie summons.*)

TWENTY ONE

June 1, 2020
(Trump disrupts a peaceful protest at Lafayette Square)

[*The setting is an underground bunker beneath the White House built to be used during terrorist attacks. President Trump is seen pacing back-and-forth in an obviously foul mood in front of his wife Melania and Chief of Staff Mark Meadows. When the door is open, chants of "I Can't Breathe" are faintly heard from a large crowd of peaceful protesters who have gathered across the street in Lafayette Park. They are outraged at the killing of a Black man, George Floyd, by a Minneapolis police officer who'd cut off the man's air supply by applying pressure with his knee until the man succumbed.*]

Scene One

(Trump) "How come the National Guard hasn't chased them off?"

(Meadows) "Barricades have been erected, Mr. President. They're on public property."

(Trump) "What difference does that make? They could start a riot at any time."

(Meadows) "It's been very peaceful so far. They have a right to march."

(Trump) "Well…put the troops on high alert. One false move and I'll…"

(Melania) "You'll do what, darling? Have them shot?"

(Trump) "This is no concern of yours. Don't you have something to do?"

(Melania) "I'm doing it. I don't want to see anyone bullied. That's my project."

(Trump, *irritatingly*) "This is about law and order, my dear. (*Raising his arms as if in victory*) And I'm the president of law and order! This is not playground stuff."

(Meadows) "By the way, I'm here because…"

(Trump, *interrupting*) "I was wondering why you were here. What is it?"

(Meadows) "We have an idea."

(Trump) "Who's 'we?'"

(Meadows) "That would be me and some cabinet members."

(Trump) "So let's hear it. What's the great idea?"

(Meadows) "We see this as an opportunity."

(Trump, *annoyed*) "An opportunity to do what?"

(Meadows, *with enthusiasm*) "An opportunity to display your courage and leadership!"

(Trump, *nodding approval*) "I'm listening. Go on."

(Meadows) "We think you should go out and meet with the protesters."

(Trump, *astounded*) "What! Me? The president? Walk straight into a gang of thugs?"

(Meadows) "It won't be like that. We can even cull a few out for the photo op."

(Melania) "I think it's a wonderful idea, darling. Show your courage and (*pauses*)…"

(Meadows, *thrusting a fist in the air*) "Leadership!"

Scene Two

[*The setting is the same but the trio has been joined by Attorney General William Barr and Secretary of State Mike Pompeo. They're about to discuss the proposal.*]

(Meadows, *to Barr*) The president has some concerns about his safety."

(Barr) "He won't be going alone; the Secret Service will accompany him, correct?"

(Meadows) "But of course. It's a very low risk high reward opportunity as we see it."

(Trump) "I'm not convinced."

(Melania) "Are you scared, darling?"

(Trump, *aroused to anger*) "Scared? Me? Nothing scares me. Nothing at all."

(Melania) "Then, why not do what they are suggesting?"

(Trump, *stumbling for words*) "Well, I'll have to walk all the way over there, right?"

(Pompeo, *chuckling*) "Too short a distance to fire up the helicopter!"

(Trump) "That brings up the matter of my bone spurs which have again been acting up."

(Melania) "Darling, you haven't mentioned that before."

(Trump) "That's because I'm tough. I put up with pesky things, like…"

(Melania, *half expecting him to say "you!"*) "Continue!"

(Trump) "Look, What about Pence? Why can't we send him?"

(Meadows) "C'mon! He's a wimp and you know it. You only keep him around as someone to compare with your own macho self. The crowd would eat him alive."

(Trump) "Then let's keep it in the family. What about Kushner?"

(Meadows) "Don't you remember? He's on assignment."

(Trump) "No, I don't remember. What assignment?"

(Meadows) "He's in charge of getting quotes for painting the border wall black."

(Trump) "How long does that take?"

(Meadows) "You ever try to find a clerk to help you in Home Depot?"

(Trump) "Okay, how about Don Jr.?"

(Pompeo) "Be for real, Mr. President. Even with a police escort he'd get lost."

(Trump) "Alright. I'll go outside. But I have a better idea."

<u>Scene Three</u>

[*The same group as before, now joined by a few cabinet members, have gathered under the White House portico preparing to walk to St. John's Episcopal Church, known for 150 years as "The Church of the Presidents" since it is so close to the White House and has been routinely visited by former presidents. The president snuggly positions himself in the midst of a phalanx of hefty bodyguards as they begin to walk toward the gate.*]

(Melania) "Something smells funny."

(Trump) "It wasn't me!"

(Meadows) "You're smelling tear gas residue."

(Melania) "Tear gas? Why tear gas?"

(Meadows) "Your husband's orders. He wanted the crowd dispersed."

(Melania) "But you said they were protesting poor Mr. Floyd peacefully."

(Barr) "They were, but the president didn't want to take any chances."

(Melania) "How can you have a great photo op with no people around?"

(Barr) "Just wait…You'll see."

Scene Four

[*The setting is St. John's Church. Alerted in advance, a swarm of photo journalists have gathered at the scene. The president and his entourage have entered the venerable church which had suffered some fire damage during protests staged the night before.*]

(Meadows, *handing him a book*) "Mr. President, hold this book aloft for the cameras."

(Trump, *confounded*) "What is it?"

(Meadows, *exasperated*) "The Bible!"

(Trump) "The Bible?"

(Meadows, *patiently taking a deep breath*) "You know – The Holy Bible; God's word."

(Trump) "Oh, yeah. Billy Graham wrote that, right? (*pausing*) Or was it Joel Osteen?"

(Meadows) "People are watching. Just take the book in your hands."

(Trump, *aside to Meadows*) "I haven't seen one of these since my swearing in ceremony. Look, I'm winging it here tonight and I'm not swearing to the truth about anything."

(Meadows) "You don't have to. Just hold it up for the pictures."

(Trump, *holding up a Bible*) "Let me tell you folks what God thinks about these protesters. He's pissed. God doesn't like hoodlums. Nor does he like governors who act like jerks by not getting tough with them, like I intend to do if they won't..."

(Barr, *aside to Pompeo*) "Do you know where he's heading with this?"

(Pompeo, *to Barr*) "I have no earthy idea. But, we'll soon see."

(Trump) "I will call out thousands and thousands of soldiers to restore order. Thousands and thousands of tremendously armed soldiers on the streets of our cities who won't hold back. It'll be a beautiful thing. Absolutely tremendous. You have to arrest people. You have to track people down. You have to put them in jail for ten years. And, you know what? I'll tell you what. You'll never see this (*hesitates while thinking*)...stuff again."

(Meadows, *grabbing Trump by the arm*) "Wonderful speech, Mr. President. But, it's time to go. They have all the photos they'll need for the news. Hurry, so we too can watch!"

(Trump, *arguing*) "But I was just warming up!"

(Meadows) "See, it's too late. They're all running off to file their stories." (*Aside*) "You've already said way too much!" (*Again to Trump*) "Let's go back to the White House. We'll break out the toy soldiers and tanks and you can play with them on your desk."

Scene Five

[*The setting is the Oval Office of White House the morning after. Awaiting the president's arrival are Chief of Staff Mark Meadows, Secretary of State Mike Pompeo, Attorney General William Barr and recently appointed Press Secretary Kayleigh McEnary.*]

(Pompeo) "Well, that was a disaster!"

(Barr) "Blame the media. Who knew they'd focus on the protesters getting gassed?"

(Meadows) "We had to clear the way for the presidential procession."

(Pompeo) "Maybe he should have taken the helicopter!"

(McEnary) "The Bible stunt didn't go over too well either."

(Meadows) "The evangelicals loved it."

(McEnary, *with a hint of sarcasm*) "And the Neo-Nazis."

(Pompeo) "Splendid! We have the 'The Earth Is 6,000 Years Old' crowd and the Klan on our side. What more could we possibly ask for?"

(Barr) "Face it, people. He looked goofy. For those of you who might go that far back, he reminded me of Dem candidate Mike Dukakis whirling around in a tank with that World War I helmet bobbing on his head. He too was trying to look tough and it backfired."

(Pompeo) "Or a Catholic priest holding up the host while threatening to shoot people."

(McEnary) "Guys, I'll make it sound like he was invoking God's blessing."

(Barr) "Good luck with that! The good news is that he didn't hold it upside down."

(Pompeo) "Quiet now! I think he's coming."

Scene Six

[*Trump has just entered the room and the discussion continues.*]

(Pompeo) "Well here is the man of the hour!"

(Trump) "You think so?"

(Pompeo) "Of course! You knocked the ball out of the park!"

(Trump) "I'm hearing about some criticisms."

(Barr) "Don't pay any attention to those wacko-bird Dems."

(Pompeo) "You did a fantastic job. I can see the campaign ads and posters now."

(Barr) "Trump: For God and for Country! How do you beat that?"

(Trump) "I can think of something."

(Pompeo) "What could that possibly be?"

(Trump) "God: For Trump and his Country!"

(Barr) "Absolutely brilliant! You are indeed a marketing genius!"

(Trump) "I think so. Last night was a great job done."

(All, *resoundingly*) "You bet!"

Scene Seven

[*Everyone has now left the room except for Barr and Pompeo.*]

(Barr) "Well, that's over. What a relief."

(Pompeo) "What a dumb ass."

(Barr) "As big a fool as they come."

(Pompeo) "What does this say about us?"

(Barr) "Just think of it as your job, Mike. Just think of it as your job."

TWENTY TWO

King Trump

(Soliloquies from a newly discovered Shakespearean manuscript)

<u>Act One</u>

[*In Act One the king has died without an heir and the noblemen have gathered to elect one of their own as his successor. Trump, known for his unscrupulous business dealings and cruel treatment of his vassals, must decide if he will nominate himself to be king.*]

"To run, or not to run? That is the question –
Whether 'tis nobler in the mind to suffer
The slings and arrows of media scrutiny as king,
Or take up arms against the king as an outsider,
Where no sea of troubles can disturb my comforts.
To rule, or be ruled by a man of lesser stature?
The heartache and the thousand natural shocks
That kings must endure – 'tis a consummation
Not devoutly to be wished upon by most men.
But I dream of being king – ay, there's the rub!
For in being king I can forge what dreams may come.
When I have shuffled off this mortal coil,
The Trump name will be immortal!
That thought alone makes me wonder why I pause.
As king I gain respect that will crown my existence."

<u>Act Two</u>

[*In Act Two we find that mainly through treachery against his peers Trump has been elected king. He must now decide if he will reform and behave like an honest ruler.*]

"The virtues of truthfulness are overstrained!
Lies – like my margin of victory;
The size of my inauguration crowd;
(*Chuckles*) And of my dagger!
My net worth, these just for starters –
Droppeth from my lips as the gentle rain from heaven,
Nurturing the adulation felt for me by my following.
Avoiding the troublesome truth is twice blest:
It blesseth the liar by creating a bloated self-esteem,
And those lied upon longing for a hero to worship.
Untruth 'tis least noticeable in the mightiest; like me.
Substituting falsehoods for facts elevates one's image.
Fake facts can boost prominence and respectability
Amongst both friend and foe.
Too much is made of being an honest man.
'Tis harder to hold power over others
When the truth might expose a human-like frailty
Unbecoming of a great monarch; like me.
Aversion to truth is enthroned in the hearts of kings
Whose scepter empowers spawning dread and fear.
Earthy power doth then show likest God's
When harmful truths are gilded by deception."

Act Three

[*In Act Three King Trump is beginning to experience the slings and arrows of his critics and has grown envious of the Russian King Vladimir who rules with an iron fist.*]

"Vladimir, Vladimir, wherefore art thou Vladimir?
'Tis but thy country that was our enemy; not thyself.
We met; you spoke the truth, swearing you had no
Role in my election or other of my kingdom's affairs.
It is just your Russian name that makes you my enemy.
What makes a Russian? Are we not made the same?
We differ not in hand nor foot, nor arm nor face
Belonging to a man. Oh to give you some other name!
What's in a name? That which we call a rose
By any other word would smell as sweet.

So Vladimir, you could be my lasting friend
With not a Russian name. You I trust and love.
Validmir, doff thy name, and that name,
Which is no part of thee, I would take for myself
If it meant I could rule with your impunity!"

Act Four

[*Although King Trump remains favored by noblemen whom he keeps at bay by slashing their share of taxes and allowing them access to royal properties where they mine and despoil the land for personal enrichment, the commoners have risen up and put the king on trial for his coziness with King Vladimir and ensuing cover-ups. The king in Act Four considers unleashing his power, but relents knowing that the jury, with its majority share of loyal noblemen, will acquit him of any misdeeds despite a preponderance of evidence.*]

"'Tis now the time for the witch hunt to begin,
When churchyards yawn and hell itself breathes out
Contagion to this world. Were I so disposed
I could drink hot blood and raise such havoc
My accusers would fall on their knees in fear.
They label them bigots, racists, white supremacists,
Misogynists, anti-Semites. That they may be, but
They are my loyal legions who would act upon my will.
Soft, it is my mother country that made me rich
With loose laws that I flaunted without fear.
O heart, lose not thy nature, let not ever
The soul of Nero, whom I hold in high esteem,
Lead me to incite violence beyond my natural cruelty.
I will speak daggers of her but keep the weapon sheathed.
My tongue and soul in this be hypocrites.
Protest I will, but to upheaval my soul will not consent!"

Act Five

[*Time has passed and, in accordance with the original charter, a second election was held and King Trump was dethroned. His tempered attitude towards civil unrest was soon replaced by a cry for vengeance and upheaval. Summoning his most ardent followers, the former king incites them to riot, but the insurrection fails and an uneasy peace reigns over the land with Trump unrepentant of his intent to overturn the legitimate monarchy.*]

"All kingdoms will ultimately collapse,
This should have died hereafter.
There would have been a time for such a word.
Tomorrow, and tomorrow, and tomorrow.
Creeps in this petty pace from day to day
To the last syllable of recorded time.
Only fools believe a kingdom has no end.
I was merely extinguishing a flickering flame,
Hastening the march to inevitable dusty death.
Out, out brief candle! My temporary demise
Is a tale told by idiots who stole my throne,
One full of sound and fury, signifying nothing.
My time upon life's center stage is not undone!"

References:

Act One: *Hamlet (3:1)*
Act Two: *The Merchant of Venice (4:1)*
Act Three: *Romeo & Juliet (2:2)*
Act Four: *Hamlet (3:2)*
Act Five: *Macbeth (4:5)*

TWENTY THREE

The Superman Trilogy
(*Part One: Great Caesar's Ghost*)

<u>Scene One</u>

[*It's October 15, 2020. The setting is the office of Perry White, Editor-in-Chief of the The Daily Planet, New York's leading newspaper. Mr. White is seen watching a news bulletin on television. Suddenly, he pounds his fist on his desk and presses a button on his intercom system to summon his secretary. As the scene opens he's very agitated.*]

(Secretary) "Yes, Mr. White. What is it you need?"

(White) "Miss Walters, are Kent, Olsen and Miss Lane in the office?"

(Secretary) "I'm not sure, Mr. White. Shall I find out?"

(White) "Yes! And if not, find them at once. I want them in my office pronto!"

(Secretary, *as she leaves*) "Yes, sir…I'll see to it right away."

(White, *to himself*) "Great Caesar's Ghost! How is this happening to us?"

The door opens and in walk reporters Clark Kent, Jimmy Olsen and Lois Lane

(Kent) "You want to see us, Perry?"

(White, *irritated*) "Why else would I call for you? Have a seat; all of you."

(Olsen) "I must say, Chief, you seem somewhat out of sorts."

(White, *angrily*) "Don't call me Chief! But how observant of you, Olsen, to notice that. Someday you might develop into a good reporter."

(Lane, *concerned*) "Did you see the latest poll results?"

(White) "See, Olsen...That's being a good reporter on top of things!"

(Kent) "It looks like Biden's lead has all but evaporated."

(White) "That's what's bothering me. How did that happen so fast?"

(Lane) "The White House claims people are coming to their senses."

(White) "Great Caesar's Ghost! Don't they realize it's the Russians?"

(Kent) "Attorney General Barr disputes that claim; says he's checked it out."

(Lane) "And Trump says he's talked to Putin who denied any involvement."

(White) "Look, this election is being manipulated by outside forces. It must be stopped!"

(Kent) "It appears to be more than that, Perry. With the Voting Rights Act disemboweled by the Supreme Court, several states in the South are resurrecting poll taxes to keep people with court histories from voting. Native family members aren't allowed to hand-deliver the ballots of their elders. Mail boxes are being removed in poor districts..."

(White) "I know...I know. Our democracy is being devoured by vermin from inside and out. When they're finished feasting, the carcass of Lady Liberty won't be recognizable."

(Lane) "Do you have any ideas, Mr. White?"

(White, *pensive*) "I wish I did…I wish I did. My scathing editorial exposing the evil doers behind the inflammatory, malicious and unfounded attacks on Biden hardly drew a whisper of response. People seem content to watch our Democracy die before their eyes."

(Olsen) "This looks like a job for Superman!"

(Kent) "I'm afraid not, Jimmy. This is an enemy that even Superman can't conquer."

Scene Two

[*The setting is Perry White's bedroom in his apartment suite. It's midnight and he lies in bed wide awake, his mind troubled by the tyranny he sees sweeping over the country.*]

(Ghost) "Perry!"

(White) "Who's calling me?…Who's there?"

(Ghost) "It is me, the one you summon so often. I'm Julius Caesar's ghost."

(White, *alarmed*) "This is absurd! I can't sleep and now I'm losing my mind!"

(Ghost) "You are not going mad, Mr. White. To the contrary, you have grown wise."

(White) "If I'm not mad and you are Caesar's ghost…show yourself."

(Ghost, *appearing diaphanous as a ghost*) "Here I am."

(White, *frightened*) "Great Caesar's Ghost! (*stammering*) I mean…It *is* you!"

(Ghost) "Who else did you expect? Crassus? Pompey? Cicero perhaps?"

(White, *calming down a bit*) "How did you get here? Why did you find me?"

(Ghost) "'Tis the Ides of October. On the monthly anniversaries of our deaths we are free to reappear, but only if we are summoned. Did you not call me?"

(White, *stammering*) "Why, it's just a phrase I use…From Shakespeare. That's all."

(Ghost) "Then you should be more careful with your choice of words and phrases."

(White, *relieved*) "I guess so…Now what is it you want with me?"

(Ghost) "I believe it's more what you want with me, isn't it?"

(White) "I don't know what you mean."

(Ghost) "You want to know what's happening to your country, do you not?"

(White) "I see our country morphing from a Republic into… into…"

(Ghost) "Imperial rule?"

(White) "I don't know. This Trump. He wants to be a Putin. He wants unbridled power."

(Ghost) "An Emperor, perhaps?…Like me?"

(White) "I don't know. It's just that if he gets a second term there's no telling what he'll do to further consolidate power. He already controls the Senate and the Judiciary."

(Ghost, *smiling sympathetically*) "Mr. White, don't you see what's happening?"

(White, *mystified*) "I guess I don't…You seem to know, however, so tell me."

(Ghost) "It's oh so familiar to me. The dissolution of democracy! The end of the Roman Republic and the birth of the Empire under imperial rule. This Trump is your Caesar!"

(White) "But, this isn't Rome! This is America! It's been this way for almost 250 years."

(Ghost, *chuckling*) "Do you know how long the Roman Republic lasted?"

(White) "I'm a well-read man familiar with the long history of your Republic."

(Ghost) "Then you must know what happened. Now you must be seeing the same signs."

(White) "What signs?"

(Ghost, *with a sigh*) "Democracies fail when the people are irreconcilably divided along class lines. In my day it was the *optimates* against the *populares*. Each faction had its leaders. The populist hero was Marius – a fine soldier and an honest man. The aristocracy, fearful of losing wealth and power, despised him. When he died, it was open season on his followers in the Roman fashion of vengeance…I doubt you'll see that."

(White) "What will we see?"

(Ghost) "Your Caesar has no rivals. I had Crassus and Pompey to deal with. Crassus was a lot like your Trump – a rather unsavory character, more of a swindler than a soldier, but the richest man in Rome. Pompey gave me no choice but to cross the Rubicon."

(White, *confidently*) "But, even with them out of the way in the end you got killed."

(Ghost) "Fools if they ever conceived the thought that the Republic would be restored."

(White) "So, after Trump another like him?"

(Ghost) "Democracies are like temples. Once destroyed they aren't easily rebuilt."

(White) "And what destroys them?"

(Ghost) "Greed! A craving for wealth and power! Once a small segment of the population has it in their grasp, and they find a leader who will champion their cause, like your Trump, the lust is all-consuming. The charade is that some of the people who aren't wealthy, who barely hang on, for some reason, stupidity perhaps, come to believe these powerful men actually care about their well being. It makes no sense, but see for yourself how many of your minions have fallen for the ruse and actually sing his praises."

(White, *irritated*) "Is there no hope? Goddamnit! Is there no hope?"

(Ghost) "Depends on what you're hoping for. An idyllic nation where class, race and religious distinctions are ignored and the people live in blissful harmony? That's a concept that people pretend to hold – how do you put it? 'That all men are created equal?' When in history has it ever happened? I say that *our* Republic came the closest."

(White, *forlorn*) "I fear that November 3rd will mark the beginning of our end."

(Ghost) "I can see the past but I can't predict the future. But, I speak from experience. There's no sweeter sound to the ears of the dictator than cheers from the oppressed."

(White, *as the ghost dissolves*) "Hail Caesar!"

Scene Three

[*It's November 10th, 2020. Editor-in-Chief Perry White has gathered reporters Clark Kent, Jimmy Olsen and Lois Lane into his office. A week now and no official winner.*]

(Lane) "Mr. White, ever since the election you've looked like you've seen a ghost."

(White) "Lois, as I've said before, you're an observant woman and a talented reporter."

(Lane) "Gee, thanks for the compliment, Mr. White…But, how so?"

(White) "You'll all think I'm crazy…but I did see a ghost."

(Olsen) "Gosh, Chief! Did you get an interview?"

(White) "Don't call me Chief! But, for once you're beginning to think like a reporter."

(Olsen) "Well, did ya?"

(Kent) "I believe, Jimmy, that Mr. White has been imagining things."

(Lois) "Yeah, Jimmy, like imagining that Kent here is Superman."

(White) "I know it sounds stupid but the ghost made so much sense."

(Kent) "What ghost?"

(White) "Great Caesar's Ghost. He came to me one night. October 15th to be precise."

(Lane) "I think he's serious…What did Caesar's ghost tell you?"

(White) "That we're damn fools to think that our democracy can't come crashing down."

(Lane) "There've been reports of people being turned down at the polls. People waiting five hours in line and being told that the polls have closed. Reports of mail-in ballots being discarded for dubious reasons in Black voting districts. All sorts of irregularities."

(White, *sighing*) "*Optimates* vs. *Populares*."

(Lane) "It's getting scary. Biden easily won the popular vote, but with him now inching ahead in the Electoral College count there are strong rumors that Trump's given orders to barricade the White House and plans to declare the election void by presidential decree."

(Kent) "He can't do that...can he?"

(Lane) "The same sources tell me that he's demanded loyalty pledges from the Supreme Court with an intent to disband Congress, declare Marshall Law, and authorize vigilante militia groups to patrol the streets and fire upon any protestors, armed or unarmed."

(White, *pounding his desk with his fist*) "That's pure anarchy! He must be stopped!"

(Lane) "But how? It appears this eventuality was orchestrated well in advance."

(White) "Kent, maybe you can check to see...Kent? Where is he? Did Kent leave?"

(Lane) "That's our Clark Kent. First sign of real trouble and he runs off and hides."

THE END...Or is it?

(*Loud voice heard from outside*) "Look! Up in the sky..."

TWENTY FOUR

The Superman Trilogy
(Part Two: A Supernatural Secret Revealed)

<u>Scene One</u>

[It's November 11ᵗʰ, 2020 and the setting is Lafayette Square across from the White House where Lois Lane, a reporter with The Daily Planet newspaper, is about to interview General Mark A. Milley, the Chairman of the Joint Chiefs of Staff.]

(Lane) "General, what can you tell me about what's going on?"

(Milley) "All I can say at this time is that the President is secure in the White House but there are reports that the Vice President and several others close to the administration have been kidnapped. They are sending text messages with photos from some very strange locations confirming they are safe but won't be reporting to duty anytime soon."

(Lane) "Can you provide any details as to the circumstances of the kidnappings?"

(Milley) "This might sound crazy, but it seems that Superman is involved."

(Lane) "I know Superman, and he's all about 'truth, justice and the American way.'"

(Milley) "Apparently Superman isn't of the feeling that President Trump and these individuals represent those values, especially the American way of electing leaders."

(Lane) "Can you tell me which individuals are involved?"

(Milley) "I guess I'm free to speak as the texts sort of went viral. Senate Majority Leader Mitch McConnell is now apparently a member of the Sri Mayapur Chandroya Mandia Hare Krishna temple in West Bengal, India. He says he chants throughout the day about peace and harmony. His orange robes remind him of the hair of the 'great oppressor.'"

(Lane) "Wow! That's a turnaround. Who else?"

(Milley) "Vice President Pence is seemingly happily ensconced in a East European plush retreat and bathhouse for inveterate nymphomaniacs. (*shows Lane a photo on his cell phone*) That's Mike, smiling and naked in a bubbly vat with six new nubile friends."

(Lane) "I heard that Jared Kushner has also been…relocated."

(Milley) "This one's a little more disconcerting as he's unharmed but serving as a personal 'attendant' – we're trying to determine what exactly that means – to Hassan Nasrallah, Secretary-General of Hezbollah in South Beirut. That diaper outfit he's wearing looks like something right out of the Gunga Din movie if you ask me."

(Lane) "Has Superman taken any other actions?"

(Milley) "You can see that as of yesterday by order of the President we surrounded the White House grounds with troops and tanks. Presumably as a prank – Superman does seem to have a sense of humor – he lifted two of the tanks and from what I hear deposited them at the Mar-a-Lago resort in Florida with their gun barrels aimed at the complex."

(Lane) "But so far Superman has had no direct interaction with the President?"

(Milley) "Hold on! I'm being told the President's on the line asking for me…I gotta go."

Scene Two

[*The setting is a bunker beneath the White House where President Trump and several armed Secret Service agents are holed up, initially in expectation of violent reprisals for his planned decision to void the November 3rd election results and now out of concern that Superman is on a rampage, his decision to void the election having been leaked.*]

(Trump) "Look, Milley, Superman hasn't blown up Mar-a-Lago has he? I seen pictures on *Fox News* with those tanks out front. Can you imagine him firing them guns?"

(Milley) "Mr. President, Superman wouldn't need projectiles to destroy your favorite retreat. Our interpretation is that it was executed as a symbolic gesture."

(Trump) "What's that supposed to mean?"

(Milley) "It means that...(*thinks*) he's letting you know that you're making him mad."

(Trump) "Well, you can tell him that he's making *me* mad as hell too!"

(Milley) "Are you prepared to tell him that?"

(Trump) "Well...sort of. I'm going to have Pence meet with him."

(Milley) "Let me just say that the Vice President is in a bit of hot water himself."

(Trump) "Okay, then I'll send Kushner."

(Milley) "Your son-in-law is...well...up to his ass in his own prickly issues."

(Trump) "Then get McConnell to convene the Senate and...outlaw Superman!"

(Milley) "Another not-so-swell option. Mitch is now known as 'Mr. Tambourine Man.'"

(Trump) "Okay, I'm feeling a bit trapped here...I'm going for the nuclear option."

(Milley, *alarmed*) "Surely you're not serious! Superman might be the only survivor!"

(Trump, *cupping the phone*) "It's more of a personal secret that I might have to explain later. When Superman shows up have him first meet with my original physician."

(Milley) "Not your current personal physician?"

(Trump, *sighing*) "No, find Bornstein. He's the one who must talk to Superman."

Scene Three

[*It's later in the day and Superman has landed in Lafayette Park where he's approached by General Milley. The two men cordially shake hands, and then speak.*]

(Milley) "It's a pleasure meeting you, Superman. But, you've caused quite a stir."

(Superman) "Not nearly the stir that Trump is about to cause if he voids the election."

(Milley) "I understand that. But, it's my job to protect him as this is beyond the scope of the Secret Service. Still, I'm not sure there's anything at my disposal that can stop you."

(Superman) "I mean him no personal harm; I'm here to make sure he doesn't disrupt the constitutional process through which power changes hands peaceably in a democracy."

(Milley) "He's a very stubborn man. I wish even *you* luck talking sense into him."

(Superman) "Talking is the first step. Maybe he'd prefer to live on an asteroid?"

(Milley) "He'd probably go for that if he could rule all the aliens on the asteroid."

(Superman) "I'm a little sensitive to the term 'alien,' General Milley."

(Milley, *apologetically*) "Sorry, Superman, I wasn't thinking."

(Superman) "Let's get on with it. Is he coming out here, or should I walk through the walls of his bunker and present myself before him? And, please tell your Secret Service guys that I'm coming so as not to waste their bullets. A ricochet could hit Trump."

(Milley, *murmuring to himself*) "If we would be so lucky!" (*and then aloud to Superman*) "Curiously, he wants you to meet first with his original physician. His name is Harold Bornstein. He took over for his father Dr. Jacob Bornstein in 1980. You'll recall that Bornstein fell out of favor and lost the job when he revealed that Trump insists on writing his own fitness reports and, get this, was being treated with hair-growth medications. "

(Superman, *laughing*) "Tell me where he is and I can be there in a matter of seconds."

Scene Four

[*It's later the same day and Dr. Bornstein has agreed to meet with Superman in his upper story Manhattan office. To ensure privacy, Superman arrives through an open window.*]

(Bornstein) "Superman, I'm thrilled to make your acquaintance."

(Superman) "The feeling is quite mutual, Dr. Bornstein."

(Bornstein) "I just got off the phone with the President. He has reluctantly given me permission to share with you some extremely sensitive information, but you must promise to share it with no one. You'll understand what I mean once you hear me out."

(Superman) "I'm good for my word, but understand that my mission is to save our democracy from someone who seems intent on destroying its very foundations."

(Bornstein) "I understand. You're originally from Krypton, are you not?"

(Superman) "That is correct. My father was Jor-El and my name was Kal-El."

(Bornstein) "So, you're more than familiar with people not being who others might think they are. You, for instance, became a different type of man on Earth with its lighter gravity. And, a man of great strength. Fascinating. It's a little different with Trump."

(Superman, *curious*) "Different in what way?"

(Bornstein) "Let me be blunt – Donald J. Trump is not a real human being."

(Superman, *shocked*) "Is he from another planet?"

(Bornstein) "Perhaps, there's some confusion. I'll do my best to explain. My father was Dr. Frank Stein – the 'Born' was added later, and he preferred Jacob as a given name for some reason, although his middle name was Nathan, usually shortened to "N." Trump's father showed up at his office one day with an infant that appeared to be human but was lacking a brain and a heart. He knew that my father was a bit of a dabbler in mysticism and chemistry – sort of a 'Mad Scientist' if you would – and you might say he saw this as an *opportunity*."

(Superman) "So, your father created Donald Trump in his laboratory?"

(Bornstein) "Not the whole body as I explained. The form was intact, though some parts, his hands for instance and…well, let's just stop at the hands, were somewhat small for his size. My father's instruction was to develop a brain with cognitive powers compatible with a normal child and a heart mechanism, a motor, to keep his body functioning."

(Superman, *intrigued*) "Really? An artificial brain and an artificial heart?"

(Bornstein) "Precisely!"

(Superman) "And this half-human, half-android became President of the United States!"

(Bornstein) "Perfectly understandable! In 2016, hardly anyone, even Democrats, was thrilled with Hillary Clinton. The Donald J. Trump that my father helped create is impervious to certain feelings we commonly associate with human beings. For example, he's completely oblivious to insults, and doesn't experience human emotions such as compassion, remorse, and sympathy. So, what we had was someone – or some *thing* – filthy rich, completely self-absorbed, of limited intellect, with no feelings toward others. You might agree with me that my father helped create the perfect Republican candidate!"

(Superman) "So, your father installed a life-sustaining device in his chest?"

(Bornstein) "That's very critical to our discussion and largely the reason you're here."

(Superman) "You're going to have to explain that statement."

(Bornstein) "I will in a moment. Another oddity is that people haven't come to the conclusion that the brain my father created was somewhat rudimentary. Programming in that day and age – even though my father was eons ahead of his time – was challenging. He was eventually able to install a vocabulary of about 200 words. He must have inadvertently typed in "tremendous" several times because it's become a staple. Trump has a fairly good mind for figures, which he's put to use in a rather corruptive fashion in his business dealings and even more so in calculating his taxes. But, due to his mental shortcomings – my father offered a certificate guaranteeing no more than 6th grade reading comprehension skills – he's, well, to use a euphemism, 'not the sharpest tack.'"

(Superman) "Dr. Bornstein, what am I to make of all this? How does what you've shared in confidence impact my meeting with Trump which I intend to commence shortly?"

(Bornstein, *stroking his chin*) "You might want to reconsider having that face-to-face meeting for *his* sake, you appearing so strong, and for *your* sake, you being so…weak!"

(Superman) "Dr. Bornstein, I could pick up this building and rest it on the moon!"

(Bornstein, *leaning forward*) "There was no Earthy element that my father could find to provide the lasting energy normally associated with the human heart, and experiments with quartz failed, but he found an element in a museum meteorite that did work."

(Superman, *suddenly very agitated*) "You don't mean…"

(Bornstein) "Yes, Superman, I do mean…Kryptonite!"

<u>Scene Five</u>

[*It's now late in the day and the setting is the office of Perry White, the Editor-in-Chief of The Daily Planet. He's meeting with reporters Jimmy Olsen and Lois Lane, just arriving from an assignment in Washington, D.C...The door opens and in walks Clark Kent.*]

(Lane) "Well, look who the cat just dragged in!"

(Kent, *removing his hat*) "Sorry, out on a little personal business. Did I miss anything?"

(White, *shouting*) "Did you miss anything? Have you been visiting another planet?"

(Lane) "There's almost too much to summarize. We have a president holed up in the White House insisting he'll never concede the election because it was fraudulent. The Army is on high alert standby. Wall Street has cancelled all trading after stocks plunged 10,000 points in an hour. Superman intercepted a squadron of Russian fighter jets that took off from a base in Cuba, and he was involved in several top administration officials fleeing the country and adopting new lifestyles inconsistent with who they once were."

(Olsen) "For example, Lindsey Graham had a gender epiphany, resigned his Senate seat, and joined an order of The Little Sisters of the Poor at a secluded convent in France."

(White, *with heavy sarcasm*) "So, you see Kent, you didn't miss a damn thing!"

At this moment, White's personal secretary knocks briefly and then hurriedly enters the room holding a letter-sized envelope clearly marked "URGENT" on the outside.

(Secretary) "Mr. White, sorry to interrupt, but a currier just dropped off this envelope. It's from the White House and addressed to Perry White, Editor-in-Chief, The Daily Planet."

(White) "Hand it to me and don't leave just yet." (*Perry rips open the envelope*)

(*Kent, Lane and Olsen all at once*) "What's it say?"

(White) "Great Caesar's Gh…No, I don't want *him* coming back! What day is this?"

(Lane) "It's November 11th, Mr. White. Is something wrong?"

(White) "What an irony…Armistice Day." (*White then removes a sheet of paper from his desk, begins writing on it in big block letters, folds it and hands it to his secretary.*) "Miss Walters, take this immediately to the Press Room. Have them stop the presses. Tell them this is tomorrow's front page. Full page! Big block print! Nothing else on that page!"

(*Miss Walters takes the folded paper and rushes out. Perry White slowly buries his head in his hands. Lane and Olsen don't say or ask anything. Clark Kent has disappeared.*)

TO BE CONTINUED

TWENTY FIVE

The Superman Trilogy
(Part Three: Showdown!)

Scene One

[*The setting is the office of Perry White, Editor-in-Chief of The Daily Planet, the nation's biggest newspaper in its largest city. The date is November 12, 2020. Gathered for a meeting are White and reporters Lois Lane, Clark Kent and Jimmy Olsen. The reason: yesterday's headline announcing that President Donald J. Trump has declared victory over his Democratic rival, Joe Biden, despite losing the nationwide popular count by over 7.0 million votes and narrowly losing the certified Electoral College tabulation, citing unsubstantiated fraud related to mail-in ballots in key districts in the State of Florida. In a startling decision, the Supreme Court has agreed to consider his claims.*]

(White) "There's more to the story than what the headline revealed."

(Olsen) "How about it, Chief, what could possibly be worse?"

(White, *pounding his desk*) "Don't call me Chief! It has to do with Superman."

(Lane, *laughing*) "But Superman removed all his close allies in Congress and the administration. They're strewn all around the world. Trump must be next on his list."

(Olsen) "Ivanka's now a seamstress in a Pakistani sweatshop. Ya gotta love that!"

(Kent, *nervously*) "Perry, what exactly did Trump's message say about Superman?"

(White) "It's odd. He didn't say why, but he implied that Superman can't touch him."

(Kent, *more relaxed*) "I can't imagine that Superman has gone over to the dark side."

(White) "Maybe Trump believes that, given Superman's indomitable respect for justice, he won't attempt to interfere in some way with the Supreme Court's deliberations."

(Lane) "Or perhaps Trump has information on Superman's real identity?"

(Olsen) "That's it! I'll bet he's trying to blackmail Superman!"

(White) "Let's not jump to conclusions. There's nothing to do now but wait to hear from the Supreme Court, packed as it is with Trump loyalists. They're meeting tomorrow."

Scene Two

[*It's the next day. The setting is a bunker beneath the White House where a camera has been installed as President Trump is preparing to address a very nervous nation in a live broadcast. One reporter, a friend from Fox News, was approved in advance to attend.*]

(Trump) "What we've seen since the bogus election earlier this month is tremendous proof that in America nobody, including all those lying and cheating Democrats, can steal an election. I urge everyone to stay calm while our Supreme Court justices take a look at the tremendous fraud that took place, especially in Florida. Ballots marked Trump found in rivers, creeks, even wastepaper baskets. I'm telling you the election was a total fraud."

(Reporter) "So you feel confident the Supreme Court will confirm your claims?"

(Trump) "Of course! That's what they're there for. They know fraud when they see it."

(Reporter) "Do you feel more confident about their decision following the confirmation of Associate Supreme Court Justice Amy Coney Barrett just prior to the election?"

(Trump) "You might say it was an added bit of security but the liberals were already outnumbered. The fight the losing Democrats put up at her hearings was shameful."

(Reporter) "You seem to be implying that politics will play a role in their deliberations."

(Trump) "It damn well better! I wouldn't call it politics; I'd call it 'getting things right.'"

At this moment, General Mark Milley, Chairman of the Joint Chiefs of Staff, who has been outside the bunker's entrance, suddenly enters the room holding a message.

(Trump, *irritated*) "What's all this about? Why are you barging in?"

(Milley, *handing him the message*) "The Supreme Court is missing!"

(Trump) "All nine of them, including our guys?"

(Milley) "No, *the* Supreme Court…With them inside."

(Trump) "Cut the cameras!" (*the broadcast is shut down*) "What are you saying?"

(Milley) "Superman, using his laser beam x-ray vision, severed the foundation of the Supreme Court building all around its perimeter and flew off with it."

(Trump) "Where'd he take it?"

(Milley) "Satellite images indicate it's in Iran."

(Trump) "No matter. I know how to handle Superman. Dare him to meet me here."

Scene Three

[*The setting is the office of Perry White the same afternoon. Reporters Lois Lane, Clark Kent and Jimmy Olsen have been summoned to discuss this latest strange development.*]

(White) "Does anyone here know how to contact Superman?"

(Lane) "I'm sure Superman's aware of Trump's challenge to meet face-to-face."

(Olsen) "But, Superman hasn't been heard from since Iran released the justices after temporarily holding them hostage and converting the building to a mosque."

(White) "I'm fully aware of that situation, although I did get a kick out of the photo the regime released of Alioto, Thomas, Kavanaugh, Gorsuch and Roberts in their fashionable thobes, ghutras and turbans posing with the Ayatollah. That's a front page photograph!"

(Lane) "I'm baffled why Superman won't meet Trump. Any ideas?"

(Kent) "Perry, you could meet with him, saying you know Superman and represent him."

(White) "Or, better yet, maybe you, Kent, could impersonate Superman and get to the bottom of what Trump has on Superman. What have you to say about that?"

(Lane, *laughing*) "What a joke! I'd make a better impersonator of Superman than Kent."

(Kent) "Well, Lois, I tend to disagree, but a cape would go very nicely with your blouse and skirt. But, seriously, if we can't locate Superman, maybe you try for an interview."

(White) "That sounds ridiculous and could be dangerous, but then again…"

(Olsen) "Then what, Chief?"

(White) "Don't call me Chief! How many times do I have to say that? One more time and I'll order *you* to meet Trump pretending to be Superman. Lois can go as a forerunner."

(Lane) "I'm all for it, Mr. White. I'd like to interview this impertinent imposter!"

Scene Four

[*The setting is the White House bunker the following morning. Informed that Superman will be coming, Trump relishes the thought that Superman might not have been informed by his former personal physician that his artificial heart is powered by Kryptonite.*]

(Trump) "When Superman arrives send him in. I'll meet with him alone. Let nobody else in the bunker. I'll be fine. I'll lock the door from the inside. Don't let anyone enter!"

(Milley) "Are you sure about that, Mr. President?"

(Trump) "What could you do anyway? The world needs to hear of me destroying the so-called Man of Steel. Once they see Superman cower the nation will elect me for life!"

(Milley) "Mr. President, an emissary, reporter Lois Lane from *The Daily Planet*, has arrived in advance of Superman. Should we allow her to enter the bunker?"

(Trump) "Has she passed through the extra-sensitive security scanner?"

(Milley) "Of course. She's unarmed."

(Trump) "I mean, does she have a nice figure? I'll tell you what, just save the image."

(Milley, *rolling his eyes in disgust*) "Yes, Sir. Do you know this reporter?"

(Trump) "I'm familiar with this Lane. Nice piece of ass. Let her in and don't disturb us."

The steel door to the soundproof bunker swings open, the Secret Service agents who were protecting the President file out of the bunker and Lois Lane enters the suite.]

(Trump, *arms spread wide*) "Welcome to my humble abode, Miss Lane."

(Lane, *looking around*) "Doesn't look too humble to me."

(Trump) "Well, after that unfortunate Lafayette Square incident – my first time being down here – I had them refurbish the place. A complete renovation. Pretty nice, huh? You'll note the bedroom has been upgraded with a luxurious king bed with silk linens and wall and ceiling mirrors. Maybe it would be more suitable meeting in there?"

(Lane) "Look, I'm here to find out why you're so anxious to meet with Superman."

(Trump, *moving closer*) "Superman is helpless near me. I'm your new Superman."

Trump reaches out and grabs Lois by the waist and pulls her firmly towards him.

(Lane) "In your dreams, Fatman!" (*She then stomps on Trump's foot with a spiked heel, kicks him viciously in the crotch with her knee, and delivers a sharp blow to his fat gut.*)

(Trump) "Whoa, little lady! All I wanted was a little feel. I knew you'd want it."

Lois Lane then delivers another swift kick to Trump's groin and then punches him hard in the chest, dislodging the couplings connected to his inhuman heart. Trump tumbles to the floor and begins hacking furiously, soon coughing up the chunk of Kryptonite that Dr. Bornstein had inserted to keep the human parts of his body functioning efficiently.]

(Trump, *panting*) "Wadaya doin'? Stop! Stop! Please call for help!"

(Lane, *with her heel on his throat*) "Tell me you lost the election fair and square."

(Trump, *in anguish*) "Okay, okay! Biden won fair and square."

(Lane) "Tell me you'll cooperate completely with the transition team."

(Trump) "Okay, okay. I'll cooperate."

(Lane) "Tell me that you knew the Russians helped get you elected in 2016."

(Trump, *gasping*) "It was all Putin's idea. We had a deal...Please get Bornstein!"

(Lane) "Tell me you lied to the country about the coronavirus."

(Trump, *feeling feint*) "It was all I could do to save my election chances."

(Lane) "Finally, Trump, admit you're a liar, a cheat and a philanderer."

(Trump, *crying*) "You got me. I'll confess. I'll write it all down. Just please let me go."

Scene Five

[*The setting is Perry White's office the following morning. After a brief hospital stay where he was privately attended to by Dr. Bornstein (who surgically inserted an artificial heart with a modern pacemaker), Trump, citing health issues related to a fall, has conceded defeat and committed to enter a sexual offender program. Perry, Lane and Olsen are discussing the previous day's extraordinary events when Clark Kent enters.*]

(Lane) Well, once again, look who the cat has dragged in."

(White) "Kent, where in tarnation have you been?"

(Kent) "Chasing a great story about a burglary on 57th Street."

(White) "Do you know anything about how Miss Lane saved the country?"

(Kent) "She did? You don't say!"

(White) "Yes, I do say! Between this woman knocking some sense into Trump and Superman taking care of the Supreme Court, America can finally move forward."

(Lane) "Not that you'd have any knowledge of it while chasing down a burglary story, but Superman, learning that the Supreme Court majority was about to expose itself as a political arm of the executive branch, took the whole bunch of them to Iran so they could get a good taste of what a corrupt court looks like – sort of their mirror image – freeing them only after obtaining a few concessions, more like confessions if you ask me."

(Olsen) "Word is that Kavanaugh will be impeached for lying under oath at his confirmation hearing and that President Biden plans to replace him with Loretta Lynch."

(Kent) "I guess I did miss a few things!"

(White) "The real story of Lois' encounter with Trump in the bunker will forever be withheld from the public. He tried groping her and she beat the crap out of him."

(Lane) "Not a big deal because he's fat, soft and when attacked cries for mercy. What came out, quite literally, was that Trump had somehow ingested a chunk of Kryptonite which explains why he not only didn't fear Superman, but wanted to meet him."

(Kent, *nervously*) "What happened to that chunk of Kryptonite? You didn't keep it!"

(White) "Harmless to you Kent, and the rest of us, but we know it's the only element that can not only weaken Superman, but could potentially kill him. Lois alertly picked it up and later threw it in the Potomac River. This woman saved Superman and America!"

(Kent, *with conviction*) "You know, Perry, I'm not sure that America needs Superman as long as we have such wise, strong, and invincible women."

THE END*

*Dedicated to the late Helen Reddy whose anthem "I Am Woman" changed forever the way women are regarded in American society.

TWENTY SIX

The Chosen One
(*Eric the Red confronts Donald of Orange*)

<u>Scene One</u>

[*The setting is a castle in Iceland near the end of the first millennium. King Olaf has summoned his two most supportive chieftains, Eric the Red and Donald of Orange, to discuss a daring expedition into the uncharted waters to the west.*]

(Olaf) "Welcome. I thank thee for heeding my call. I have a bold plan to announce."

(Eric) "We are all ears, sire. Share with us your noble wishes."

(Olaf) "The land and seas to the east of our beloved homeland are fully explored. We know where our friends live and where our foes can be found. But, what might lie beyond the ocean to the west remains a mystery. There might be lands to discover, kingdoms to conquer, and riches to be found. I want to solve these mysteries in the name of Iceland!"

(Erik) "A noble initiative indeed, sire. But, we'll need ships and men worthy of the task."

(Olaf) "I have been secretly building a small fleet made of the stoutest of timbers. These ships are almost ready to sail. What I need is a leader; someone to command the expedition."

(Donald) "Are we to assume that's why we have been summoned, sire?"

(Olaf) "Precisely. But, only one of you must go, and knowing full well that you'll both want to be chosen, I have brought you here to plead your cases before me and each other."

(Eric) "Fair enough, sire."

(Olaf) "Let me be honest and straightforward my countrymen. No man has endeavored to sail west. If the Earth is flat, as some scholars say, you could fall off the edge! If no edge is to be found, as others maintain, suggesting the world is round, you could encounter dragons and beasts like none ever seen before as speculated in some Norse writings."

(Erik) "You have made yourself understood, sire."

(Olaf) "There's more to warn about. Those are but speculative concerns. We've seen how the seas erupt furiously at times against our shoreline. Villages are swept away; no sign left of them. Imagine facing such tempests while afloat. Even the sturdiest ships might be swallowed up by a gigantic wave and reduced to splinters. The sea gods can be cruel."

(Erik) "We are god-fearing men but the gods will soon be aware of our bold spirit."

(Olaf) "Well spoken, Erik the Red. Proceed with your argument to lead this expedition."

(Eric) "Thank you, sire. I am an unlearned man when it comes to studies, but I am a man of the times who knows men. I have sailed the known waters of the world and my crews have always trusted and respected me; I am a leader. I know not the names of the stars but I have studied their movements; I am a skilled navigator. I have faced hardened warriors in hand-to-hand combat; and I have conquered the innate fear of war. I am undaunted."

Chorus off to the side chanting (always heard only by the audience; not the characters):

"His name is Eric the Red
And of him it is widely said,
That he never rests his head
Until the task has been put to bed.

A respected leader is he
Who has commanded men at sea.
Upon sight his enemies flee.
Who then could be more wor-thy?"

(Olaf) "Those are ideal qualities. A chieftain gains fame by being victorious in battle and earns respect by being generous with his followers, to 'feed carrion to the ravens' as we say. You have made a strong case for yourself, Erik the Red...Now Donald, speak."

(Donald) "Ah, yes, sire. This expedition has my name, Donald of Orange, written all over it. I feel like I was born to fulfill such a mission. I am indeed 'The Chosen One.' Make no mistake, there's no one more suited for the job. No one. But, if full disclosure be the better part of valor, I must admit that these bone spurs of mine have been acting up badly of late. Very badly; and no Nordic man of medicine nor sorcerer can seem to find a remedy to this ailment. I can deal with the pain, of course. No one deals with pain like me. It's just sure footing aboard ship that's an issue. I'm one to climb the highest mast."

(Olaf) "So, Donald of Orange, you are deferring to Eric the Red?"

(Donald) "Yes, I must; but I can be of great service to the expedition here at home. You see, I build things. I'd like to have a look at those ship plans. I might, probably will, discover a flaw in the design that could jeopardize the journey. There's nothing I'm not good at."

Chorus off to the side chanting:

"His crown is bright orange on top,
But see how his belly does flop.
His boastful words are mere slop;
Best to bring a pail and a mop!

> He brags of being so bold
> But if the blatant truth be told,
> Of the facts he has no hold;
> As a liar he has broken the mold."

(Olaf) "Erik, I hereby designate you the supreme leader of the expedition. Your charge is to sail west as far as the winds will carry you. Report back what you have found. So be gone, chose your men wisely, and may the gods that rule the sea look favorably upon you."

Scene Two

[*Three years have passed. The wise old king has died and Donald of Orange by questionable accession now rules the Icelandic kingdom. The setting is the royal hall where the king is in session with his high level courtiers and the Legal Assembly. A messenger suddenly bursts into the chamber with the incredible news that Erik the Red, the mariner long thought lost with his ships and men, has returned to the homeland.*]

(Messenger) "Sire, I come with startling and welcomed news…Erik the Red has returned from his long voyage! Some ships were lost in savage storms, but most of the men are back safely, thanks they say to his skills as a mariner…Shall we prepare for him a hero's welcome?"

(Donald) "My heroes don't lose any ships or men, but I shall acknowledge his return in due time."

(Messenger) "He encountered no tribes or enemies, nor did he find gold, but he discovered a new land, a land of rare contrasts – fertile soil and rivers of ice. He deemed it 'Greenland.'"

(Donald) "Rather nasty of him not to name it after me, wouldn't you say, I being his sovereign?"

(A courtier speaks) "My lord, a gentle reminder that Olaf was king when Erik departed."

(Donald) "Well, maybe so, but what I'm sayin' is that the expedition was my idea. My idea alone. And I wanted to lead it myself but Erik the Red must have bribed the king to get the job."

(Courtier) "As you say, sire."

(Donald) "And here's another thing. If I had led the expedition I would have been back a lot sooner, a lot sooner, and I wouldn't have lost any men or ships like he did, and I'll guarantee you that I'd return with more than news of finding dirt and ice."

(Courtier) "Of course, sire."

(Donald) "Big, big mistake sending Red. He's a loser. What else can I say? He's a loser."

(Courtier) "You are right, sire."

(Donald) "You bet I'm right. And that land he claims he found, if his story is true, it won't be called 'Greenland,' I'll tell you that. I'll build on it. You know. Nice castles where people can stay and we can make a lot of money. Maybe something more like... Mar-a-Lago."

(Courtier) "That's a fine name, sire."

(Donald) "Where's Pence? Where is the little scamp? Someone please fetch me my jester."

A courtier scurries out of the great hall to find Pence. Meanwhile, the chorus chants:

> "How many lies can you say in a sentence?
> How many lies can you tell in a day?
> And when you lie without repentance
> You're letting the devil have his way."

The courtier returns with jester Pence in tow

(Donald) "Ah Pence my boy, I have an assignment for you. Go find Erik the Red and bring him here. Take no one with you. I don't want to make it seem like anything special."

The chorus resumes its chants:

> "How do you deal with a jealous mind
> That takes all credit for another's find?
> How long must a nation endure this guff
> When no one dares to call his bluff?"

(Donald) "When jester Pence arrives, let Erik the Red cool his salt-worn heels here. I'll be in my private chamber with my lady Melania, coming down when I'm good and ready."

The king leaves the hall as his courtiers and the Legal Assembly remain behind

Scene Three

[*The setting is the king's private chamber where he sits pensively, his crown laid on the floor at his feet. Lady Melania, now Queen of Iceland, notes his troubled spirits.*]

(Melania) "What troubles my master?"

(Donald) "Would that the world had an edge, or that the dragons had been justly fed, or that the wind and waves had conspired to swallow his ships…Eric the Red has returned."

(Melania) "Why is that something to fret about? You have risen above the other chieftains to become king. You are no longer equals in the eyes of the Assembly. You are his lord."

(Donald) "All that transpired while he was away. Given his brutishness, I fear the worst from him."

(Melania) "You have the law on your side. Your courtiers, those closest to you, are loyal servants. The Assembly has grown fearful of you, lest they suffer reprisals. They don't speak out."

(Donald, *breathing deeply*) "I wish it was bedtime and all was well."

(Melania) "Don't speak so foolishly, my Lord. Your staff is not false, but true. Erik the Red will probably drop to his knees and seek to kiss your ring if he's a true countryman."

The chorus chants:

> "What is the choice for a tyrant
> Who always relies on his rant,
> When someone dares to oppose him
> Whom he'd like to dispel but can't?"

Scene Four

[*The setting is the great hall while the king is absent. Erik the Red, his sunburned visage barely visible beneath a tangle of red hair and beard, storms into the chamber with jester Pence, wailing and kicking, tucked under a muscular arm. He's followed by a throng of commoners chanting his name. The Legal Assembly parts down the middle to clear a path to the vacant throne, into which he dumps Pence, instructing him not to move.*]

(Courtier, *in trembling voice*) "Welcome...Welcome back, Erik the Red."

(Eric) "Welcome back to *what* I might ask? I've yet to observe the sun set twice on my beloved home soil and the story has been related to me many times of what has occurred since I set sail and ventured west. How our kind and generous king has died, and how Donald of Orange ascended to the throne, not by the will of the people, but at the power of the Danish king, our erstwhile enemy, and continues with the feeble acquiescence of you, the Legal Assembly. Can anyone from his clan in this assembly explain the circumstance?"

(Courtier) "The other chieftains, numbering digits from three hands, fell to his will."

(Eric) "And what was his persuasion? The same as why he, and not I, should go to sea?"

(Courtier) "That was part of it. He swore you bribed your way into the assignment; that he was more than prepared, even anxious to go, but that Olaf owed unspoken allegiance to you."

(Eric) "What blasphemy! While standing before the king his tongue was a-wagging but his knees were a-knocking at the mere thought of a voyage beset with danger. His ship wouldn't pass beyond the breakwater when fish would be feeding on his last meal."

(Courtier) "What would you have us do?"

(Eric) "Act like men! Act like men elected to the Legal Assembly to steer the ship of state into safe harbors when the captain has no compass. You are like sheep herded into a corral, bleating softly while the wolf has his way. Is there not a man of conviction among you?"

(Courtier) "Do *you* want to be king?"

(Eric) "No, that is not my purpose for coming here. I will say though that jester Pence, pathetic pissant that he is, would bring more honor to the throne of Olaf than this interloper who makes friends of enemies and enemies of friends, (*pointing at the frightened courtiers*) surrounds himself with spineless mimics, and lies to his people. What say you to that?"

(Courtier, *timidly*) "He says he is 'The Chosen One.'"

(Eric) "And I ask you, chosen to do what? To bring shame upon our nation? I hear the Danes laugh at us. King Vlad fed him sweet words from the font of flattery and now he eats out of this enemy's hand. The Viking Way is gaining respect and honor through generosity to countrymen and bravery in battle. I'm told that Donald of Orange favors the nobles and dishonors war heroes – he who was breast fed on the milk of family prosperity and now begs for a Medal of Honor for what?...For cowardly shirking his duty to serve?"

(Courtier) "You speak boldly to us, Erik the Red. We await what transpires when the king arrives."

Scene Five

[*The setting is the same great hall filled with the king's courtiers, members of the Legal Assembly from the two rival clans, and throngs of commoners filling every available space. Erik has thrust jester Pence from the throne and stands before it as Donald of Orange makes his entry, again a path opening so the two men soon stand face to face.*]

(Donald) "Hail, Erik the Red."

(Eric) "Hail, Donald of Orange."

The chorus chants:

> "Two combatants girded for glory,
> Who will the victor be?
> There is no conclusion to this story,
> As the decision is up to thee."

BOOK FOUR

Aftermath: Divisiveness, Discord, Dysfunction and Despair

*Beyond his well-planned effort to overturn election results and
remain in power and inciting his followers to stage an insurrection,
Trump continued in the election aftermath to claim, without
a shred of evidence, that the 2020 election was stolen. This
emboldened his blind but loyal core of believers who have never
accepted the outcome, causing distrust in government and the
electoral process, and resulting in the great national divide we
sense today that tears at the core fabric of American politics and
domestic life.*

TWENTY SEVEN

Animal Barn
(A hog attemps to take control of the family farm)

<u>Act One, Scene One</u>

[In the opening scene, Dorothy Honeysuckle, a matronly woman of about 65 years, who prefers being called Mrs. Thurman Honeysuckle, is drying dishes at the kitchen sink looking out a window at their farmhouse barn. Mr. Honeysuckle arrives in the kitchen through the door to the shed wiping his hands which had been cleaned of motor oil.]

(Dorothy) "Thurman, what in tarnation is goin' on out there in the yard?"

(Thurman, *looking over her shoulder out the window*) "Damned if I know."

(Dorothy) "Well, you'd better go have a look. Somethin's botherin' the animals."

(Thurman) "Oh, it could be ol' Gent stirrin' 'em up for no reason a-tall."

(Dorothy) "Darlin' don't look now but ol' Gent is sound asleep on the hamper."

(Thurman, *sighing*) "Useless hound. Ok, I'll go have me a look. Probably nuttin."

<u>Act One, Scene Two</u>

[The scene is the sty-filled barn on the Honeysuckle farm. Truman, the eldest

and fattest boar hog, is upright on all fours (not his preferred position) holding a meeting of the senior hogs – Domino, Rhubarb and Pinky. Also invited and present are Godfrey the farm's senior goat, Old Baxter the plow horse, and Rudolph (Rudy) the red rooster.]

(Truman) "This is outrageous! How did I get voted out of being barnyard president?"

(Domino) "Truly a calamity, sir. It's unthinkable that you could lose reelection."

(Truman, *angrily*) "I didn't lose!"

(Rhubarb) "And to a *duck* no less!"

(Pinky) "I suspect foul play!"

(Godfrey) "I can assure you all that every goat voted for the president."

(Baxter) "Mind you, the *former* president. That duck is about to be sworn in."

(Rudy) "This cock will not announce the winner until an investigation is ordered."

(Truman) "Don't be a sucker, Rudy. There's no time for an investigation."

(Rudy, *stammering*) "Ah…Let me think. An insurrection! We'll revolt!"

(Truman) "Now you've got your feathers on straight. I like that idea!"

(Baxter) "But, let us remind ourselves, the election was lawfully executed."

(Truman, *shouting*) "Lawfully! Hell no. *I'm* the law around here!"

(Pinky) "That you are indeed, Mr. President…And always will be."

(Truman) "It was stolen! I tell you it was stolen!"

(Godfrey) "The little ones are behind this outrage – the ducks, the chickens, the mice."

(Baxter) "I don't mean to be obstreperous, but they are allowed to vote."

(Truman) "Damn it! Would you speak English! The minor animals *should not* be voting."

(Domino) "Of course not. They're…Unrefined!"

(Rhubarb) "They're…Dangerous!"

(Pinky) "They're…Socialists!"

(Baxter) "Let's face it. They might be all of that…but they're the winners."

(Rudy) "Not yet! We gotta stop the steal. C'mon patriots! Onward to the duck pool."

Act One, Scene Three

[*Farmer Honeysuckle is seen following the commotion to the net-covered duck pool next to the barn where he observes dozens of pigs and goats splashing in the water amidst the startled ducks. He runs to the barn, grabs his pitchfork, and enters the skirmish.*]

(Domino, *breathless*): "Where's Truman? Isn't he with us?"

(Rhubarb) "Yes, of course, but he's back at the barn. Bone spurs, remember?"

(Godfrey) "Take the plunge fellow patriots! Victory awaits our noble cause!"

(Pinky, *shivering*) "I'd wade in but the water's too cold!"

(Godfrey, *alarmed*) "Hurry! Here comes the upright creature with his pitch fork."

(Rudy) "He's of high constitution. We'd better run. The swine courts will redeem us!"

Act Two, Scene One

[*Farmer Honeysuckle has returned to the farmhouse kitchen; his wife is waiting.*]

(Dorothy) "For heaven's sake, Thurman. You're soaking wet and all muddy."

(Thurman, *catching his breath*) "You shoulda seen it. They was all in the pool."

(Dorothy) "Who was all in the pool?"

(Thurman) "Lots of pigs and goats. They ripped a hole in the netting and went in."

(Dorothy) "Any idea why they might do that? Did they need a bath?"

(Thurman) "That pool's fer ducks; it ain't fer them and they knows that."

(Dorothy) "Now, how would they know that?"

(Thurman) "There's a fence ain't there! Won't be doin' it agin. I stabbed one of 'em."

(Dorothy) "A pig or a goat?"

(Thurman) "Pig…Guess we'll be havin' ham come Sunday."

Act Two, Scene Two

[*The invaders have now retreaded back to the barn to report to Truman.*]

(Godfrey, *wet and breathless*) "Mission went as planned until that man came out."

(Baxter) "I watched from here. That man owns this farm. Name's Honeysuckle."

(Godfrey) "How do you know so much?"

(Baxter) "Easy. I pull his wagon into town every now and then and he talks a lot."

(Truman) "Baxter's onto something. Restoring me to my rightful office is only a temporary fix. Even if I control the barnyard I don't control the farm. The man that lives in the two-story shed with all the windows is the real boss...We must get rid of him!"

(Pinky) "Whoa! Are you sayin' we get rid of the boss man who feeds us every day?"

(Truman) "Look at it as obliterating our oppressor. Besides, he's just the middleman. I know from a crow that flies by on occasion that there's a field we can't see from here that is full of food. There's rows and rows of cabbages. Paw the ground a bit and you'll find beets, and turnips and potatoes. He says there's rows of corn stalks as far as you can see."

Domino: "And he's the one who brings in all them ducks and chickens. We get rid of him, we can banish all the minor animals. They can't vote if they ain't around no more!"

Rudy: "I have a plan. Gather 'round and I'll tell you how we take over the whole farm."

Act Two, Scene Three

[*It's now three weeks later – a beautiful fall afternoon and the pigs and goats are sprawled in the big house with all the windows having abandoned the barn.*

They're drinking whiskey and feasting on all the ripe vegetables found in the big garden.]

(Truman, *now close to 400 pounds*) "I do say this is indeed the good life!"

(Godfrey) "Should have done this long ago. I can still picture you rolling on that Mr. Honeysuckle after I butted him in the buttocks when he bent over. He couldn't breathe!"

(Rudy) "And, the chickens loyal to our cause plucked the life out of his female companion when she was gathering eggs. Hollered and hollered but the coop door was locked."

(Pinky) "Anybody seen Baxter? Where's he been off to?"

(Truman) "Screw Baxter. He's a horse with no damn horse sense. Forget about him."

(Domino) "What I still don't understand is where all the corn, turnips, cabbages and such come from. I went back where we'd cleared some out and they hadn't grown back."

(Truman) "You worry too much. That garden is endless. The minor animals have been banished. The big house belongs to us. We're the government now. We're in charge!"

(Pinky) "I just hope and pray it stays like this forever."

Act Three, Scene One

[*Two months have passed and a harsh winter has set in. The ground is frozen solid and once verdant trees are bare and the fields are dry and covered with ice and snow. Life is not good at the former Honeysuckle Farm. The pigs and goats that once feasted on nature's bounty are now starving and in a rebellious mood. Truman and his top advisors have sequestered themselves in the big house, banishing the others to the leaky barn.*]

(Godfrey) "Truman, we hoarded the food for ourselves but we're as cold as the others."

(Truman) "I've been thinking. We'll take down the barn and burn the wood for heat."

(Domino) "What about our fellow patriots who find there what little comfort it offers."

(Truman) "What about them? They're minor animals now. Their fate is their own doing."

(Godfrey) "What's happened to us? What have we become? Our life wasn't all that bad but we got greedy and wanted more. The farmer ruled with impunity. He fed us and kept us warm. The duck ran an honest campaign. He won, but we still would have had our rights and freedom. We could block his reforms and prepare for the next election with some restrictive laws. What good is power when there is no one left to rule? We failed."

(Truman) "Fellow swine. Do away with this traitorous goat. Then set fire to the barn!"

<u>Act Three, Scene Two</u>

[*It's the following morning. The county sheriff, a fireman and two neighboring farmers have gathered at the smoldering ruins of the Honeysuckle barn. The pungent smell of burnt carcasses permeates the air along with the acrid odor of burning motor oil.*]

(Fireman) "Do you know if Thurman and Dorothy were home or away?"

(Sheriff) "Apparently away…and for good. There's a note scratched on the kitchen wall, hard to read, but says 'Gone Forever D + T.' Looks like it had been there some time."

(Neighbor #1) "They did keep mostly to themselves and I haven't seen 'em fer awhile."

(Neighbor #2) "Looks like they jus up an' left and the pigs were free ta roam."

(Fireman) "What'll happen to all the pigs found in the house?"

(Sheriff) "Already taken care of; shipped to the slaughterhouse over in Conroy. One big ol' boy weighed 450 pounds and did he ever squeal. You'd think he owned the place."

(Neighbor #1) "Still don't make any sense. Honeysuckle Farm been here seemingly forever. Thurm's great granddaddy was one of the founding farmers in these parts. Both him and Dot were pillars in this community. Good folks. Honest folks. Hard workers. Kept high standards and expected the same of others. People of solid constitution. I never dreamed that the day would come when Honeysuckle Farm would be no longer."

(Neighbor #2) "I guess that's the way it is. You think that somethin' is here forever and then all of a sudden it's gone. There's a lesson in there somewhere I reckon."

(Fireman) "I guess we'll never know how or why it happened. 'Tis a shame though."

(Sheriff) "Well lookie there. If it ain't Baxter. There's your answer if only he could talk."

TWENTY EIGHT

Down on the Plantation with Miss Lindsey Graham:
The Trial

(Trump loyalists unite to prevent an impeachment conviction)

Act One, Scene One

[The time is the late 1850s. As the scene opens, Miss Lindsey Graham (ML), a senator from South Carolina, is seen sprawled on a swinging chair suspended from the roof of the veranda that runs the entire length of the front of her white-columned plantation house. She's seen feverishly fanning herself before summoning her personal servant.]

(ML) "Oh, Charles, do fetch me an ice cold lemonade. Tomorrow I return to that dreadful capital where the former president is being put on trial for...insurrection!"

(Charles excuses himself and returns with her drink)

(Charles) "Beg pardon, Miss Lindsey. But, what's he bein' 'cuzed of?"

(ML) "Charles, it's all nonsense is what it is. As you know, our beloved president wasn't reelected, or so they say. He claims, with reason I believe, that the election was stolen by the opposing party. Some of his more ardent supporters paid a visit to Washington to voice their disapproval of the election results. The president, of course, was glad to have them there and in a speech innocently suggested they let Congress know their feelings."

(Charles) "So lettin' someun knows yo feelins is dis 'inerection?'"

(ML) "No, it's more than that. As can happen when good folks sense that something isn't right, isn't fair, isn't the way it should be, things got a bit out of hand during the protest. Dear me, it did get a bit ugly (*waves her fan more vigorously*) but that's because no one would listen to them. Can you imagine how it must feel to know that something isn't right, isn't fair, isn't the way God wants it to be and being helpless to do anything?"

(Charles, *doffing his straw hat*) "Well, ta be honest, Miss Lindsey…"

(ML, *not listening*) "They really have a nerve! (*Takes a long sip through her straw*) As if taking over the White House isn't enough, they now want to put the poor man on trial for the…um, *disordliness* that followed. Can't they just rest on their laurels and move on!"

(Charles) "Them laurels a lot like our hay? Chester down the bunkhouse was tellin' folks that dere was a riot dat took place in Washinton and dat some folks got kilt. Is dat true?"

(ML) "Chester should select his words more judiciously; I'll make a point of talking to him about that. It's true, there was a, um, *disturbance* and injuries did occur, but that was just a few people getting carried away with the cause, most likely provoked by some infiltrators from the other party anxious to embarrass the president."

(Charles) "Dis president da one wit da orange hair who don like colored folk?"

(ML) "Charles, where did you ever get such a notion? I think I know so you don't have to snitch and tell me…Looks like I'll be having a more serious conversation with Chester."

(Charles) "Miss Lindsey, please d'own do dat. All Chester was wonderin' when we was gathered 'round after day's chores was done was if iny of us kind was in dat protest."

(ML, *sternly*) "You mean people of your color?"

(Charles) "Yessum. We was wonderin' what mighta happen if a whole lot of us kind was ta start such a 'dis-tur-bance' to maybe git somethin' God might wan fer all of usuns."

(ML) "Charles, what on Earth has gotten into you? God is happy with where you are. It's the natural order. Mess with that order and, goodness knows, we'll have a civil war!"

Act One, Scene Two

[*The setting is poolside at a sprawling estate in south Florida where the former president has reluctantly taken up residence after leaving the White House. He has gathered his closest advisors — his two sons, Don Jr. and Eric, and son-in-law Jared Kushner — to discuss his upcoming impeachment trial. The former president (FP), emerging from the shallow end of the pool, his wet belly bulging over the waistband of his Sponge Bob swimming trunks, has ordered a towel be brought and coffee for all the participants.*]

(FP, *grinning*) "At least here there are no rules about not peeing in the pool."

(Don Jr.) "I haven't worn a tie since we arrived."

(Kushner) "Such a shame…All those clip-ons going to waste?"

(*An orderly arrives with coffee and a beach towel under his arm*)

(FP, *wrapping the towel around his waist but unable to make the ends meet to tie into a knot*) "Remind me to fire someone's ass over the itsy-bitsy size of these towels."

(Eric) "I still think you should have fired every cabinet member and department head."

(Don Jr.) "Hell, yes! A bunch of friggen' wimpy traitors. They should have *led* the charge on the Capitol! Left that up to a bunch of goofs with horns and fur hats."

(FP) "I've always said you should never do anything half-assed. You can chant and hold up signs like pussy's protest, or (*loudly*) you break in, take hostages, and demand the stolen election be overturned. For a while it looked like justice might be had, but…"

(Kushner) "I guess that leads us into why we're here, huh?"

Act Two, Scene One

[*The setting is a conference room in the Senate wing of the U.S. Capitol. Minority Senate leader Mitch McConnell has reserved the room for a private meeting with three of his Republican colleagues – Ted Cruz, Josh Hawley, and freshman Senator Tommy Tuberville – to discuss the forthcoming impeachment trial of the former president.*]

(McConnell) "Thank you, gentlemen, for agreeing to meet. You'll agree these are unprecedented times and that there's more at stake than the fate of the former president."

(Tuberville) "I want ya'll ta know that this is bigger than bein' in a huddle fer a game winnin' drive in da Soup-a Bowl. Golly, I'm jus like a pig in slop bein' here with ya'll."

(McConnell) "We're happy you could join us, Tommy." (*Aside, to himself*) "This guy's dumber than they said he was. I'm almost beginning to miss Jeff Sessions…"

(Cruz) "Mitch, you said that the president had committed an impeachable offense. Down in Texas they'd have you branded on your ass end with the word 'traitor' fer sayin' that."

(McConnell) "Take it easy, Ted. We're here to discuss what needs to be done. We'd have lost all credibility if we didn't condemn the mob and acknowledge that the president had lit a fire under them. Being impeached isn't the same as being convicted as we all know."

(Tuberville) "I don't mean ta in-tar-upt when the quarterback is callin' the play, but kin someone tell me what this 'im*peach*ment' means? Is it got sometin' ta do with Jaw-ja?"

(McConnell, *sighing*) "Tommy, it's an old term; probably of French derivation…"

(Hawley) "Tommy, consider it as a personal fowl for unnecessary roughness."

(Tuberville) "I git it now! (*Pretending to blow a whistle and then gripping his wrist*) "Personal foul, Number 45, fifteen yards and loss of down fer impeachament."

(McConnell) "If there are no more questions, let's proceed…"

(Hawley) "If I can be so bold, Ted here has a point. On that fateful day, he and I were the only ones who challenged the Electoral College vote, that hopefully everyone in this room believes was riddled with improprieties. Now (*pausing*)…What's that Tommy?"

(Tuberville) "Sorry, fellas…but can ya'll speak a little clearer? What's an 'improperty?'"

(McConnell) "It means that something bad happened that wasn't right."

(Hawley) "Tommy, think of it as a bad penalty that caused Auburn to lose the game."

(Tuberville, *angry*) "Fer cryin' out loud, we can't let that happen. I smell a fix!"

(McConnell, *wiping his brow*) "Josh, you were about to say…"

(Hawley) "I was about to say, and you might not take kindly to this, that while you were playing patty-cakes with the opposition party, Ted and I were standing up for the president and doing what was necessary in order to ensure that he remained in office."

(McConnell) "Mr. Hawley. That 'patty-cakes' is known among senior senators as 'decoy diplomacy.' You're a little too green to understand so I can appreciate your annoyance. As I mentioned, there's much more at stake here than the fate of the president in this upcoming trial. We need to be mindful that the future of our party hangs in the balance."

(Cruz) "Mitch, c'mon, you've been whoopin' like a wannabe cowboy sittin' in a saddle on a fence post. The future of our party *was* at stake, and while you were hootin' and hollerin' we were busy riding herd protecting the president."

(Tuberville) "Yahoo! Ridin' herd! Ya'll count me in. (*begins singing*) Rollin', rollin', rollin'. Keep them doggies rollin'...Keep them doggies rollin'...."

(McConnell) "Tommy, please! We could use a little inspiration here. Why don't you be real quiet and think about some of our great southern legends and maybe they'll speak to you. I'm thinking of recent heroes like Andrew Jackson, James Polk and Henry Clay."

(Tuberville) "I kin do that. I kin think real hard. I'm gonna begin with Coach Dye."

(Cruz, *aside*) "You handled that better than a marshal caught in a Texas cat house."

(McConnell) "Since we're not pulling punches here, I think it's pretty obvious that your valiant efforts to derail the Electoral College vote, which you both knew full well was doomed to fail, was less about the president and more about your own political futures."

(Cruz) "Well, if that ain't the sheriff pullin' a gun on his own deputy!"

(Hawley) "Me? Politically motivated? Sure! And so was Ted! I was just honoring my duty as an 'up-and-coming party luminary.' Unlike Ted here whose name is well-known, and respected I might add, no one ever heard of me outside of Missouri before all this."

(McConnell) "Okay, we've each had our say. The bottom line is we're all Republicans and we need to decide if there's greater risk to the party in exonerating the president or affirming his complicity. That's where we are. That's what we have to decide."

(Tuberville) "I was up ta concentratin' on Johnny Rodgers and

Frank Broyles but at the same time I was also listenin' in ta ya'll. Kin I break off my thinkin' 'bout legends ta speak up an' say that I'm fer honorin' da president rather than confirming his afflicity.' "

(McConnell) "Let's break, gentlemen...I couldn't have summarized it better myself."

Act Two, Scene Two

[*We're back at poolside at the former president's private retreat in south Florida where he's meeting with his two sons, Don Jr. and Eric, and son-in-law Jared Kushner to discuss strategy for the upcoming impeachment trial. They're seated around a large circular table shaded by a bright red MAGA umbrella. A waiter has just arrived.*]

(Waiter) "May I take your drink orders, gentlemen?"

(Eric, *speaking up first*) "I think I'm gonna have one of them Bud Lights."

(Waiter) "Very good. Bottle or chilled glass?"

(Eric) "The bottle's fine."

(Waiter, *turning toward Don Jr.*) "And for you, sir?"

(Don Jr.) "I'll have the same thing; only make mine a light Bud Light."

(Waiter) "Um...Of course. Bottle or chilled glass?"

(Don Jr.) "The bottle's made of glass, right?

(Waiter) "Ah...yes, of course."

(Don Jr.) "Well, since I don't like warm beer I'll have the chilled glass bottle."

(Waiter, *holding his pad in front of Jared Kushner*) "And what would you like?"

(Kushner) "I'm going to have a daiquiri."

(Waiter) "For $10.00 more would you like to make that a Stormy Daniels?"

(Kushner) "I don't understand."

(Waiter) "Same drink but bottomless."

(Kushner) "Ah, I'd better not go there."

(Waiter, *turning toward the former president*) "And for you, Mr. President?"

(FP) "I'll have a Jack Nicklaus."

(Waiter) "You mean an Arnold Palmer, don't you?"

(FP) "Same thing, only I prefer to call it a Jack Nicklaus. He's a big supporter of mine."

(Waiter) "Yes, I understand."

(FP) "We have a lot in common, Jack and me, ya know." (*Extends his arms outward*). "We both take big strokes resulting in those deep drives that get your balls closer to the hole."

(Waiter) "I see…"

(FP, *grinning*) "Of course, when it comes to *golf* he's a much better player."

(*As the waiter leaves to fill the orders, the former president makes an announcement*)

(FP) "I've invited the new attorney who'll represent me at the trial to join us for lunch."

(Kushner) "New attorney? I thought Miss Lindsey had recommended someone."

(FP) "She did, a guy named Butch Bowers. Pretty weak, a low-key sort who shudders in front of the press. He musta been up her skirts. Anyway, no loyalty there so I fired him."

(Kushner) "Who's the replacement?"

(FP) "You know, this case is so simple I could try it myself and have it dismissed on day one. But, I don't wanna go near the place. His name is David Schoen and he's great."

(Kushner) "The name's familiar. I think my father knows him."

(FP) "Makes sense. I hope your old man is happy with the pardon."

(Kushner) "I recall his clients include the alleged head of the Russian mafia, two Italian underworld bosses and several accused mobsters…Won't the media be all over this?"

(FP) "You mean the *fake* media? It takes a guy like Schoen to cut through all the crap."

(*At this point the waiter returns with a tray of drinks and lays them out*)

(Waiter) "Mr. President and gentlemen guests, would you care to order at this time?"

(FP, *setting aside the menu*) "We're expecting one more so you can bring up another chair and put out a fifth place setting…but we'll go ahead and order."

(Waiter) "We'll begin with you this time, Mr. President."

(FP) "Why change? I'll have the usual POTUS Special – loaded triple cheeseburger, extra fries, side of rings and a double chocolate malted shake. No ketchup; I'm dieting."

(Waiter, *quill poised*) "And your preference, Mr. Israeli Ambassador Kushner?"

(Kushner, *examining the menu*) "What do you have that's light but not a green salad?"

(Waiter, *placing a finger on the menu*) "I would recommend the lightly breaded Schumerschnitzel that comes with sides of Pelosi prunes and Susan rice."

(Kushner) "Can't have pork; but can you describe the sides for me?"

(Waiter, *glancing slyly at the former president who obviously suggested names for some of the retreat's menu offerings*) "Why, of course. The Pelosi prunes are simply shrunken dried prunes. The Susan rice, pronounced 'Sue-san,' is a small brain…ah, little slip, I meant to say small *grain* brown variety with likely connections to China."

(Kushner) "On second thought I'll have the Massachusetts Dems mixed fruit salad."

(Waiter, *turning to Eric.*) "And for you, sir?"

(Eric) "I'm in the mood for a big hero sandwich, any recommend-ations?"

(Waiter) "Of course. Our favorite heroes are the 'Putin' with Russian dressing, the 'Kim' with big buns and hair-raising soy sauce, and a killer 'Saudi Prince' drizzled with oil."

(Eric) "Oh my gosh! This is tough. I love them all…I'll have one of each!"

(*As the waiter turns to Don Jr., David Schoen suddenly arrives. The waiter quickly pulls out a newly arrived chair and sees to it that the newcomer is comfortably seated, hands him a menu, places a large white linen napkin on his lap, and then addresses Don Jr.*)

(Waiter) "Have you thought things over?"

(Don Jr.) "I think I'll continue posting on my Twitter account and maybe get married."

(Waiter) "I was actually asking about your lunch preference."

(Don Jr.) "Oh, yeah. I'll go with the McCain platter of wings."

(Waiter) "Excellent choice. One McCain POW." (*facing Mr. Schoen*) "A verdict?"

(Schoen) "That's easy, thanks fer askin': 'not guilty!' That's why I'm here…I'll have a bottle of your *best* Italian red and a steaming plate of linguini with two meatballs."

(Waiter) "Very good, sir. I recommend the exquisite Bruono Giacosa Collina Rionda from Barolo to complement our herb spiced steaming hot linguini and…"

(FP, *interrupting*) "Two meatballs – Obama and Biden! And, waiter, until we're finished talking here, and have our little deal worked out, make that the house Chianti."

Act Three, Scene One

[*We're back at Miss Lindsey's South Carolina plantation. Her house servant Charles is awaiting the arrival of her carriage from the train depot as she's returning to her mansion during a recess in the former president's impeachment trial. Seeing a cloud of red dust at the far end of the long magnolia-lined lane he gets up to await the arrival.*]

(Charles, *helping her down from the carriage*) "Welcum back, Miss Lindsey. Yous right on time. Didya have a nice trip?"

(ML) "Thank you, Charles. That trip is always dreadful, but this time I had the most delightful companion. (*Senator John Cornyn alights slowly from the carriage wearing polished high boots, tails and a gray top hat*) Charles, this is my esteemed colleague, Senator Cornyn from the great state of Texas. (*Charles bows*) I had no way of warning you that I'd be inviting a guest but I'm sure you can make proper accommodation. Have Bessie help you with the trunks; and have Winnie pour my hot bath as I'm all dust."

(Charles) "Greetins Mr. Senator, sir. You be stayin' long?"

(Cornyn) "It's a short recess, sad to say. But just getting out of that damn town is worth the trouble, and Miss Lindsey was kind enough to invite me to spend the weekend."

(Charles) "We see to it that you be welcom'. Let me take yo valise. (*Charles groans a bit lifting the heavy satchel*) "Look like you brought sum work wit you."

(Cornyn) "Not really. (*whispering*) "Just a few little trinkets for my generous hostess."

(ML) "Don't you two be whispering to each other. Charles, you can prepare the room down the hallway from mine on the second floor. That room gets a nice breeze."

(Charles) "Yessum. (*to Cornyn*) "Dat a room fer *special* guests. Flos don't squeak!"

(Cornyn) "I'm sure I'll be perfectly comfortable…Please draw me a bath as well."

Act Three, Scene Two

[*It's later but before dinner. Miss Lindsey is relaxed, looking quite refreshed from her bath and a change into a multi-layered southern belle hoop dress and fashionable hat. She's sitting in the swinging chair on the veranda fanning herself opposite Senator Cornyn who's seated cross-legged in a white wicker chair padded with a soft cushion, looking dapper in a spotless and freshly pressed white suit with gold watch chain, matched by polished white boots and a white hat with a band featuring a lone star.*]

(ML, *ringing a small bell*) "I believe drinks are in order, don't you agree, Senator?"

(Charles, *emerging from the house through the screen door*) "You rang, Miss Lindsey?"

(ML) "A round of mint juleps, Charles. Heavy on the bourbon as usual."

(Cornyn, *as Charles reenters the house, making sure not to let the screen door slam behind him*) "This is a perfect setting, indeed, Miss Lindsey. Such a contrast, huh?"

(ML) "Made more perfect by your presence, I must say, Senator. *(fanning herself vigorously)* I'm so pleased that you accepted my invitation on such short notice."

(Cornyn) "How could I refuse? Besides the opportunity to spend time with my favorite colleague *(bows in Miss Lindsey's direction)*, the only other choice was remaining in that infernal city crawling with vengeful Democrats like hyenas on a steaming carcass."

(ML) "Correction, Senator. They only *wish* they were feasting on a carcass. They'll be licking their bruised paws when this so-called trial is over. How did we ever get here?"

(Cornyn) "Spite. That's all. They claim they won the election and they're afraid the truth might come out and the former president will again be the president next time around."

(*Charles carefully backs through the screen door holding a silver tray with two drinks*)

(ML, *reaching out to accept her drink*) "I've been looking forward to this moment all day." *(waits for the Senator to be served then raises her glass)* "To justice and acquittal!"

(Cornyn, *as they touch glasses*) "To justice and acquittal!"

(Charles) "Mine if I ask how it's goin' wit dat trial? He guilty of dis in-sur-rection?"

(ML) "You have a fine memory, Charles." *(leaning towards Cornyn and whispering)* "I told Charles about the charge against the president and he remembered. He's got a fine mind but no education. Best to keep it that way." (*speaking out loud*) "The trial, Charles, is a total sham. You wouldn't believe what the prosecution has concocted! Just pitiful!"

(Charles) "So dere no reason ta go back?"

(ML, *sighing*) "If only that were true. We're taking a recess – a short break. We'll have to go back and put up with some questions and answers. Then we'll vote and it'll be over."

(Charles) "It gonna be foun he done no wrong?"

(ML) "Of course! We have a few strays in the party – lost senators who don't seem to understand that their voting their way out of Congress. They'll be crucified back home."

(Cornyn) "I'm pleased to say that one of those strays isn't my esteemed colleague from Texas. Ted Cruz is a straight-up man. He'll defend the president like it's the Alamo."

(Charles) "Sorry ta keep askin' 'bout it, but Chester an' the rest down the bunkhouse was hopin' ta git sum de-tails. Dey had heard peoples got kilt in dis in-sur-rection thing."

(ML, *laughing*) "Details? I guess some were presented, and a constable was killed for getting in the way. On the wrong team you might say. As for details (*takes a long sip*), I don't recall any. (*winks at Cornyn*) The Senator and I sat together in the balcony off by ourselves...If there was something going on down below (*titters*) I could hardly say!"

(Cornyn) "It was warm and uncomfortable in the chamber, you see. (*laughs*) Especially with all that hot air coming from the mouths of the prosecution...We moved upstairs."

(ML, *blushing*) "Where I could raise my dress and get some ay-r circulating underneath."

(Cornyn) "Is that right? I don't believe my eyes noticed that."

(ML) "That might be true…But your wanderin' hand certainly knew of it!"

(Cornyn, *clearing his throat*) "You see, Charles. There was no reason to pay attention. We were being kind not dozing off. After all, it's not interesting if you know the ending."

(Charles) "Dat seem bit strange cuz Chester say some real bad tings happin. Say that yousun senators had ta duck unda yo desks and run fer cuvva ta not git hung."

(ML) "Chester exaggerates. I wasn't afraid; were you afraid, Senator?" (*Cornyn shakes his head while finishing his drink*) "Now, I will say that the Vice President was in a bit of a panic. Every right to be! Imagine, him disappointin' the president the way he did."

(Chester) "Wha he do, Miss Lindsey?"

(ML) "I'll tell you what he did…But first, our guest needs a refill. Me as well."

(*Charles, who'd been standing, slips into the house, making sure not to slam the door*)

(Cornyn) "Your Charles asks a lot of questions…and you let him. Why?"

(ML, *fanning herself*) "They're curious like children. They don't understand the issues as we adults do so I feel obliged to straighten out some of their queer notions."

(Cornyn) "They?"

(ML) "All the servants. Charles, Bessie, Winnie, Chester and the rest. They've been with me for a long time. Father bought them as a lot when they were children."

(Cornyn) "I'll tell you something, my dear. Beware of this new president. Talk about strange notions. There are rumors that he'd declare all slaves free if he had his way."

Act Four, Scene One

[*The setting is poolside at the former president's* (FP) *Florida retreat. He's alone, stretched out on his back on a cot, his mountainous white belly exposed to a brilliant afternoon sun. He forms a stick man with the index and middle fingers of his right hand and walks him up the mound. He calls him "Hand Man," or sometimes "Nero" after the Roman Emperor he admired from stories his grandmother read from a children's book.*]

(FP, *talking to his hand*) "What do you see from up there, Nero?"

(Nero, *FP talking to himself*) "From here I can see your feet…wiggle your toes."

(FP, *wiggling his toes*) "Now turn around and what do you see?"

(Nero) "The handsome head of the greatest president in American history!"

(FP) "You got that right!"

(*FP continues indecipherably chatting with hand man when a shadow crosses his face*)

(Schoen) "Talking to yourself, Mr. President?"

(FP, *keeping his eyes shut*) "Who let you in, Schoen?"

(Schoen) "I thought you'd be expecting me."

(FP) "Cruz wired me with the news; said you butchered your day one presentation."

(Schoen) "The House Managers made a strong case; I decided to change tactics."

(FP) "Wouldn't have mattered anyway; I knew I had the votes."

(Schoen) "You know that seven in your party voted for conviction."

(FP) "Yeah, seven traitorous losers. We'll take care of them...Pull up a chair."

(*Attorney David Schoen retrieves a chair and sits next to the former president*)

(Schoen) "You won, why were you talking to yourself?"

(FP) "I'm the only one I can talk any sense with around here."

(Schoen) "I thought the boys were down."

(FP) "Schoen, you know what I mean. They got my dick and their mother's brains."

(Schoen, *aside to himself*) "Shorted on both!" (*then aloud*) "You upgraded in every department with Melania."

(FP) "Maybe too much. She's become a reader. Calls me 'Moby Dick' after some great white whale in a book that came out a few years ago by a Melvin something-or-other."

(Schoen, *looking at the bloated white figure in front of him*) "Pretty harsh!"

(FP) "You can say that, but (*opening his eyes and lifting his head slightly*) I need more work on my diet. Down to a double cheeseburger and regular fries and no ketchup for lunch but Nero (*making a stick man with his fingers*) still has a hill to climb."

(Schoen) "Nero a hero of yours?"

(FP, *eyes closed*) "Sort of. Him 'n Henry the Eighth and Napoleon I'd say. Men of girth."

(Schoen) "So, you read history."

(FP) "No, learned about them from children's books when I was a kid. I don't need ta read. Ya see, my instincts are so tremendous there's no reason to trust anything else."

(Schoen, *again examining the white bulge*) "Gut feeling, huh?"

(FP) "Funny, Schoen, very funny. You're lucky I'm paying you."

(Schoen) "I delivered the goods, didn't I?"

(FP) "I think the goods delivered you. From what I learned a lot of the votes to acquit were based on me bein' out of office. A constipational issue."

(Schoen) "Regardless, I have a piece of advice. I think you should head back up to Washington. They need to see that you're still the face of the party. Still in charge; calling the shots. As for the traitorous seven, sink their ship like Moby Dick did."

(FP) "Moby Dick sunk a ship?"

(Schoen) "Only one survivor…fellow named Schumer."

(FP, *bolting upright with his eyes agape*) "Schumer!"

(Schoen) "Settle down; I was making a little joke. His name was Ishmael."

(FP, *fire in his eyes*) "I'm a survivor, too! Call me Ish…Ish…whatever!"

Act Four, Scene Two

[*The setting once again is the veranda at the plantation house. David Schoen had delivered an invitation that the former president spend a night at Senator Miss Lindsey Graham's South Carolina mansion on his long trip back to Washington, D.C. Miss Lindsey is wearing her finest frilly dress and flowery oversized hat while brandishing an unopened parasol that matches her outfit. He is formally dressed in top hat and tails.*]

(ML) "How delightful to see you in such a fine mood, Mr. President, after all that has happened to blemish your legacy. (*fanning herself*) It was such a terrible travesty."

(FP) "That's all behind us now, many thanks to you, Miss Lindsey. Time to look ahead."

(ML) "The things that were said and insinuated! That *you* inspired an insurrection."

(FP) "In a way I blame myself; I should have been more precise with my instructions."

(ML) "Why, Mr. President, you most certainly didn't condone the violence…did you?"

(FP) "I don't know if I did or not. What's 'condone' mean?"

(ML) "Well, in simple terms, you agreed with it."

(FP) "You do believe, Miss Lindsey, that the election was rigged against me?"

(ML) "You've said that many times."

(FP) "You saw my rallies. People as far as the eye could see hanging on to my every word, cheering for me, chanting when I urged them to. That told me I could never lose."

(ML) "You certainly have a following. But that mob that stormed the Capitol…"

(FP) "Good people. I love 'em. They had it in their grasp, but didn't finish the job. What they wanted was justice. Rightin' a wrong. Gettin' back what was stolen…What a strange circumstance that the fella who stole the election has the nickname 'Honest.'"

(ML) But, if I dare say, weren't you concerned about the risk to the country? A coup, however it might seem justified, is nonetheless a coup. Our democracy might not have survived; our freedom gone with the wind. Weren't you concerned about a civil war?"

(FP) "Frankly, my dear, I don't give a damn."

TWENTY NINE

It's All in the Family: The House Hearings
(Archie Bunker refuses to watch the January 6 Congressional Hearings)

<u>Scene One</u>

[*The setting is the home of Edith and Archie Bunker at 704 Hauser Street in Queens. The date is June 9, 2022. Archie Bunker is seated in his easy chair smoking a cigar and sipping on a beer facing the television tuned to Fox News. His wife Edith and daughter Gloria are in the kitchen cleaning up after the evening meal. The front door opens and in walks Gloria's husband, Michael. Edith and Gloria rush in to see who has stopped by.*]

(Gloria) "Michael, what are you doing here? I thought you had class tonight."

(Michael) "We did, but it was cancelled so we could watch the hearings."

(Edith) "Did ya have ya dinna, Michael?"

(Michael) "No, Ma, I was in a big rush to get home so I wouldn't miss anything."

(Edith, *wiping her hands on her apron*) "Come in da kitchen an' I'll fix ya a san-wich."

(Michael) "That would be great, Ma. I'll help you."

(Archie) "Nose you don't. We had roast beef and you'll pile it a mile high."

(Gloria) "Daddy! Don't say things like that. You had three helpings yourself."

(Archie) "But I'm the head of the household, little goyl...He's a freeloader."

(Gloria) "Might I remind you that he's my husband and he lives here."

(Edith, *fretting*) "You jus stay here, Michael. Gloria and me will fix you your san-wich."

(Archie, *to Michael*) "So what's this reason we're honored with your company tonight?"

(Michael) "Archie, tonight the House Committee investigating the January 6 attack on the Capitol holds its first public hearing. We're going to learn what really happened."

(Archie) "I can tell you what really happened. Yous liberals wit some feds help roused up some peaceful protestors and it got a little out of hand, dats what happened."

(Michael, *holding a hand to his forehead*) "You don't really believe that do you Arch?"

(Archie) "Of course I believe it. Yous all was jus tryin' to embarrass our president."

(Michael) "Arch, they stormed the Capitol, people got killed and injured, your president incited them to riot, they wanted to hang Mike Pence and overturn the election!"

(Archie) "That's all part of the nonsense coming from yous liberal types."

(Edith, *entering the room with Gloria*) "Here's ya san-wich, Michael, an' some patayta salad that you like so much. You mus be star-vin' if ya haven't eaten anathin.'"

(Archie) "Him starving? Does he look like one of them consecration camp victims?"

(Gloria) "Daddy, that's enough. Now turn the channel so we can watch the hearings."

(Archie) "I'm already watchin' the 'real news' station. Let's leave it right here."

(Michael) "Archie, Fox News isn't covering the hearings. They're the only hold outs."

(Archie) "Well don't that jus say it all! It's only on them socialist stations is it?"

(Edith) "Archie, you kin watch your Fox News afta it's ova."

(Archie) "Geez, Edith. Why do ya always have ta side with the Meathead?"

(Edith) "Not always, Archie. Rememba, I root fer all your sports teams and Michael is too busy to watch all them games. He's got betta things ta do, doncha Michael."

(Michael) "Ma, between part-time jobs and school I just don't have the time, that's all."

(Gloria, *changing the channel*) "It's time...Look, tonight's hearing has already started."

(Archie) "No it hasn't. They must be cleanin' up the room from somethin' else. See, some colored guy, probably a security guard or janitor, is splainin' the delay."

(Michael, *exasperated*) "Archie, that happens to be Representative Bennie Thompson who's the chairman of the committee."

(Archie) "Now I've seen it all! You mean some colored guy is runnin' all this hoopla!"

(Gloria) "Daddy! Representative Thompson is a well-respected, articulate, honorable *Black* man who chairs the committee with Republican Liz Cheney serving as co-chair."

(Archie) "Ain't she one of them HIPPO Republicans?"

(Gloria) "Huh?"

(Michael) "I think he means RINO Republicans."

(Archie) "Whateva…HIPPO, RINO, she ain't really what she claims to be."

(Michael) "And what might that be, Arch?"

(Archie) "Geez, don't ya know, that she's a *Re-pub-li-can*. She's no more thinkin' straight nowadays than the Meathead here."

(Gloria) "She's an honorable woman willing to stand up to Donald Trump's lies!"

(Edith) "That's true, Archie. She is."

(Archie) "Edith, don't you have somethin' ta do in the kitchen where ya belong."

(Gloria) "Daddy! Ma has every right to speak and have her opinions heard."

(Archie) "My opinions is her opinions. That's the way it's supposed to be."

(Michael) "Arch, you're hopeless. But, we're missing the opening statements."

Scene Two

[*The setting is the same living room but it's an hour or so later and the hearing is in recess. Throughout the session, Archie has busied himself reading a newspaper.*]

(Michael) "Arch, have you been paying any attention at all?"

(Archie) "I don't need to pay no attention ta dat liberal nonsense."

(Gloria) "Well you should 'cause you might just learn something. I didn't realize that the committee was going to place *all* the blame for the attack at the feet of President Trump."

(Michael) "Not only that, they have irrefutable evidence that Trump tried to overturn the election in what they're calling a multilayered scheme...Archie, he tried to stage a coup!"

(Archie, *putting his newspaper down*) "A what?"

(Michael) "A coup...A revolution! He wanted to remain in power at any cost."

(Archie) "And deservedly so Mr. Know-It-All. I have it from a very reliable soice dat the election was stolen. President Trump was only demandin' his constapational rights."

(Michael) "Okay, Arch, I'll bite. Who's this 'reliable source' you're referring to?"

(Archie) "Henry Fishbauer."

(Edith) "Ain't he one of the men down on your loading dock?"

(Archie) "That's right, Edith. But, he ain't the main soice. He lives across the street from Howie Witherspoon who loined it straight from the man himself."

(Michael) "And who's 'the man himself' if I might ask?"

(Archie) "President Trump! Rememba when the president came by our neighborhood before the election and stopped in to chat with a few chosen families ta get their opinions on stuff...I still can't figya out why he didn't come here. I mean, it was all set up wit them social security fellows. I was all but guaranteed he'd come by but he neva did."

(Michael, *winking at Edith and Gloria*) "Yeah, Arch, that remains one big mystery."

(Archie) "But, he did stop by Howie Witherspoon's and later on Howie told Henry that Trump said that if he loses the election it would only be 'cause it was rigged."

(Michael) "That's your proof! Archie, that's what the committee is exposing. Trump was afraid he'd lose and began laying the groundwork for 'The Big Lie' months in advance."

(Archie) "Well there's more to it than that I'll have ya know. One of the boys at the dock saw a suspacious-lookin' unmarked truck pick up a load of boxes that he's convinced was stuffed with Biden ballots headed over ta Pennsylvania…How do yous splain that?"

(Michael) "If that's the truckload of New York ballots that conspiracy theorists put out, that story was checked out on both ends and it was proven to be completely bogus."

(Archie) "See, that's the problem here. Ya can't trus the people checkin' things out."

(Edith) "Let's discuss this late-a. Toin up da sound, Gloria. They're startin' ta talk again."

Scene Three

[*The same location but now the hearing has ended.*]

(Michael) "Did you at least hear the part where several of Trump's own cabinet members were convinced he'd lost his mind and was too dangerous to be left alone?"

(Archie) "I didn't hear that or nuttin' else. I'm tellin' yous all the election was stolen."

(Gloria) "And your only proof is that Trump told Mr. Witherspoon who told some guy on the loading dock who told you and this other guy who buys into conspiracy theories?"

(Archie) "Look here, little goyl. President Trump was a great president. Don't ya knows he put that MAYO deal on hold makin' them Krouts and the others pay their way…"

(Michael) "It's called NATO, Arch."

(Archie) "Whateva. And then he called out them Chinks for startin' that pamblemic by releasin' bats from a lab…they eat them bats ova dere don't ya know. And, he built a wall as promised to keep dem invaders out ta say nuttin' 'bout the towel heads."

(Michael) "Come on, Arch! It's NATO that's preventing Putin from invading more countries than Ukraine. Trump was so slow in responding to COVID that it got out of control. That wall that Mexico was supposed to pay for was all symbol costing taxpayers billions. Archie, the election wasn't a fraud. The only fraud is Donald Trump himself."

(Archie) "Don't you go talkin' like dat around here! You'll see. This here committee with Bernie the (*looking at Gloria*) *Black* guy and Liz Cheney Jr. the traitor will make a big splash and then sensible folks like Rudy Giuliani will be valipated and it'll all blow ova."

(Michael) "You think so, Arch? Then what happens in 2024 in the next big election?"

(Archie) "Lemme tell ya somethin.' Peoples gonna return to dere senses, Trump gets hisself reelected in an honest 'lection and America is great again. It's dat simple."

(Michael) "Archie, the man belongs in jail; not the White House!"

(Archie) "You know Meathead, you really need to ferget all that schoolin that's doin your head no good and go out an' get a real job…And look at the time! I'm goin' ta bed."

(Edith, *as Archie heads upstairs*) "Gloria an' Michael, ya really shouldn't get Archie all upset. He's got his mind all made up on these things and nuttin's gonna change him."

(Michael) "I know, Ma. But, that's the problem, isn't it? Trump's nothing but a con man spreading all these lies to protect his ego and good people like Arch believe him."

(Gloria) "And Ma, think about all the respectable Republicans who are no different than Daddy. They've got their heads in the sand as well. Trump tried to overthrow the election and stay in power. He caused a riot. He's a dangerous man…I'm really worried."

(Edith) "Maybe we should all go an' have some pie before we go to bed. Ya know, pie fixes everythin'."

THIRTY

Rush to Judgment

(Rush Limbaugh nervously awaits his final judgment)

[*Time is immaterial; the setting is inconsequential. This is the afterlife, at least the beginning of the afterlife. People who lived on Earth and had recently died are seen on a great groundless expanse, their human forms covered up to their knees by a cloud-like vapor. Some are in one of three lines leading to platforms and gates in the distance. Others, newcomers, are moving about in a confused state, trying to get a grip on what is happening, what the meaning is of what they're observing. In the foreground a man is slowly turning in circles, his arms raised, as if pleading for some sort of explanation. Suddenly, a figure approaches and greets the man cordially. They begin to talk.*]

(Man) "Thank goodness, someone to talk to. Can you tell me what's going on?"

(Figure) "That's indeed my job. I'm here to assist you."

(Man) "I'm dead aren't I? I mean, I don't recognize where I am. Where am I?"

(Figure) "Your time on Earth is indeed over, Mr....?"

(Man) "Limbaugh, Rush Limbaugh."

(Figure, *looking at a tablet he has produced, the electronic variety*) "Let me check."

(Man) "What are you doing?"

(Figure) "I'm looking you up to see if you've been pre-assigned."

(Man) "Pre-assigned to what?"

(Figure) "To an afterlife destination, of course. Surprised there's an afterlife?"

(Man, *confidently*) "No, not at all. See, I'm a Christian."

(Figure, *busying himself on the tablet*) "That's nice...Let me see now."

(Man) "Doesn't being a Christian mean something? Isn't Paradise automatically mine?"

(Figure, *now looking straight at the man*) "Let me explain. What you see around you isn't Paradise or Heaven; nor is it what you would call Hell. Compare this to a triage station. I'm here to process you for judgment. Behind us is where judgment is rendered."

(Man, *peering into the background*) "I see people in what seem to be three lines...I get it! One of them lines is for Christians, like me. I can join the Christian line, right?"

(Figure) "Not exactly. You see, how you labeled yourself while on Earth doesn't matter. What matters here is how you lived your life. Belonging to a religion helps, of course, if that religion inspires a person to live a good life; but nothing is automatic."

(Man) "So, what are the three lines?"

(Figure) "You're getting ahead of me but I'll explain. I like to refer to the line on our right at the 'B' line, sort of a double entendre for 'bee' as in fast, and 'B' short for Beatitudes. We find your Christian Beatitudes come closest to defining a 'good life.'"

(Man) "Beatitudes?...Yeah, of course. But, remind me a little, will you?"

(Figure) "Poor in spirit, meek, righteous, merciful, peacemaker..."

(Man, *nervously*) "As a fundamentalist Christian, I'm all of those, right?"

(Figure) "There you go again, Mr. (*looks at his tablet*) Limbaugh. Whatever brand you wear on your sleeve or forehead is, to use your term, 'fundamentally' meaningless. In the 'B' line you'll find Christians, Jews, Hindus…all the denominations, as well as atheists, agnostics, non-theists, humanists. Again, all that counts is how you lived your life."

(Man) "So, what are the other lines for?"

(Figure) "On the far left are those who pretty much lived polar-opposite lives. On Earth you would condemn them as murderous, torturers, rapists. Seemingly intrinsically evil."

(Man) "You mean guys like Pol Pot, Stalin, Hitler, Idi Amin, Pontius Pilot?"

(Figure) "Notoriously evil, yes. But, note the long line. It's not just the famously bad types. And, the delay at the gate is that they're pleading their cases, claiming that they always were that way, that they didn't have a chance. It was what they were born into, the way they were raised, what they were taught that led them to lead the lives they did."

(Man, *sounding a bit hopeful*) "Does that ever work? Can they repent?"

(Figure) "It's not my privilege to know, but I would assume so, yes, in some cases."

(Man) "The longest line is in the middle. Who's in that line?"

(Figure) "I call that the 'P' line, for 'phonies.' These can be the worst offenders, those who committed evil deeds in the name of religion or who liked to consider themselves holier-than-thou persons but were nothing but hypocrites. Over the eons I've seen in that line popes, ayatollahs, rabbis, faith healers, spiritualists…lots of evangelical preachers."

(Man) "Over the eons? By the way, who are you?"

(Figure) "My Earthy name was Hunon. I lived before most religions were formed."

(Man) "We're you among those considered meek, merciful, and righteous?"

(Figure) "Yes, not perfect, of course, but I was ultimately judged to have lived a good life without the help of any religion. I entered Paradise through one of the middle gates."

(Man, *looking at that platform with its twin gates*) Who's up there now?"

(Figure, *following the man's eyes*) "The one in the middle is the person being judged. On his right, that's the Angel Gabriel on duty. The 'Your Saved' side switches off. He relieved the Angel Moroni. On the 'Your Damned' side the Devil never delegates."

(Man) "What are they doing now?"

(Figure) "They're arguing over the man's merits for salvation. One will concede."

(Man, *shielding his eyes for a clearer view*) "The *Black* fellow on the right is the Angel Gabriel? Isn't he supposed to be white, sport a halo and have big wings?"

(Figure, *laughing*) "You're all hung up on artist renditions; sheer fancy made to make both simple and sophisticated minds form an image of what goodness looks like. You'll also note that the Devil isn't red, doesn't have wild eyes, horns or even a forked tail."

(Man, *nervously*) "What line am I to join?"

(Figure) "As a volunteer triage coordinator, that's what I'm here to determine."

(Man) "I think I belong in the expedited 'B' line, don't you?"

(Figure, *tapping on his tablet*) "We get to use all the most up-to-date devices and they don't need to be powered up. Sure beats the old heavy log books and endless scrolls."

(Man) "What do you see there? Are you looking at my history?"

(Figure) "Yes, sort of. Not all the details, of course. You can help me."

(Man) "How so?"

(Figure) "Mr. Limbaugh, did you ever rape anyone?"

(Man, *insulted*) "No! Never! Everything was always consensual."

(Figure) That's good, sort of. Did you ever murder anyone?"

(Man) "Now you're being crazy. Of course not!"

(Figure, *reading*) "It says here that you are accused of being a 'once-removed accessory' to multiple murders. Can you explain that to me?"

(Man, *agitated*) "I have no idea what you're talking about."

(Figure) "What did you do for a living, Mr. Limbaugh?"

(Man, *proudly*) "I was a famous talk-show host."

(Figure) "Nice! One of those late-night hosts who gets to interview celebrities?"

(Man, *pausing*) "No...I had a one-man show as a conservative political commentator."

(Figure, *reading and grimacing*) "That could explain a few things I'm seeing here. You were accustomed to making racist, sexist and homophobic remarks. Is that true?"

(Man, *greatly agitated*) "Look, you need to understand. I had a huge following. Millions of people tuned in to my show every day. They were mostly white men and women, and they didn't like what they saw going on in our great country. God loves America, right?"

(Figure, *dismissively*) "God loves people; not countries. What are you getting at?"

(Man, *sweating profusely*) "What I'm getting at is that it was my role to say what they wanted to hear. It was my job, damn it! These people needed to be fed and I fed them. They didn't like illegal aliens taking their jobs. They didn't cotton to welfare moms. They knew that God created marriage for a man and a woman, not for fags. Sure, I said some things that could be considered racist, sexist and homophobic, but how do you know I believed that stuff? They loved me for it! I was their hero! I was just doing my job!"

(Figure, *raising his eyes*) "I'm not your judge. Bring that up when you're up there."

(Man, *whimpering*) "I will, I will...But how can I make them believe me?"

(Figure) "Uh oh!"

(Man, *still whimpering*) "What do you mean, uh oh? What are you reading now?"

(Figure) "There's page after page under 'purveyor of falsehoods.' Did you lie?"

(Man) "Not intentionally. All I said was what my listeners wanted to believe."

(Figure, *scrolling down*) "This last entry is highlighted by bold lettering. It says that you spread the false rumor that a certain election was stolen. Can you explain that?"

(Man) "Of course. That was just recent. Democrats stole the presidential election."

(Figure) "And you know that as a fact?"

(Man, *stammering*) "The man whose election was stolen said it was stolen."

(Figure) "And you were satisfied by that? Did you try to get at the truth?"

(Man) "That wasn't my job. He said it was true and I trusted him."

(Figure) "Who's *he*?"

(Man) "Donald J. Trump."

(Figure) "Is he known to be an honest, truthful, 'B' line type of man?"

(Man, *squeamishly*) "Ah, let's see. I'll say he 'plays around the edges.'"

(Figure) "But you believed that the election was stolen because he said it was?"

(Man) "That's right. He said it was and millions of others said it was as well!"

(Figure) "And they had proof? Did this ever go to court?"

(Man, *dispirited*) "The courts couldn't find any fraud based on the evidence presented."

(Figure) "Seems like there was no evidence."

(Man, *shouting*) "The evidence is that the president said it was stolen. That's all!"

(Figure) "Was anyone harmed by these 'false' claims, if I presume to call them that?"

(Man) "Okay, there were some disturbances. The Oath Takers, Proud Boys, QAnon conspirators staged a few protests and once stormed the Capitol; people were killed."

(Figure) "I guess that would make you a 'once-removed accessory' to murder?"

(Man) "No! It wasn't *me*. It was *him*! It was *them*! I...I...I'm not to blame!"

(Figure) "Oh, I see you're being waved for. Join the middle line, Mr. Limbaugh."

(Man) "Up here, or wherever I am, I can suddenly hear. I was deaf for a long time, you know. But my damn back is still aching. You wouldn't have any pain pills would you?"

(Figure) "Mr. Limbaugh, if all goes well for you on the platform you won't need pain pills anymore. And if it doesn't go well, pills aren't allowed. Pain is the Devil's middle name."

THIRTY ONE

Leave It To Beaver 2023
(The Cleaver family tries to adjust to Republican manifestos)

<u>Scene One</u>

[*It's April, 2023. In November, the Republican Party had gained majority control of the U.S. House of Representatives in the midterm elections and state Republican-controlled legislatures are passing measures to protect gun rights. The setting is the kitchen of the Cleaver residence located in a middle class suburban white neighborhood in Texas. Ward and June have two children: 15-year old Wally and his 10-year old brother Theodore, also known as Beaver. June has just poured Ward, dressed for work in business attire and tie, a refresher cup of coffee. The door opens and Beaver enters.*]

(Ward) "Well, good morning, Beaver. Did you sleep well?"

(Beaver) "Yeah, I guess so. I was asleep most of the time so couldn't really tell."

(June) "Have a seat next to your father as your breakfast is almost ready."

(Ward) "Anything special happening today at school?"

(Beaver) "Not really. Same ol' stuff. We're slowly gettin' used ta all the new rules."

(June, *putting down Beaver's plate*) "It's *me* that's not getting used to all the new rules."

(Ward, *looking up from behind his newspaper*) "Everything new takes some time."

(June) "I suppose. But multiple cameras in the classrooms, topics that can't be discussed, and not only the teachers having firearms but the kids as well...that to me is too much."

(Ward) "Now, dear, you know that classroom shootings are almost a weekly occurrence, and ever since the Supreme Court ruled last June that people have the right to carry unconcealed firearms to protect themselves, this seems like the logical thing to do."

(June) "But Beaver's only ten years old. Does he really need a gun?"

(Ward) "That's really not for me to decide. Our Republican leadership has mandated it."

(Beaver) "But we can't play with them on the bus or during recess."

(June) "You don't *play* with guns, Beaver. They're...they're...too dangerous"

(Ward) "What your mother means is that they're lethal weapons that must be handled with care and caution by everyone, especially by fifth-graders."

(*At this moment Beaver's teenage brother Wally enters the room*)

(Ward) "Well good morning, sleepyhead. Have a rough night?"

(Wally) "Aw shucks, dad. A guy's gotta get his rest."

(June) "You barely made curfew last night. What kept you out so late?"

(Beaver) "I'll bet he was making out with Mary Ellen Rogers."

(Wally) "Who told you that? You don't even know what 'making out' means."

(Beaver) "It's sorta like hangin' out only with girls which doesn't make any sense."

(Ward) "One of these days you'll understand, Beaver. But Wally, answer your mother."

(Wally) "Me, Eddie, Lumpy and some of the guys went to the new firing range to get in a few hours of training. You know, we have to put in at least 10 hours to get certified as volunteer School Guards. They've installed some pretty neat new targets down there."

(June) "What kind of targets, Wally?"

(Wally) "Well, they useta just have ordinary bullseye targets that were stationary, but since they know that any gunman isn't going to stand still they've introduced life-size moving cardboard cutouts of some people they think we might enjoy shooting at."

(June) "Who would it be that someone would want to shoot at?"

(Wally) "Oh, they have Obama, Pelosi, Biden, Harris, Schumer and a few others."

(June) "Wally! That's awful. You mean at the practice range you pretend to shoot them?"

(Wally) "No, mom, we don't pretend. We're using real bullets."

(*At this moment Wally's classmate Eddie Haskell who has let himself in arrives*)

(Wally) "Hi Eddie, I was just telling mom and dad about the new targets at the range."

(June) "And I find the whole idea despicable!"

(Eddie) "Mrs. Cleaver, I find it rather despicable as well. Tasteless you might say. And, might I add that you look stunning as usual this morning. What a smart-looking outfit."

(Wally) "Knock if off, Eddie. You know you enjoyed shooting at those cutouts."

(Beaver) "Yeah, knock it off Eddie."

(Eddie, *to Beaver*) "Pipe down, squirt." (*Then to Mrs. Cleaver*) "I'll be sure to mention our concerns to the firing range manager, Mrs. Cleaver."

(Ward) "As much as I'd like to continue following this discussion, I must get going. Dear, while shopping yesterday did you remember to pick up my bulletproof vest?"

(June) "Do you really have to wear that thing?"

(Ward, *slipping on a suit jacket*) "It's not mandated. Congress considers it 'wise advice.'"

(June) "I expect soon we'll all be encouraged to drive around in armored vehicles!"

(Beaver) "That would be really cool. Maybe have gun turrets. Pow! Pow! Pow!"

Scene Two

[*It's the same morning and the setting is Beaver's fifth grade classroom at the Grand Avenue Grammar School. His teacher, Miss Landers, calls the class to order.*]

(Landers) "Okay boys and girls, settle down. Now, what is it we all do next?"

(Class, *in unison*) "We put our side arms in our desk holsters."

(Landers) "Very good, class…And what must we remember to do?"

(Class, *in unison*) "Do not snap shut the strap over the gun handle."

(Landers) "And remind me why we don't do that according to the manual."

(Class, *in unison*) "So it won't interfere with pulling our weapons out rapidly."

(Landers) "But what is it that we should always do?"

(Class, *in unison*) "Make sure the safety lock is engaged."

(Landers) "Perfect! And now I'm putting my AR-15 underneath my desk."

(Beaver, *raising his hand*) "Miss Landers, I left my Glock in my lunch box."

(Landers) "That's not an authorized toting device, Theodore. But, go get it now."

(Beaver) "I really can't, Miss Landers. See, I left my lunch box at home."

(Landers) "Theodore, you mean you got on the bus unarmed against regulations?"

(Beaver, *as the class titters*) "Yes Miss Landers."

(Landers) "I should report this infraction to Mr. Brittingham. But, since it's you're first offense you can remain in place for today's first lessons. Now, open your history books."

(Judy, *raising her hand*) "The rule book says that such an infraction should be punished."

(Landers) "I realize that, Judy. But we're all adjusting to the new rules. Now please sit."

(Judy) "And I saw Larry Mondello…"

(Landers) "Judy, let's just say that you've already earned your $10.00 Ted Cruz award for reporting rule infractions. You only get one a day so save that one for tomorrow."

(Judy, *sticking her tongue out at Beaver before sitting*) "Thank you Miss Landers."

(Landers) "Now class, please turn to page 102 in your history books. We're up to the Civil War. Who can tell me why Americans took up arms against each other?"

(Judy, *first with her hand up and recognized*) "It was all about states' rights."

(Landers) "Very good, Judy. Thank you. And what rights were in question?"

(Gilbert) "The southern states were slave states and the northern states were not."

(Landers, *pulling down a map showing all the states*) "Yes, these states here…"

(*Suddenly a piercing alarm is heard and red lights flash around the room's cameras*)

(Robotic Voice, *coming from classroom speakers*) "Our automated outlawed word recognition device has detected a rule infraction. Immediately stop all classroom activities until authorities can infiltrate the premises and conduct an investigation."

(Landers) "I will not! What is causing this interruption to my lessons?"

(Principal Brittingham, *on the speaker*) "Miss Landers, the device is programmed by the state Department of Education so it's out of our control. It detected the 'S' word."

(Landers) "The 'S' word?"

(Brittingham, *whispering*) "S-L-A-V-E."

(Landers) "My children can hear and spell and this is ridiculous! What *is* the infraction?"

(Brittingham, *reading from a guidebook*) "Slavery is associated with Critical Race Theory that since the Republican takeover of Congress and the state legislature in January is hereby prohibited from being taught in schools for the worthy goal of preventing white students from feeling guilty about what happened eons ago."

(Landers) "Eons ago! Racism exists now! You can't pretend it doesn't exist."

(Brittingham) "Miss Landers, stand down. I'm sorry, but the School Guard will be arriving soon to restore order to your classroom. You are dismissed for the day."

Scene Three

[*It's the same day but late in the afternoon. The setting is a lush conference room in a church complex. The Church Council is getting ready to hold its monthly meeting.*]

(June, *on her cell phone*) "Ward, will you be home soon?"

(Ward) "I guess in my rush this morning I forgot to tell you. The Church Council is meeting tonight so I'll be late but you can hold my dinner. Is everything okay?"

(June) "I guess so. Beaver got sent home at noon with a note from his principal. He forgot his lunch and I guess I'm the one who put that awful gun he has to carry in his lunch box so he wouldn't forget it...or hurt himself. He also said that Miss Landers got in trouble for allowing the 'S' word to be uttered in her classroom. Things are so crazy."

(Ward) "So Miss Landers was discussing sex with her fifth graders?"

(June) "No, some boy in the room mentioned 'slave' and that activated an alarm."

(Ward, *sighs*) "That 'Critical Race Theory' ban. Sorry, I'm being waved in. Gotta go now."

(Fred Rutherford) "Ward, how's your boy Wally doing in school?"

(Ward) "Fine, Fred, just fine. Looks like he'll letter in three sports."

(Fred) "That's nice. My Clarence doesn't have time for sports. Of course, he'd letter too if he was interested. I warn him never to lose focus on that Princeton scholarship."

(Ward) "Lumpy...er, Clarence is thinking about applying to *Princeton?*"

(Fred) "A formality, of course. If not Princeton he might choose Yale or Harvard."

(George Haskell, *another Board member*) "Mind if I cut in? I thought I heard you talking about our boys. My boy Eddie certainly enjoys hanging around with Wally and Lumpy."

(Fred) "That's Clarence if you don't mind. Wally and Eddie sort of look up to my boy. They make a good threesome. They went out hunting Democrats last night I hear!"

(George) "Eddie told me all about it. Up pops Obama in a tree top, then Bang! Bang! And down he comes. Biden...Bang! Bang! They all took turns blasting away at Harris."

(Fred) "Harris, Lord help us! Best insurance plan Biden could ever have. You'd have to take 'em both out at once. Bang! Bang! That's why we need multi-round magazines."

(George) "Well, things are now back in order after two years of chaos. Biden is still around, but his nuts are caught in a vice. With Republicans controlling the House no Marxist bills will ever pass and in two years we can welcome back Trump."

(Fred) "Let's not forget that we own the Supreme Court. And in June we can celebrate the one-year anniversary of overturning Roe v. Wade. Down with the baby killers!"

(George, *tugging at his tie*) "I wholeheartedly agree. I'm all against abortion; don't get me wrong about that. But, between us girls, I gotta confess that I got myself into a little jam back in my seed-sowing days. She ended up pregnant and said I was the papa. What was I to do? I'd been accepted at college and she was nothing but a joy ride so I arranged for her to go outta state and get rid of the evidence, so to speak. I really had no choice."

(Ward, *who'd just been listening*) "But you're all against abortion now?"

(George) "Oh yeah! I'm a God-fearing Christian and proud member of our Church Council. These cases we're hearing about nowadays aren't like mine. Mostly Black girls getting knocked up by their boyfriends who notch the bedpost and then run off. As I said, I really had no choice. I was getting ready to start my college career."

<u>Scene Four</u>

[*It's the same day but dinner is over and Beaver has been given permission to go outside and play. What he does is go to the firehouse to have a chat with his elderly pal Gus.*]

(Beaver) "Hey, Gus, I need to talk to you. See, there are just a lot of things I don't understand. I know us kids aren't supposed to know anything, and that grownups are supposed to know everything, but it seems to me that even more than us kids it's the grownups that can't get along. Is there ever a time when people can just get along?"

(Gus) "I'm long retired as a fireman, but since the missus passed I like coming down and spending time at the old firehouse. The people you see here are all different – different backgrounds, different religions, different politics, different personalities. But when that alarm sounds they all come together united as a team to go out and fight a fire and perhaps save a house or the lives of people they don't even know. It's a thing of beauty."

(Beaver) "Golly, Gus. Is there a chance a big alarm could go off and change things?"

(Gus, *puffing on his pipe*) "Sure, Beaver. It has happened and could happen again."

(Beaver) "Gee whiz, Gus. Can we make that happen again? When did it last happen?"

(Gus, *puffing*) "Could. Not sure if we'd want to though...It took World War II."

THIRTY TWO

Veepstakes
(Trump hosts a gathering to discuss 2024 running mate options)

<u>Scene One</u>

[*The setting is poolside at Trump's spacious and walled private pool/whirlpool complex at his Mar-a-Lago residence in Florida. The day is sunny with warm, almost hot temperatures – definitely pool weather. The former president is stretched out on a recliner at the edge of the glistening pool, the back raised at a 45 degree angle. From that position he can lift and wiggle his toes and just see the tops of them over the white mound of his hairless belly that wife Melania has come to refer to as "Mt. Baldy" owing to his daily luncheon diet of a one-pound Mar-a-Lago Burger with fries. He's wearing his tailor-made Stars & Stripes Speedo swimwear briefs with the secretly sewn-in padding in the front. The recliner is draped with a large beach towel featuring his image as a muscular superhero created for his digital trading cards. On each side of him, sitting on all-weather chairs, are his close friends and advisors Rudy Giuliani and Steve Bannon. Because he came unprepared for a poolside meeting, Giuliani has been outfitted with a pair of Sponge Bob boxer shorts borrowed from his host and a gaudy loose-fitting Hawaiian shirt. Bannon arrived wearing baggy camouflage shorts and a black tank top that doesn't quite stretch over his waistline. All three are sporting Polaroid sunglasses.*]

(Bannon) "Short notice, Mr. President, but as always I'm happy to oblige."

(Giuliani) "Is this meeting about a possible indictment on the hush money payments?"

(Trump) "No, that witch hunt isn't going anywhere. I've got another team on that one."

(Bannon) "That new AG seems determined to make a case."

(Trump) "Who is the grand jury going to believe, a liar like Cohen or the president?"

(Giuliani) "If you were still the president none of this would be happening."

(Trump) "I'm the legitimate president *now*, but in 2025 we'll get to start all over."

(Bannon) "Of course, Mr. President, but why did you summon us here?"

(Trump) "Pretty soon I'm going to have to pick a running mate and I'd like your advice."

(Giuliani) "Have you set any parameters?"

(Trump) "I don't know. Maybe I have…What are those things?"

(Giuliani) "What I mean is, are you looking for a certain kind of person?"

(Trump) "I am. I want a female running mate. Has to be a woman."

(Bannon, *taking notes*) "So, criteria #1 -- no balls!"

(Giuliani) "He's already had one of those. Pence had no balls." (*They laugh*)

(Trump) "If he had balls we'd now be meeting in the Oval Office."

(Bannon) "Okay, I'll throw out a name…Marjorie Taylor Greene."

(Trump) "Ah…she's…ya know…a big supporter…but…but…"

(Giuliani) "Out with it, Mr. President. She's what?"

(Trump) "I...I want someone whose pretty face will look perfectly matched with my handsome one on our campaign posters, if you get my drift."

(Bannon) "I think what he means is that she's a bit of a dog."

(Giuliani) "I get it. Woof! Woof!"

(Bannon) "Okay, she's out. Who else do we have?"

(Giuliani) "How about Lauren Boebert? She's not bad looking."

(Bannon) "Not at all! And, she's a big Trump supporter. Put her on the list."

(Giuliani) "Talking about big; how about Sarah Huckabee Sanders?"

(Trump) "Did you hear what I just said a moment ago? Be for real!"

(Bannon) "I think he means 'beef' for real!" (*They laugh*)

(Giuliani) "There's that gal governor up in South Dakota, Kristi something-or-other."

(Bannon) "Won reelection in a landslide; would look good on posters too."

(Trump, *raising his hand*) "Hold on a minute; it's time to order lunch."

(*A gate swings open and a man in full waiter regalia arrives with place mats, utensils wrapped in linen napkins, and a pad for taking orders. He meticulously lays out three place settings at an umbrella-shaded table and then turns his attention to the men.*)

(Waiter) "Mr. President, are you and your guests ready to order?"

(Trump) "I believe so, why don't you start with Mr. Giuliani."

(Giuliani) "I don't see any menus; are there any specials?"

(Waiter) "We don't typically use menus but I can recite today's specials."

(Giuliani) "Well, let's hear then, tell us what's on special today."

(Waiter) "We have the Schumerschnitzel with sauerkraut. That's sauerkraut spelled S-o-u-r K-r-a-u-t on the menus – the President's idea – and it comes with a small wiener."

(Bannon, *laughing*) "Anything else?"

(Waiter) "We have the Biden Budget Burrito – an oversized burrito stuffed with pork."

(Trump, *grinning*) "Keep going, there's more."

(Waiter) "Our latest addition is the DeSantis Burger. It's a vegetarian imitation of the House specialty Mar-a-Lago Burger only made much smaller for delicate constitutions."

(Giuliani) "DeSantis. All bone meal; no meat. That makes sense... Got any desserts?"

(Waiter) "Yes! We now offer the Santos Ice Cream Sundae. It's comprised of three heaping scoops of the day's featured flavor smothered in chocolate or caramel sauce topped by strawberries and walnuts with a large homemade chocolate chip cookie on the side."

(Bannon) "I had a big breakfast so I'll have the Santos Sundae with caramel sauce."

(Giuliani) "Can't eat pork and the names of those other choices don't sound appetizing so I'll have the big Mar-a-Lago Burger cooked medium-rare; but you can hold the fries."

(Trump) "My usual."

(Waiter) "Thank you. I'll bring pitchers of ice water, ice tea and lemonade. Meanwhile, make yourselves comfortable at the table. I'll adjust the umbrella to block the sun."

(*The waiter leaves and the three men move over as suggested to the circular table*)

(Bannon) "What's with these place mats, Mr. President?"

(Trump) "I knew you'd notice. I had some White House documents laminated and converted them into place mats. Something for guests to read while they wait!"

(Giuliani, *aghast*) "Mine is stamped 'TOP SECRET' in red ink!"

(Trump) "All declassified! Here (*he borrows Giuliani's mat*), I'll show you how it's done." (*Trump holds it up in front of his face*) "You are now officially declassified."

(Bannon) "Are you sure that's on the up-and-up?"

(Trump, *smirking*) "Of course it is. I'm the legitimate president, aren't I?"

Scene Two

[*Thirty minutes have passed. The men have delayed further discussion of the potential running mates, swapping off-color jokes and engaging in "locker room" banter.*]

(Trump) "And then this gal tells me, 'Mr. President, you can grab my'... Hold on."

(*The waiter has arrived balancing a large tray on one arm and proceeds to set down plates in front of the three men – a super-stacked Mar-a-Lago Burger with a double order of fries for the president; the same minus the fries for Giuliani; and a small dollop of vanilla ice cream topped with a single cherry in front of Steve Bannon.*)

(Waiter) "Bon appétit, gentlemen. Anything else before I take my leave?"

(Bannon, *in disbelief*) "Yeah, didn't you say the Santos Sundae was three scoops of ice cream smothered in chocolate or caramel sauce with a layer of strawberries and nuts?"

(Waiter) "I did say that…But I was lying, ha, ha!"

(Trump, *laughing so hard he shakes loose the padding in his Speedo and has to reach under the table and readjust it*) "I couldn't wait for someone to fall for that one!"

(Bannon, *annoyed*) "Well, I don't find it so funny!"

(Giuliani) "Take it easy, Steve. (*Removing the lid off his bun*) Here, have my bacon."

(Trump, *passing the huge bowl of fries*) "And help yourself to some of my fries."

(Bannon, *still somewhat agitated*) "That's okay. I had a big breakfast. Let's talk."

(Giuliani) "Have we mentioned Nikki Haley?"

(Bannon) "For chrissakes, Rudy, she's running against us!"

(Trump) "Not so fast, Steve. She's flipped more than a steak ordered well-done. She's a nothing. She was nothing until I gave her that UN dead-end job and she's been nothing since then. She needed to do something to gain attention, so she announced that she's running. Trust me; she'd leap into my lap if I offered her a place on the ticket."

(Bannon) "Then do you want her on your short list?"

(Trump) "Let's wait to see her reaction when she sees all the gals being interviewed."

(Giuliani) "I know you have notion to consider Kari Lake. Still feel that way?"

(Trump, *adjusting his padding that just flinched*) "I think she'd be a good...f...fit."

(Bannon) "She lost the Arizona gubernatorial race to some chickenshit Democrat, correct?"

(Trump) "No, she won big time. Like me in that state the election was rigged."

(Giuliani) "That's true – a Mexican drug cartel ran the Hobbs campaign."

(Trump) "Happened to all of my candidates. But, Kari hasn't given up. She's a fighter."

(Giuliani) "I'll vouch that that bitch has fire in her belly and can throw a verbal punch!"

(Bannon) "True, Rudy, but she's a news reader with no experience in government."

(Giuliani) "Hey, what experience did the greatest president of all time have?"

(Bannon) "But he (*nodding to Trump*) had business experience and other great assets."

(Trump) "Lemme tell you, Kari Lake has a great ass...not sure about the 'ets' though!"

(Giuliani, *amidst laughter*) "And, she's really high on you, Steve."

(Bannon) "Wadaya mean she's high on me?"

(Trump) "You haven't been paying attention, Steve. Last week at CPAC she called you a 'modern-day George Washington.' That's the *second* best compliment a man can get."

(Bannon, *so puffed up his tank top slips higher on his belly*) "You don't say?"

(Giuliani) "That's settled. Lake's in. But I still say we should interview MTG."

(Bannon) "If for no other reason than she'd be insulted by the oversight."

(Trump) "Fine by me. But, know from the start that she's not my type."

(Giuliani) "Perfect! That'll make it a true *dog* and pony show!" (*Laughter*)

THIRTY THREE

Donald Trump and the House Fly
(Following an FBI search of Mar-a-Lago, a fly comforts Trump)

<u>Scene One</u>

[*The setting is Trump's library in his home at the Mar-a-Lago resort. There are no books on the shelves, just photographs in stand-up frames of Trump posing with various celebrities, movie stars, and national and global leaders. The man himself is snoozing in a soft leather chair before going to bed, wearing his typical nighttime garb – an oversized Superman T-shirt and Sponge Bob boxer shorts. The safe in the room is open and porn photos, ladies panties, fifth grade histories with big print and lots of pictures labeled "DEBATE PREPARATION" once safely stored in the safe are strewn about.*]

(Fly) "Hey there Mr. Trump! Why are you looking so glum?"

(Trump, *startled and stirring*) "Who's there? I didn't hear the door open."

(Fly) "I don't need a door. You see, I'm a house fly."

(Trump, *mumbling*) "A talking house fly? I must be out of my mind."

(Fly) "No you're not. See I'm right here on the lip of your lampshade."

(Trump) "I must have dozed off with the light on."

(Fly) "You weren't reading."

(Trump) "I know. I don't read. I like to think with the light on."

(Fly) "You look pretty down if I can say so. We're you thinking sad thoughts?"

(Trump, *perking up*) "Wait a minute! Am I talking to a fly?"

(Fly) "Yes, you are. You always say you'd like to be me. Here I am!"

(Trump, *now wide awake*) "What do you mean I want to be you?"

(Fly) "You always say it. Here's one for you, remember saying 'I wish I was a fly on the wall in the changing room of the Miss Teen USA contest.' Does that sound familiar?"

(Trump, *chuckling*) "Yeah, then I bought the show and would walk in all the time when the girls were dressing. I thought they'd enjoy meeting the man who owned the show."

(Fly) "Did they like it? That was well before my time."

(Trump, *smiling his rubbery-faced smile*) "I don't know but *I* sure did!"

(Fly) "So, getting back to business, why so glum?"

(Trump) "Look at this room. Stuff strewn about, my safe wide open, pictures turned."

(Fly) "We're you robbed?"

(Trump) "Worse! I was raided. Raided by the FBI no less. It's a terrible injustice."

(Fly) "What were they looking for?"

(Trump) "I can talk since you're just a fly and nobody but me is going to listen to you. Frankly, I don't know why *I'm* listening to you. I must be dreaming. But, that aside, I took a few documents when I left the White House that they say I shouldn't have taken."

(Fly) "What kind of documents?"

(Trump) "I don't know. I was in a hurry and filled a few boxes with papers and personal notes. They say all that stuff belongs in the national archives. I say that's pure bullshit."

(Fly) "Looks like they left quite a few other things behind."

(Trump) "How'd you like someone rummaging through your hidden stash? (*Points to the floor*) That pair of pink panties came from that changing room. Pretty girl. She was covering up her top and I handed her the bottoms but she shook her head and ran off. So, I kept them as a souvenir. (*Gesturing*) I had quite the collection of souvenir panties."

(Fly) "You were quite the ladies man!"

(Trump) "It's easy when you're a celebrity and have lots of money to throw around."

(Fly) "Enough reminiscing! Since you always wanted to be me I'm here to cheer you up."

(Trump) "What are you going to do? Buzz around Garland's head 'till he freaks out?"

(Fly) "No, but I can listen in on what people are saying about you and report back."

(Trump, *glumly*) "I already know what they're saying. They say I'm a liar. They say I'm a cheat. They say I lost the election…I won in 2020, you know. I won by tens of millions of votes…If only I was a fly on the wall in those ballot counting centers I could prove it!"

(Fly) "See! There you go again; wishing you were me. It's time to cheer you up. Give me the names of some people who really like you and I'll go hang around them and let you know all the great things they have to say. I can get around easily. I know how to board and hide on airplanes so I can travel long distances. Gimme some names and sleep well."

Scene Two

[*The setting is the War Room in the Kremlin. President Vladimir Putin is meeting with his top two military commanders: General Aleksandr Dvornikov and General Vitaly Gerasimov. As the fly arrives they are discussing setbacks on the Ukrainian front.*]

(Putin) "How can this be happening? Why isn't this special military operation over?"

(AD) "We thought that President Zelenskyy, a former comedian, would run when the first shot was fired and that his countrymen would put up no defense. They are now fighting admirably, well equipped with weapons from NATO and the United States."

(Putin) "Damn! If only Trump had won."

(Fly, *to himself*) "Perfect timing!"

(VG) "What exactly do you mean, Mr. President?"

(Putin) "Trump was a pawn! I could hand him a loaded pistol to put to his head assuring him that it was unloaded and he would pull the trigger, he was that trusting of me."

(VG) "And would you have wanted him to pull the trigger?"

(Putin) "Hell no! He was one of us. If not exactly one of us he was someone I could mold in the fingers of my hand like soft clay. He'd believe anything that I told him. I'd have him sending arms to *us* as opposed to Ukraine. It's a fact: a fool is easily fooled!"

Scene Three

[*The setting is Republican Senator Lindsey Graham's office in Washington, D.C. When the fly slips into the room the senator is just about to begin a morning briefing with Senior Advisor Bob Heckman and Communications Director Brittany Bramell.*]

(Graham) "Good morning, Bob. Good Morning, Brittany…I only wish it was good!"

(Heckman) "I assume we need to respond to the FBI searching Trump's Florida home."

(Graham) "Yes, that's why I asked Brittany to join us. We must post a statement."

(Bramell) "I assume you want to blast the FBI for raiding a former president's home."

(Graham) "Of course that will be the public position…But, what an idiot!"

(Heckman) "Beg pardon?"

(Graham) "Look, Bob, I know the rules for home searches. The FBI can't just barge in any ol' time and have a look around hoping to find something. It doesn't work that way. They had to go to a federal judge and get a warrant, arguing convincingly that they had probable cause. The fact that the warrant was issued means that they were certain Trump had run off with highly sensitive documents and they knew exactly what to look for."

(Brittany) "So you're saying that the FBI did nothing wrong and that Trump did."

(Graham, *frustrated*) "It did set a precedent since the target was a former president."

(Heckman) "But no man is above the law, right Senator?"

(Graham) "If Trump wasn't so boneheadedly ignorant this would have never happened."

(Fly, *to himself*) "Ouch!"

(Brittany) "So, what are we going to post?"

(Graham) "We're going to blast the FBI, of course, just as you said."

Scene Three

[*The setting is former Trump advisor and confidant Steve Bannon's rowhouse on Capitol Hill in Washington, D.C. – a very short flight for a fly from Senator Graham's office. Bannon is found meeting with defense attorney Evan Corcoran to further discuss a court ruling holding Bannon in contempt of Congress for ignoring a subpoena to appear before the House Select Committee investigating the January 6 assault on the nation's Capitol.*]

(Corcoran) "Looks like the FBI's spotlight has swerved from you Steve back to Trump."

(Bannon) "I've issued a statement saying that the FBI is the Gestapo and funding for the agency should be cut off until we get to the bottom of who was behind the break in."

(Corcoran) "I saw that. Good job. Trump needs to know that you have his back."

(Bannon) "Protecting his fat ass is about all I do nowadays. Just you wait and see. He'll get away scot free and I'll end up in jail. You know, the guy only cares about himself."

(Corcoran) "But, you still defend him in public and refuse to testify."

(Bannon) "He might be a stupid jackass, but he's my kind of stupid jackass. I'm loyal."

(Fly, *to himself*) "I've heard enough! I'm getting out of here before they see me."

Scene Four

[*The fly is now back at Mar-a-Lago and finds Trump's son Don Jr. and son-in-law Jared Kushner sitting by a glimmering pool in swimsuits sipping on frosty pina coladas.*]

(Don Jr.) "I'm so mad I'd like to blow up fucking FBI headquarters."

(Kushner) "Chill my friend. Take a long sip. Your dad will wiggle out of this."

(Don Jr.) "He acts defiant but you gotta know it's gnawing at him."

(Kushner) "Look, if he accidently took some documents home he should say so."

(Don Jr.) "You think it was an accident? I guess he could pull a Britney Griner and claim that he was in a big hurry and didn't pay attention to what he was putting in his bags."

(Kushner) "Your dad knew what he was doing. He didn't want evidence left behind."

(Don Jr., *perplexed*) "So you think he stole some stuff?"

(Kushner) "Stole is a tough term. He was constantly tearing up and flushing away papers at night. You knew that. It's the way he does business. Your dad's a pro at covering up."

(Don Jr.) "They stole the election from him so I guess fair is fair, huh?"

(Kushner, *exasperated*) "Look, Don, your father *lost* the election. It wasn't stolen. Bill Barr liked your dad. He wanted your dad to win, but there was no evidence that the election was stolen and he had to tell your dad that. Your father simply refused to listen."

(Don Jr.) "You sound like a traitor!"

(Kushner) "Calm down. I didn't appear before the House Committee to get my ass in trouble for lying under oath. Between you and me and that fly on your head your dad made a lot of mistakes. He didn't know what he was doing but he loved being president. He loved the attention. He loved fan adulation. He loved getting gifts and hobnobbing with dignitaries, especially Kim and Putin. He just didn't like the job that came with it."

(Don Jr., *flailing at the fly*) "Gosh, Jared, you're makin' it sound like he was unfit."

(Kushner) "Your dad was fit for a lot of things. Being president just wasn't one of them."

(Fly, *avoiding the hand swipe*) "This isn't going quite like expected!"

<u>Scene Five</u>

[*The scene is once again the library at Trump's Mar-a-Lago home. The room has been swept clean of items left behind by the FBI. Trump, dressed for bed, is slumped in his soft leather chair – his starched orange-dyed hair a bit askew – when the fly awakens him.*]

(Fly) "Hey there Mr. Trump. It's me. The fly on the wall. As you can see I'm back!"

(Trump) "How come you don't address me as 'President Trump' like all my friends do?"

(Fly) "I'll fix that! (*Looking around*) Looks like the big mess has been all cleaned up!"

(Trump) "I cleaned it up right after you left. Couldn't have the first lady pop in and find all those panties and porn star pix lying around now could we? Talk about evidence!"

(Fly) "You, Mr. President, are the supreme master of crimes and cover up!"

(Trump) "I trust that's meant as a compliment?"

(Fly) "Talking about compliments, the people whose names you gave me all love you."

(Trump, *perking up*) "Putin still loves me?"

(Fly) "More than anyone! He *really* wishes you were still president."

(Trump) "I am still the president. There's an imposter in the White House!"

(Fly) "Senator Graham is going to release a statement damning the FBI for the raid."

(Trump) "Ah, Miss Lindsey. What an ass-kissing sissy, but good to know he loves me."

(Fly) "Steve Bannon says he'll gladly go to jail rather than testify before Congress."

(Trump) "That isn't Congress. That Leftist Select Committee is a partisan sham."

(Fly) "And your son-in-law Jared Kushner, he said you loved being president."

(Trump) "Good job. Now come down from the lampshade and sit on my armrest."

(Fly) "Sure thing Mr. President. My wings could use a rest after all that flying."

(Trump, *quickly swatting the fly with a scrolled centerfold*) "Sorry to have to do that."

(Fly, *dying*) "But why?"

(Trump) "Two reasons. You now know too much and you know how I hate liars."

THIRTY FOUR

Scary, Scary Night
(Following his arraignment in New York, Trump must subdue his conscience)

[*The setting is Donald J. Trump's bedroom suite at his Mar-a-Lago residence. It's 2:00 a.m. on April 5th, 2023. The former president lies in his luxurious bed trying to sleep after one of the most tumultuous days of his life – his arraignment in New York on charges brought forward by the Manhattan District Attorney relating to hush money checks he signed to prevent a porn star from going public with their affair on the eve of the 2016 presidential election; the long flight home in his giant jet; and his speech a few hours prior to a pre-selected gathering of his most ardent MAGA worshipers and loyalists.*]

(Voice) "Trouble sleeping Donald?"

(Trump, *jerking upright, startled and frightened*) "Who's there? Where are you?"

(Voice) "It's me, Donald, your conscience."

(Trump, *angrily*) "Not *you* again! I thought I left you at the hospital."

(Voice) "So, you remember my visit when you were stricken with COVID-19?"

(Trump) "How could I forget; they sent me to the psycho ward."

(Voice) "You were screaming and acting erratically."

(Trump) "All because of you I might add."

(Voice) "Just doing my job."

(Trump) "So your job is to torment me?"

(Voice) "You talk like I'm someone else; I'm part of you as you know."

(Trump) "A part that I'd just as soon put a bullet in."

(Voice) "You'd be shooting yourself. A lot of people might like that."

(Trump, *greatly irritated*) "What's it you want this time?"

(Voice) "Oh, just a little chat after quite the busy day."

(Trump) "Busy, I should say so! Go away. I need my sleep."

(Voice) "I'm keeping you awake, am I?"

(Trump, *burying his head under the covers*) "Damn right you are. Now get lost!"

(Voice) "Are we playing hide-and-seek? How childish (*singing*)...I can *seeee* you!"

(Trump, *peeping out*) "Okay, say what you have to say and then go away."

(Voice) "Let's start with the indictment."

(Trump) "Worst thing in the history of the country. A sad day for Americans."

(Voice) "For Americans...or for *you*?"

(Trump) "When they go after me they go after everyone who loves America."

(Voice, *chuckling*) "Ah, yes. Trump, the sacrificial lamb – pure, innocent and crucified."

(Trump) "Go ahead, make fun. I didn't commit any crimes."

(Voice, *laughing louder*) "So you didn't cook the books to hide the payouts?"

(Trump, *indignant*) "It's a crime to clear the way for my election? They needed me."

(Voice) "Who needed you?"

(Trump, *defiantly*) "The country, that's who! Can you imagine if Hillary got elected?"

(Voice) "So, the end justified the means?"

(Trump) "Always does! My dad said it's just following Michael Velli's sage advice."

(Voice) "You mean Machiavelli?"

(Trump) "Whatever! Some Italian guy who wrote the book on getting things done."

(Voice) "Have you read *The Prince*?"

(Trump) "You know I don't read, but I might be tempted if he wrote *The King*."

(Voice, *exasperated*) "Besides doctoring the books, is lying justified?"

(Trump, *confidently*) "Politicians don't lie; they manage the facts for a noble purpose."

(Voice) "So you were 'managing the facts' in denying your tryst with Stormy Daniels?"

(Trump) "That's right. And, I might add, I was doing her a small favor."

(Voice) "No denying that! She said everything about you was 'small.'"

(Trump) "Enough of this! What else is on your mind if you have one?"

(Voice) "Do I need to remind you that my mind is your mind?"

(Trump) "That makes you a genius. A genius knows when to fly away."

(Voice) "On that subject, how much did that flight cost you?"

(Trump) "More than I'd like to admit. More flights like that and I'll soon be broke."

(Voice) "A smaller private jet would suffice, don't you think?"

(Trump) "I'm used to Air Force One and have to keep up presidential appearances."

(Voice) "Talking about appearances, what have you to say about last night?"

(Trump) "I pretty much said it all. Yesterday was the worst day in American history. Democrats hate this country and are driving it to destruction. They hate me because they know that only I can save America, taking all the glory. Russia, China, North Korea and Iran are forging an alliance while we are only getting weaker. This war in Ukraine would never have happened if I was the president. The economy is in shambles. Patriots are being prosecuted. Gun rights are under siege. Whole industries are going under to spare the world from phony climate change. A Soros-backed animal is falsely charging me with crimes I didn't commit while the Biden family atrocities remain shielded from scrutiny. It can only end with me being restored to the office that was stolen from me by fraud."

(Voice) "Whew, that was quite the oration...All of it a crock, of course."

(Trump, *defiantly*) "It's the truth, every bit of it!"

(Voice) "Donald, do you believe in the afterlife?"

(Trump, *pausing before speaking*) "You mean that heaven and hell stuff?"

(Voice) "Yeah, in a way I'm not at liberty to explain."

(Trump, *nervously*) "But there is a judgment day?"

(Voice) "My understanding is that all people will be held accountable for their actions."

(Trump) "So, I'll have to stand in front of St. Peter at the Purple Gates?"

(Voice, *laughing*) "I guess you mean 'Pearly Gates.' But not quite like that."

(Trump, *focused*) "So, there's no a face-to-face recombiliation?"

(Voice) "No, that's just time-worn Christian imagery. St. Peter isn't involved."

(Trump) "That's too bad. I know that I can explain myself. I'm the great negotiator."

(Voice) "What you need to understand is that I, your conscience, will be talking for you."

(Trump) "But whose side are you on?"

(Voice) "The side of eternal truth."

(Trump, *sweating*) "If not St. Peter, then who's the judge?"

(Voice) "That would be A-O-C."

(Trump, *alarmed*) "My god, you don't mean that!"

(Voice) "Why, yes I do, what's wrong?"

(*Trump throws off his bed covers, heads for the door, unbolts it, and runs down the corridor in his Sponge Bob boxer shorts screaming "It can't be! Please...It just can't be!" Secret service agents intercept him and administer a shot to settle him down.*)

(Secret Service Agent #1) "What the hell came over him?"

(Secret Service Agent #2) "I have no idea. He acted as if he'd seen a scary ghost in the night."

(Voice, *who'd followed, to himself*) "I'm at a loss as well. I can only figure that he had a mystical vision of A-O-C – the All Omnipotent Conscience."

THIRTY FIVE

The Trump Zone – The Eternal Genius
(In the afterlife, Trump is matched with his peer group)

(Rod Serling's voice over theme music for *The Twilight Zone*) "You are traveling through time and space into a new dimension – a place where the boundaries of truth and reality are blurred and distorted to conform to one man's ego-driven desired outcomes. Brace yourself, our destination is just ahead, you are about to enter *The Trump Zone*."

Scene One

[*The setting is the afterlife. On Earth the date is March 15, 2023. Broadcasts worldwide are being interrupted with the news that former President Donald J. Trump has died. In this opening scene, Trump is being welcomed into the afterlife by Dr. Albert Einstein.*]

(Einstein) "Welcome to the afterlife Mr. (*pauses to check his clipboard*) Donald Trump."

(Trump, *confused*) "Who are you and where am I?"

(Einstein) "You've entered the afterlife, Mr. Trump. Your time on Earth has ended."

(Trump, *looking down at himself in disbelief*) "You mean I'm dead?"

(Einstein) "In Earthly terms, yes. But, as you can see, there *is* an afterlife."

(Trump) "Dead, huh? Are they mourning me? I had planned to run again you know."

(Einstein) "Here we don't look back; we only look forward. You can forget the past."

(Trump) "So, where am I? Am I in heaven? Are you St. Peter?"

(Einstein) "This isn't what you expected, is it? There really isn't a heaven or even a hell, simply an afterlife. No angels playing harps floating on clouds, no devils with pitchforks in flames. Just an afterlife based on how you described yourself while living on Earth."

(Trump, *looking around*) "So, I'm in an afterlife with presidents and world leaders?"

(Einstein) "No, not like that at all. In the afterlife there are no titles or social classes."

(Trump) "What then? I'm here with other great real estate moguls?"

(Einstein, *laughing*) "No, professions don't matter either. It's how you see yourself."

(Trump, *confused*) "How did I see myself?"

(Einstein) "As a genius, of course! (*Checks his clipboard*) "You said that many times."

(Trump, *smiling*) "I guess I did…And when I did I was telling the truth!"

(Einstein, *again checking his notes*) "Truth wasn't your strong suit, Mr. Trump. But it says here that you've been awarded certain dispensations for your indiscretions."

(Trump) "I've received lots and lots of awards but I haven't heard of that one."

(Einstein) "For a genius you do have a remarkable sense of humor. What you are asking of course is how you merited dispensations for a lifetime full of…transgressions."

(Trump) "I guess you mean transactions? I did them. What are transgressions?"

(Einstein) "Ah, you continue to tease me! But, no need to *disguise* your genius here."

(Trump) "No, of course not…whatever it is *dos guys* meant about my genius."

(Einstein) "You see, Mr. Trump, the panel of judges decided to overlook a lifetime of moral and ethical misbehavior in recognition of your upbringing. You were born into a corrupt family, presided over by a corrupt father, so your own corruptness in your business dealings and while serving in public office, though not excusable, was all but predestined. The panel favored forgiveness and focused on your genius claims."

(Trump) "Are you a genius? You look familiar with that wild hair and bushy mustache."

(Einstein) "They say I am. I was a physicist who developed some interesting theories."

(Trump) "Yeah! You came up with a formula, E Equals Plurious Umoon or something."

(Einstein) "You are such a comic! We'll certainly enjoy your everlasting company!"

Scene Two

[*Dr. Einstein has walked Trump down a long corridor and has swung open a door leading into a large, lavishly decorated ballroom featuring a dozen well-spaced round tables sized to convenience cross-table conversation among six seated participants.*]

(Einstein) "Mr. Trump, you are a lucky man. Your timing is impeccable."

(Trump, *smirking*) "Thank you. My pecker was renowned for its timing."

(Einstein) "Your wisecracking will add an element of humor to the discussions."

(Trump) "Discussions?"

(Einstein, *looking at his clipboard*) "You've been assigned to Table 11. Perfect!"

(Trump) "Is it time for lunch?"

(Einstein, *chuckling*) "You just had your lunch, remember? You were halfway through that second Mar-a-Lago monster cheeseburger when you suffered a fatal heart attack."

(Trump) "So, what's it we do at this table if we don't eat?"

(Einstein) "You talk! You listen! You converse! You share ideas! You debate!"

(Trump, *unimpressed*) "What are we goin' ta talk about?"

(Einstein, *reading from his clipboard*) *"The Rise of Humanism in Western Thought."*

(Trump) "The rise of what from where?"

(Einstein) "There you go again. Stop pretending. Here you can let your genius shine."

(Trump, *as they approach Table 11*) "Who are those guys?"

(Einstein) "Your discussion circle!" (*Five men rise as they approach.*) "I'll introduce you."

(Trump) "They're dressed kind of weird, aren't they? What's with the leafy headgear?"

(Einstein) "In the afterlife, you dress as you did while living on Earth. You're referring to Petrarch, your team discussion leader. He was crowned poet laureate in Rome in 1341."

(Trump) "Who are the others?"

(Einstein, *as they arrive at the table*) "Gentlemen, to spare you testing your humility, allow me to introduce each of you to your new discussion participant, Mr. Donald J. Trump, a 'self-proclaimed genius.' Donald, please meet Francesco Petrarca, better known to you I'm sure as Petrarch. To his immediate right is Coluccio Salutati, a friend and disciple of Petrarch. To his right I'm sure you recognize Sir Thomas More (*More bows*); then Martin Luther of course, and last but certainly not least, Desiderius Erasmus."

(Trump, *taking a seat as Einstein pulls out his chair*) "Real good to meet you guys."

(Petrarch) "A genuine honor! Only the brightest dare speak of their own genius."

(Salutati) "Indeed, it's a term usually affixed by others as an honor. Welcome!"

(More) "We look forward to your 21st century views, especially on *civic humanism*."

(Luther) "I presume a perfect substitution for Mr. Machiavelli. Genius for genius!"

(Erasmus) "We'll be astutely instructed by this modern personification of humanism."

(Petrarch) "Where did you attend university, Mr. Trump?"

(Trump, *boastfully*) "Attend university? I founded a university – Trump University!"

(Luther) "How impressive! I'm not quite recalling...In Cologne was it?"

(Trump) "Oh, you like my cologne? It's from my daughter Ivanka's inspired collection of beauty products…She's another genius; 'chip off the ol' block' you might say."

(Einstein) "Wonderful! I'll now take my leave and let you begin your discussions."

(Trump, *grabbing Einstein's arm and whispering*) "How long does this go on?"

(Einstein, *whispering to Trump*) "Time isn't measured in the afterlife."

(Trump) "Okay, okay, but how long do we sit here and talk about husbandism?"

(Einstein, *pulling out a small calculator*) "You're engaged for eternity, of course, but you do rotate to other discussion groups. The chart indicates that your next opportunity seats you with Hobbes, Locke, Descartes, Pascal and Rousseau on the topic of *Reasoned Dissent*. In Earth time that would be (*checking his calculator*) 84 years from now."

Scene Three

[*Flags back on Earth haven't yet been ordered flown at half mast when Trump is seen bursting through the doors of the ballroom and wobbling (his version of breakneck speed) down the corridor where he slides on his knees landing at Einstein's feet.*]

(Trump) "Thank goodness you're still here. Look, Einstein, I need your help."

(Einstein, *alarmed*) "What's the matter, Mr. Trump? You're all worked up and red faced. You know, you can't die from a heart attack. If you have one, you're instantly cured."

(Trump, *breathless*) "Look, I'm not the genius I said I was. Not like those guys anyway. You were wrong. I've never heard of them. When the guy with the leafy wreath started talkin' – the poet laminate guy – I didn't understand he word he said. All the others were listening and nodding their heads, getting ready to speak. I almost peed in my pants!"

(Einstein) "First, pee dries up instantly in the afterlife. Great place; no dry cleaning required. Go ahead and let it loose. As for you feeling uncomfortable, there's not much that I can do at this point. The panel only meets once and you were deemed a genius."

(Trump) "I know, I know. But, to me, Yogi Berra was a genius with all those wise sayings of his. Guys like Mort Walker who comes up with a four panel strip for Beetle Bailey every day and the writers behind the Sponge Bob movies. They're my geniuses."

(Einstein) "I see. You're here for good, but perhaps I can execute a lateral transfer."

(Trump, *clutching Einstein by the knees*) "Yes! A transfer! Anywhere! With women!"

(Einstein, *examining his clipboard*) "A transfer perhaps; but no women. Interesting point, though. Throughout history there have been just as many female geniuses as male geniuses, perhaps more, only the men suppressed the women almost completely until current times and women are still regarded in many ways and cultures as inferior intellectually. Doesn't make sense, but that's the way it has been and still is. That inequity has been corrected here, fortunately. The genius section is full of women."

(Trump, *crawling up Einstein's leg while pleading*) "Please, please, send me there."

(Einstein, *reading*) "We do have integrated areas. All the men at your table have enjoyed intellectual exchanges with female geniuses, most sadly unknown to history. But, the panel made a specific notation that although they were willing to overlook your corrupt business practices and scandalous political behavior – something about trying to overthrow a democracy – they couldn't overlook your blatant and demeaning sexism."

(Trump, *sighs*) "Well, okay, but there has to be a place where I'm not so over my head."

(Einstein, *flipping some pages*) "Nothing perfect, but I think I have an idea."

<u>Scene Four</u>

[*Einstein is seen leading Trump into a big room filled with pre-school playthings – toy cars and trucks, building blocks, coloring books, beach balls, a sand box, etc. The room is occupied by infants, toddlers and tots amusing themselves in highly ingenious fashion.*]

(Trump) "Why are you taking me here? Am I returning to my childhood to start over?"

(Einstein) "As I said, there's no starting over. You're in the afterlife and your fate has been determined, not so much by the judgment panel – half of whom are women by the way – but by you. It was *you* who made such a big splash about being a genius."

(Trump, *watching a three-year old build a Lego skyscraper*) "So, who are these kids?"

(Einstein) "All geniuses who died very young. (*Pointing*) We had to bring in a miniature Steinway so that three-year old could play Beethoven. You're good at building, right?"

(Trump) "Well, I was a developer. I put deals together and arranged the financing."

(Einstein) "But, you like buildings, correct? Over there they're building amazing castles."

(Trump) "You're suggesting I spend eternity here with these kids building sand castles?"

(Einstein) "In a sense, that's the way you spent your life on Earth, isn't it? It's here or back at the roundtable where you started. I could give you a few Earth years to read up on humanism. In the afterlife, a few Earth years is nothing but a nanosecond of time."

(Trump, *whimpering*) "But, you don't realize. I don't read. I don't like history. I like to talk but I can't stand to listen. I like being around people who believe I'm a genius."

(Einstein, *patting Trump on his orange head*) "Here now. It's not all that bad. (*Pointing*) Look, that group of toddlers wants you to come and play with them. They've never seen anyone as big as you. They might be smarter than you…but you'll always be bigger!"

Scene Five

[*The camera pulls back revealing a man in a black somewhat ill-fitting suit smoking a cigarette and walking into the stage set where Donald J. Trump – a former President of the United States – is busily building sand castles with a group of two-year olds.*]

(Rod Serling) "You have just witnessed what happens when a man starts believing his own lies, not only about others and events, but lies about himself. Donald J. Trump was an insecure and barely literate man who sought refuge and comfort throughout his life by calling himself a genius. He fooled others, and even fooled himself until his time of reckoning in the afterlife when his brash and unfounded boasts came to haunt him, forcing him to be recognized as a big man in size only in a far off place we call…'The Trump Zone.'"

THIRTY SIX

Colossus
(A triumphant Trump orders monuments to his legacy)

The date is January 20, 2028 – exactly three years since Donald J. Trump took the oath of office beginning his second term as President of the United States. That election, in retrospect, represented a critical turning point in American history as victory was declared only after what was then known as the U.S. Supreme Court – now referred to as the Executive Judiciary Approval Board – ruled by majority decision to disallow tens of millions of mail-in ballots based on the challenger's contention of vast voter fraud. Unrest, marked by riots, followed, but was quickly and firmly suppressed by the military supported by free-roving bands of white supremacist militia. Marshall Law was invoked, the Constitution was temporarily suspended, a massive reorganization of governmental entities was initiated, and the nation gradually transitioned into an era of imperial rule.

COLOSSUS
(A Play in One Act)

[The setting is the new Oval Office on the recently completed upper story of the White House in Washington, D.C. The gleaming new addition, constructed of stainless steel and black-tinted glass, houses the working quarters of President Donald Trump as well as a series of rooms for entertaining and providing luxurious quarters for overnight guests.

As the scene opens, it's January 20 of 2028. The members of his NPRP (National Parks Reclamation Program) – created early in his second term through an Executive Order authorizing the disposition and privatization of the nation's National Parks and Monuments – are awaiting the President's arrival for their scheduled meeting.

The members of the committee include the heads or directors of three former governmental agencies, now disbanded under the Governmental Reorganization Act instituted by Executive Order that also significantly reduced the role of Congress in an effort to ensure continuity, efficiency and speed in the execution of presidential decrees.

Those seated awaiting the President's arrival are loyalist David Bernhardt of the former Department of the Interior, William Perry Pendley of the former Bureau of Land Management (BLM), and Andrew Wheeler of the now defunct Environmental Protection Agency (EPA). Also present is top presidential advisor, Dr. Jared Kushner, pre-ordained to succeed the President at the end of his term, appointed to chair the committee.]

(Bernhardt) "Dr. Kushner, has the President reviewed the agenda?"

(Kushner) "He simply wants progress updates and has some additional ideas."

(Pendley) "More ideas? My goodness, we're swamped already!"

(Kushner) "Calm down. He's mainly interested in the Yosemite project."

(Wheeler) "Remember, gentlemen, always refer to it as Mighty Joe's, not Yosemite."

(Bernhardt) "Good point. That's proven to be an embarrassing tongue twister for him."

(Kushner) "The President, as you are well aware, has decided not to seek a third term, preferring to spend more time relaxing with President Putin, President Erdogen, Prime Minister Orban and other leaders of the New World Alliance. So, you can understand why he's insisting that these testimonial monuments be completed or underway before the seamless transition takes place. These monuments have become his top priority."

Chief of Staff Mark Meadows opens the door to announce the President's arrival.

(Kushner) "Good morning Mr. President."

(Trump) "Good morning, gentlemen. I hope you have good news for me?"

(Wheeler) "As you know the privatization of Yosem...er, Mighty Joe's National Park was finalized in 2025. To recap, work was immediately undertaken to design a relief commemorating your presidency on the face of Half Dome, one of the former park's signature landmarks. The winning contract called for a massive relief sculpture, the world's largest, covering the entire flat façade of the mountain featuring your distinguished head in profile. We have 10,000 men working around the clock on the sculpture. It's challenging given the monolith's height and near perpendicular surface, but great progress is being made and only 538 workers have died or been permanently disabled from falls or other accidents. I'm pleased to report that completion is scheduled for June with grand opening ceremonies attended by all Alliance partners on July 4th."

(Trump) "That's tremendous. Are we coming in on budget?"

(Wheeler) "The initial estimate was $2.0 billion, and it did balloon to $5.0 billion, but, thanks to a great idea by our committee Chairman Dr. Kushner (*Kushner nods*), we executed an ingenious strategy providing sufficient funds to offset the cost overruns."

(Kushner) "Under Section 12: Clause 24 of the NPRP, we sold Great Smoky Mountain National Park and used a portion of the proceeds to cover the budget overruns."

(Trump) "I like it. Where is this Great Smoky Bear National Park?"

(Kushner) "It's big and straddles two states, Tennessee and North Carolina, that helped power your reelection, (*aside to himself*) 'once we outlawed mail-in ballots.' (*resuming speaking to all*) Nice land and well-timbered; the sale brought in a pretty penny."

(Trump) "Who bought it?"

(Bernhardt) "An all-American conglomerate of timber and mining interests."

(Trump, *whispering*) "Fair to ask if Trump Enterprises is part of that conglomerate?"

(Bernhardt, *mouthing*) "O-f c-o-u-r-s-e!"

(Trump) "That's good. Now tell me, what's the decision on Mt. Rushlimbaugh?"

(Kushner) "Mr. President, before we move on to that assignment, let me share with you a truly exciting possibility. As a condition of sale, once the forests within the former Great Smoky Mountain National Park have been clear-cut, mining operations firmly established, and its waterways damned for power generation, we're proposing that the land within the former park boundaries become a model all-Aryan state, state number 51!"

(Bernhardt) "As envisioned, people would have to apply to a special Tribunal to be granted residency in the new state that we're thinking should be named 'Trumpopia.'"

(Trump) "Tremendous...But what's with this Trumpopium? Why not just Trump?"

(Pendley) "It's a combination of 'Trump" and 'Utopia.' Pretty clever, huh?"

(Trump) "What's a U...Whatever you called it?"

(Pendley) "Utopia in this context means 'the perfect place.' People will be lining up!"

(Trump) "I like it. But, that's a long ways off. Let's get back to Mt. Rushlimbaugh."

(Wheeler) "Mr. President, our experts have determined that there's no more space for another head on Mt. Rushmore, which is the project I believe you're referring to."

(Trump) "Well they can't be very good experts if they can't figure that one out. I was there you know. Gave a tremendous speech over the Fourth of July back in 2020. The place was packed despite that China Virus. My first look at the mountain. Lots of people go to see it, so I should be up there with the Funding Fathers as they call 'em – Washington, Jefferson, and Lincoln – and that other guy that I didn't recognize."

(Pendley) "Teddy Roosevelt. He represents the nation's conservation movement."

(Trump) "Well, as you know, we're done conserving. These parks can be put to much better economic use. How much trouble would it be to replace his face with mine?"

(Pendley, *scribbling notes*) "We'll get on that, sir, and report back promptly."

(Trump) "That's good. And I suggest you begin by finding some better experts."

(Bernhardt, *putting papers in his valise*) "I guess that wraps us up?"

(Kushner) "Not quite. I'll let the President outline his new idea."

(Trump) "Guys, don't get me wrong. I'm really excited about that Half Moon carving. It'll be great and people will flock to see it. But, they're gonna have ta go a long way. It's out there in California, right? What's that…10,000 miles from New York? And, when I replace that conservation guy on Mt. Rushbaugh, that's in the middle of nowhere too."

(Bernhardt) "So, what do you have in mind?"

(Trump) "I asked Jared here to do a little checking. I'd heard that way back in time there were some big, and I mean *big* statues. Bigger than our Liberty gal. Jared, tell 'em."

(Kushner) "The Colossus of Rhodes is considered one of the wonders of the ancient world. It stood at the entrance to the harbor at Rhodes and was dedicated to the sun god Helios. There are no descriptions but it's estimated to have been about 108 feet tall."

(Trump) "So, you couldn't find any photos?"

(Kushner) "No (*sighs*), and no descriptions. But, we know it existed and was something to behold. Now, centuries later, the Roman Emperor Nero created another huge bronze statue that stood outside the colosseum. Again, history has left us no descriptions (*pauses*)...or photographs, but archeologists estimate its height at about 98 feet."

(Trump) "See, puny things because they likely didn't have the cranes and helicopters we can use today in putting up big statues. My statue can easily be twice the size of those."

(Wheeler) "Where do you propose we put your statue?"

(Trump) "That's a no-brainer, Andy. New York harbor, of course!"

(Pendley) "But, we already have the Statue of Liberty."

(Trump) "That works perfectly. She'll look like Miss Midget next to my collosomy."

(Kushner) "One consideration would be the former Ellis Island National Park."

(Bernhardt) "Makes sense I guess since we've pretty much stopped all immigration."

(Trump) "The more I think about it, why not have me straddling Miss Liberty? You know, one giant foot on each side and me towering above her. She has her little spiked crown – well below my crotch of course – and I'll be wearing a much bigger crown."

(Pendley, *scribbling notes and sketching a mock-up of a giant naked bronze man looming over a miniscule Statue of Liberty.*) "Okay, we'll add this to the list."

(Trump) "Can I see what you've drawn up there?" (*Bill hands over his sketch*)

(Pendley) "I was just doodling. I think it's a great idea. A modern world colossus! America's colossus!"

(Trump) "Am I supposed to be naked?"

(Kushner) "Many speculative renderings of the Colossus of Rhodes and of the Statue of Nero present them as naked, which would be fitting for *those* times based on smaller statuary, mosaics and wall art. Pant-less was quite the fashion it would seem back then!"

(Trump) "Okay, just make sure that *every* body part is truly colossal in size!"

About the Author

Edward H. "Ned" O'Hearn holds a BA in English from The College of the Holy Cross and a Master's Degree in City Planning from San Diego State University, between which he served as the Gunnery Officer on a Navy destroyer in the South Pacific during the Vietnam War. Now retired from a career as a commercial real estate executive, he and Carol, his wife of 48 years, live in Scottsdale, Arizona. This is his first book.

Acknowledgements

This book could not have happened without the assistance of James A. Clapp, Ph.D. who contributed the title, inspired the character Miss Lindsey, and guided me through the production process, and Laura A. Rodil, who patiently applied her multiple talents in converting the text into book form and designing and creating the cover. I would also like to thank my many readers – friends who encouraged me to publish these satires, written as a form of personal therapy that I shared with them over the past five years.

Finally, I want to recognize the writers, producers, and lyricists whose creativity provided a platform for many of my satires, including: T.H. White; Rod Serling; Herman Melville; Christopher Guest; Eddie Holland; John Hughes; Ned Washington; Robert B. Sherman; Henry Wadsworth Longfellow; Sheldon Leonard; Norman Lear; Stephen Vincent Benet; William Shakespeare; Jerry Siegel; George Orwell; and Joe Connelly/Bob Mosher.